MW00579036

HOME FIRES

Also by Claire Booth

A Sheriff Hank Worth mystery

THE BRANSON BEAUTY
ANOTHER MAN'S GROUND
A DEADLY TURN *
FATAL DIVISIONS *
DANGEROUS CONSEQUENCES *

* available from Severn House

HOME FIRES

Claire Booth

**SEVERN
HOUSE**

First world edition published in Great Britain and the USA in 2024
by Severn House, an imprint of Canongate Books Ltd,
14 High Street, Edinburgh EH1 1TE.

severnhouse.com

British Library Cataloguing-in-Publication Data
A CIP catalogue record for this title is available from the British Library.

ISBN-13: 978-1-4483-1080-7 (cased)
ISBN-13: 978-1-4483-1081-4 (e-book)

This is a work of fiction. Names, characters, places and incidents are either the
product of the author's imagination or are used fictitiously. Except where actual
historical events and characters are being described for the storyline of this novel,
all situations in this publication are fictitious and any resemblance to actual persons,
living or dead, business establishments, events or locales is purely coincidental.

All Severn House titles are printed on acid-free paper.

Typeset by Palimpsest Book Production Ltd.,
Falkirk, Stirlingshire, Scotland.
Printed and bound in Great Britain by
TJ Books, Padstow, Cornwall.

Praise for the Sheriff Hank Worth series

"Balances well-developed characters and dry humor with a solid police procedural"
Library Journal Starred Review of *Dangerous Consequences*

"Booth knows exactly what she's doing . . . a deeply satisfying conclusion"
Booklist on *Dangerous Consequences*

"Many moving parts ultimately reward the reader's attention"
Kirkus Reviews on *Dangerous Consequences*

"Fascinating . . . Readers of Steven F. Havill's 'Posadas County' mysteries may want to try this series"
Library Journal Starred Review of *Fatal Divisions*

"Booth skillfully combines police procedural elements with a sharp focus on the families and professional lives of her protagonists. This superior regional series reliably entertains"
Publishers Weekly on *Fatal Divisions*

"Compelling . . . it really feels like [Booth] is writing about real people and events"
Booklist on *Fatal Divisions*

"Strong . . . a fascinating and complex plot. Readers will hope Hank has a long career ahead of him"
Publishers Weekly on *A Deadly Turn*

About the author

Formerly a crime reporter for daily newspapers throughout the United States, **Claire Booth** has used this experience to write five previous Sheriff Hank Worth mystery novels based on small-town American life. She is also the author of one non-fiction book, *The False Prophet: Conspiracy, Extortion, and Murder in the Name of God*. She lives in California.

www.clairebooth.com

For
Joe Booth
1950-2023
Thank you, Dad

ONE

Michael Whittaker lay on cream-colored satin and polished oak, a far cry from the cold steel beds he'd used during a forty-year career serving southwestern Missouri's dead. For his own exit, the medical examiner had given himself the priceless gift of not dying suspiciously. Instead, he passed away unexpectedly two days after a massive stroke sent him to Springfield CoxHealth Medical Center. So no metal table and floor drain for him. Just an intact corpse and a dignified service with command appearances by law enforcement from more than a dozen counties.

Hank Worth glanced around the church. No one looked much upset. Whittaker had been an odd duck. Staring a little too long, laughing a little too hard. Cracking jokes just off-center in their subject matter or timing. You came to his morgue because you needed answers, not because you enjoyed his company. And you came to the funeral because your second-in-command made you.

He texted Sheila Turley.

You're missing out. You should've come.

Medical leave, remember?

You have a wheelchair, so what's the problem?

She shot back with several emojis too caustic to be shared in polite company. Or read in church. Hank put his phone away as the pastor walked in and stopped to clasp hands with the widow. After a well-honed mournful pause, he continued to the pulpit, placed slightly to the side so the good doctor's casket could sit front and center. Bouquets of lilies lined the front and bullied their way into every nose in the room. The Stone County sheriff next to him shifted uncomfortably in the pew and muttered apologetically about his bursitis.

'When did you see him last?' Hank nodded toward the casket.

'About two months ago. Motor vehicle accident out near Galena. Two fatalities. How's about you?'

'Had a homicide earlier in the spring.'

'I can imagine the chuckles he had with that.'

'Yeah. He was always, well . . .'

'Yep. Exactly.'

Two seats down, Webster County's eyes started to water. Ozark County, an affable barrel of a man he'd talked to as they waited outside for the doors to open, was clearly trying to stifle a thunderous series of sneezes. The pastor waded through the lily scent and arrived at his destination. Hank tugged at his uniform sleeve and told himself to pay attention. But the sermon was bland and boring. Say what you would about Whittaker, he at least wasn't either one of those things. The reverend obviously hadn't known him at all. Hank's mind shifted to the robbery investigation currently on his desk. He tuned back in for a mildly interesting eulogy from a work colleague and stifled a groan as the pastor asked them to stand and open their hymnals.

The church filled with rustling paper and creaking knees as the audience of senior law enforcement officials – mostly old, even more mostly white, definitely mostly men – rose to their feet. Hank sighed and flipped to the right hymn number. The pastor waited a beat and then raised his arms. Fifty people took a breath.

And Hank's phone went off. It was set on vibrate, but the buzz filled the negative space and seemed to echo off the high ceiling. He shoved the hymnal under his arm and grabbed for it. It kept buzzing. Then Ozark's went off. And Webster County's. And the Springfield police chief's. Hank dropped the hymnal altogether as the sounds rolled through the pews in a wave. He read the screen just as Stone County turned to him, his own lit phone clutched in his hand.

'Oh my holy God.'

The fires still burned. And the firefighters stood on the perimeter, watching. And weeping.

'Do we know how many people were inside?' Hank asked a man he didn't recognize.

'No. Command won't let us near it.' He nodded toward an SUV off to the right and wiped again at his streaming eyes. 'My cousin works . . . worked . . .'

Hank turned away from the blazing crater and walked over to the West County Fire District SUV.

'What the hell did you do, Sheriff? Bring the entire state with you?'

The caravan that followed Hank the thirty-five miles from Springfield was still pulling into the clearing. The vehicles' whirling emergency lights were no match for the pulsating flames that tinted even their blue and red beams a hazy orange.

'We were all at a funeral,' Hank said. He looked at the twenty-odd squad cars. 'You can put them to work.'

'Oh, I plan to,' Bart Giacalone said. The fire chief stepped on to the SUV's running board and turned to face the group. 'Y'all grab the fire extinguishers out of your vehicles and start fanning out. Spot fires all over the place. Mop up as many as you can. See something bigger, give a holler. I'm keeping my guys here in case the main blaze starts to expand, but I'll send one to you if you need.'

They were gone without a word and within seconds, melting into the woods in the morning heat. Giacalone looked down at Hank. He was a big man, solid but not fat, with buzzed gray hair and a ruddy face that sported a horseshoe mustache bristling all the way around the corners of his mouth and down toward his chin. Right now it was coated with soot and dirt.

'It's gonna explode again. There's no way that it's not. There were so many damn fireworks in there.'

Hank nodded. It was a big warehouse. And one of Branson County's more prominent employers. Until today. He closed his eyes against the heat and the orange and the thought of it all.

'Any injured?'

Giacalone shook his head. 'Nobody that lucky, I'm guessing.' He coughed up a ball of smoke-induced phlegm and sent it sailing into the bushes next to his car. 'You know how many employees they got?'

Hank shook his head. 'The only thing I know is who isn't. The newspaper had a blurb last week about a local kid joining the Marines. The job he quit was at this warehouse.'

'Marines, huh? Already the smartest decision that kid'll ever make and he ain't even to boot camp yet,' Giacalone said. 'I bet his mama's thanking her lucky stars right now.'

She'd be the only mother in this section of Branson County who was. Hank turned back toward his cruiser and the computer file that laid out the procedure. He was required to call in the state and the feds. And hell, bringing in a few local pastors wouldn't be a bad idea, either. He was opening his car door when he heard yelling from the access road to the site. A woman came running at him, her face so white with fear that the orange glow from the flames didn't darken it at all. The shouts came from his deputy as she tried to chase the woman down.

Hank stepped away from the car and directly in front of the woman, wrapping her in a hug. Her momentum staggered him back a few steps before he caught his balance and loosened his hold.

'She . . . she slipped through the line.' Deputy Molly March leaned against the cruiser and put her hands on her knees as she caught her breath. She was a decent runner, but the woman was a lot taller and naturally faster. 'I'm sorry, sir.'

They were both close enough now to see the fire, the flattened trees, the stunned firefighters. The woman stopped struggling and sagged into his arms.

'Ma'am, you can't be here. It's not safe. We're going to take you back to the main road now.'

'No, no, no, no.' It was more a moan than a word. Hank tried to turn her around but she sank to her knees. The moaning kept on. He knelt in front of her. 'We're going to get you out of here and we're going to find someone to be with you.'

Now it was a wail. 'No, no. Someone? No. No one, no one. No one left. Why didn't he wait?'

Hank motioned to March and together they lifted the woman to her feet. Hank walked with them most of the way back to the road. He stopped short when he saw what was there. Dozens more like her, pressing against the caution tape and begging his deputies to let them through. He relinquished his hold on the runner and let March lead her the last little way to the rest of the devastated group. He forced himself to walk away slowly. They didn't need to see an authority figure running from their grief. Once he was out of their sight, he pulled out his phone. Screw the requirement for calling the state and the feds first. He'd start with the clergy. As many of them as he could get.

TWO

Sam hated this part. Trying to get people to follow his instructions while looking like a high school student. Usually he had his uniform on and that helped him look older, but today was an off day and he'd come straight from his girlfriend's house. In jeans and a T-shirt. At least he had his badge with him. He pointed at it on his belt.

'Again, ma'am, I need to ask you to step back. I'm with the sheriff's department, I swear. My name's Sam Karnes and—'

'Anybody could have one of those badge things,' someone in the crowd yelled. People were jostling closer and closer. He could see the fear and worry on their faces. What could he say? *It's quite likely your loved ones are dead.* That didn't seem like a good idea. He took a step back and held out his hands.

'Folks. We're all going to stay right here. They're working on getting you some information, but until then, I need for everyone to step over to the other side of the road.'

No one moved. Sam fought the urge to ball his hands into fists and instead spread them wide and flapped them forward, like he was shooing Canada geese off a lawn. It was just about as effective. He sighed.

'We're not going anywhere, boy.'

'No one's asking you to, sir. All I need is for everybody to get out of the roadway.'

'No.' This was a different man, off to the left and surrounded by young adults who looked so similar they had to be his children. 'We're not moving. You don't know anything. You haven't shown us anything.' He started waving his hands in the air. 'How do we know you're not the one who set the bomb?'

Sam gaped at him. He couldn't even find the breath to respond. He fought for air as the muttering edged toward panic and the crowd pressed forward. 'There's no . . . no bomb.' He managed to swallow. 'Nothing to . . . no indication that there was a bomb at all. Please, everyone step back.'

By now they'd backed him up against the caution tape that blocked off access to the lane leading to the warehouse. Another step and he'd bust right through it. He heard footsteps behind him but didn't dare turn around.

'On your six,' a familiar voice said, and the tape lifted so a distraught middle-aged woman and a petite deputy no older than Sam could duck underneath. Molly March, all five foot three of her and gloriously in uniform, gave him a business-like nod. 'Deputy Karnes.'

He nodded back.

Their arrival had sidetracked talk of a bomb. Instead, people were gravitating toward the woman, who sank to her knees right in the middle of the road.

'Faye, are you all right?'

'Were you there?'

'How bad—'

'Did you see anyone?'

'Was Ron working?'

'—really explode?'

Sam and Molly looked at each other. This woman was more than just a panicked relative. Many in the crowd clearly knew her. Everyone was pressing in. Too much and too quickly.

'Whoa, whoa,' Sam shouted. He waded in, with Molly right behind him. 'Give her some air. C'mon, folks. Back up.' The two deputies managed to get her to her feet, but the crowd kept hemming them in. They were frantic for answers.

'For God's sake . . .' someone sobbed. 'Please just tell—'

The blip of a siren cut through the pleading. Sam turned to see an ambulance stopped at the outskirts of the crowd. The siren blipped again and the lights went on. Sam seized the moment.

'Everybody move! Side of the road. Let's go. Out of the way. He needs to get through.'

People ceded the roadway, but the questions didn't stop. Sam kept the woman next to him and waved the ambulance forward so that it stopped in between him and the crowd on the far side of the blacktop. He waited as Larry Alcoate rolled down his window.

'Having some issues with crowd control, Karnes?'

'You have no idea. Stay parked right there until we get the

perimeter expanded, would you?' Molly was already rolling out more caution tape to block off the road as well as the warehouse's entrance lane. Without Molly to hold her up, the woman slumped against Sam. He staggered a little and thought of something. 'And I need you to take her.'

'Well, she certainly don't look right, that's for sure.' Larry never was one for pulling his punches. 'I can check her out.'

'Not here,' Sam told the paramedic. 'Put her in your rig, take her down the lane. She's getting mobbed here.'

Larry gave him an arched eyebrow but did as asked. He skipped the rear access and let her in the side door, which was blocked from the crowd's view by the way he'd parked. Once he closed the door on her trembling form, he rounded on Sam.

'What the hell, man?'

'She's connected somehow. A witness, maybe? We need to keep her isolated. I don't want her and that crowd interacting.'

'You're thinking like a cop, man. This is a fire, not a crime.'

Sam thought of the bomb comment and cringed. 'Don't I know it. That's what I've been telling these folks for the last fifteen minutes.' He pointed at the ambulance. 'I'd rather be too cautious with her than leave her here and have it be a mistake I can't take back.' Plus, he knew Hank would back him on any decision he made in that regard. Keep witnesses separate. Get interviews done as soon as possible.

Larry, who knew that side of Hank, too, nodded his head knowingly and started to climb back into his rig.

'Why are you the one here? You're not at the closest station.'

Larry took off his ball cap and swiped at the sweat on his forehead. 'That station has people who know warehouse employees. I said I'd come out so they wouldn't have to.' He glanced toward the fire. 'But it doesn't look like I'll need to take anyone to the hospital. I don't think anyone could've survived that.'

He slammed his door and drove slowly down the lane, leaving Sam to turn and face the crowd still clinging to hope.

The pastors wheedled and charmed and prayed their way through the perimeter, helped along by a call from a higher power to the state patrol officers manning the roadblocks.

'Let 'em through,' Hank said over the radio. 'They can go as far as the area where the families are waiting.'

Sam watched them pull up, five cars full of solace and hydration. The Baptists – the van said Second Baptist of Bradleyville – whipped out a folding table and cases of water. The Lake Baptists of Forsyth did the same, only they brought to-go urns of coffee. The reverend from Shepherd of the Hollows Lutheran started pulling out pop-up shade tents. Sam and a broad-chested man who'd pulled up in a battered minivan took one and started to work on it together. After a brief struggle with the nylon canopy, they managed to set up.

'Thanks for your help.' Sam introduced himself and shook the man's hand. He must be clergy – he was too calm to be a family member.

'Tony Morales. I'm the priest at the Catholic Church in Branson.'

'Thanks for getting here so quick.'

'There're more coming. With food. From what Hank said, there won't be any answers for quite a while. Which means these poor families aren't going anywhere. And there are the firefighters. People will need to be fed.'

That explained how he'd gotten here so quickly. Hank. Guess it didn't hurt to have a priest on speed dial. One who was eyeing him carefully.

'And how are *you* doing?'

'Who, me? Um . . . I'm fine?' Sam looked around. People were settling under the tents, sipping their drinks, murmuring to one another. This little bit of tending to was settling them down. Fear and the anguish were still there, but wrapping hands around a warm drink was allowing them to take a much-needed breath. Which meant Sam wasn't holding back an angry mob any more. So yeah, he was just fine now. Then the breeze shifted, and he caught a lungful of smoke. 'Oh. You mean because of the fire. I haven't been down there. There's nothing we can do. Until it's put out.'

Father Tony nodded, but that look stayed on his face. 'Well, you let me know. If you need anything.'

Instead of responding, Sam grabbed another pop-up tent and started wrestling it out of its storage bag. He looked around for a place to put it. The firefighters would need one, too. 'We should have two food stations.' He stopped. Think like Sheila. How would the department's chief deputy/organizational mastermind handle this? They would need to be separated. No mingling. The firefighters might pass on information that civilians shouldn't be hearing. Especially once the fire died down and they gained access to the facility. And what was inside. Who was inside.

He caught himself tugging at his ear and quickly turned back to the tent, which Father Tony now had out of the bag. He pointed down the lane, past the hard-won inner perimeter tape he'd put up with help from Alcoate and his ambulance. 'Just down around that curve, until it's out of sight from here. That way nobody sees each other. I think that would just get them worked up again.'

They both looked at the families. Father Tony started to say something but was interrupted by a squawk from Sam's radio.

'I got more people here. Saying they're part of the relief effort. What relief effort? I'm not a check-in service. Nobody else gets through.'

Sam waited for Hank's response to the trooper, but none came. He tugged his ear again and then reached into Molly's squad car for her radio. 'I'll be up there in a minute. Keep 'em there until then.'

'Great. Now I'm a babysitter.'

Sam sighed and replaced the handset. Father Tony smiled at him and started down the lane with the tent. Molly tossed Sam the car keys and turned back to the line of folks waiting for coffee. He'd like to stay here – have a cup, look at the scenery – instead of going to argue with another law enforcement agency. Then he watched Molly hug a sobbing woman. He quickly started the car. A cranky state patrol officer was better than an inconsolable relative.

Because what could he say?

THREE

'**A** whole gaggle of them. Pissed off as anything that I won't let them closer. And they keep trying to stick their cameras in my face.' Ted Pimental paused as someone shouted a question. Hank couldn't make out the words over the phone, but the response from one of his favorite deputies made him groan.

'Yeah, the sheriff is on scene,' Ted called out. 'No, he's not available right now.'

Hank looked over at the line of firefighters standing vigil. There was nothing to do. Not until the fire burned out and they could get in there and figure out what happened.

'How many of them?'

'All three Springfield stations and a couple people who obviously work for newspapers,' Ted said. 'And they've been talking about expecting more folks from the network affiliates in St Louis and Kansas City.'

'So basically, the longer I wait, the worse it's going to get.'

'Yep.'

'OK, give me ten or fifteen minutes and I'll be there.' That was well before any federal or state officials were due to arrive. He'd like them at the press conference, too, but there was no way Ted could hold those reporters off for that long. He walked over to Bart Giacalone, who was working two phones and a laptop simultaneously. Finally, one phone went jammed in a pocket, the other tossed on the driver's seat of his SUV.

'Sorry. Getting some fire crews from next door in Stone County to come over and help out in shifts. I got a feeling this thing is going to burn for a mighty long time.'

Hank nodded. 'The press is asking for an update. I think we need to get something out there soon.' He looked at Giacalone's harried expression. 'I know you're busy. That's why I'll do it. Hopefully it'll tide them over until the feds get here.'

Giacalone gave him a relieved thanks and went back to his laptop. Hank's phone buzzed again.

'Ted, hi. I'm just finishing up with Chief Giacalone and—'

'You need to get up here now. They're starting to . . .' He stopped as the questions in the background got louder. 'There's mutterings about it maybe being a bomb. And one guy is doing a live shot about the possibility of terrorism.'

Hank felt the blood drain from his face and then come back in a rush that left his head pounding. Giacalone's mouth fell open. 'What the hell? That ain't the case at all.'

But Hank was already running for his car.

The Easy Come & Go on Highway 65 had been overrun. There were six TV news satellite vans and a number of economy rental cars haphazardly parked next to the convenience store and along the grassy shoulder of the access road. Hank had to resort to blipping his siren to get a St Louis station to move its logo-emblazoned ass away from the entrance. He parked by the gas pumps and straightened his uniform as he got out of the car. Reporters started to swarm, but the look on his face had them backing away. He chided himself. He needed to do a better job of hiding how he felt. He walked over to an area of the grass not yet claimed by camera cables or tripod stands. *It's not like you're fighting the fire, asshole. You got the easy gig. You're just talking to reporters. Suck it up and do your job.*

'My name is Hank Worth, and I'm the sheriff of Branson County. The incident that occurred today is within my jurisdiction, so I'm here to let you know as much as possible about what's happened.'

Deep breath.

'First of all, there is absolutely no evidence that this was anything other than an accident. The Skyrocket company facility was a distribution warehouse for fireworks. It served locations statewide and throughout the Midwest. We as yet don't know what caused it to explode, but there is no indication that it was anything other than an accident.'

There was no way he was going to say the word 'bomb'. Or 'terrorism'. Those would be the only words to show up in the nightly news promos. Even if he put a giant 'not' in front of them, those words would be what stuck in people's minds. So, only 'accident' and whatever synonyms he could think of.

'This was an unintentional ignition. And our county fire districts, in conjunction with state and federal authorities, will be investigating. That can't start, however, until this accidental fire has been extinguished.' He hadn't used this many five-dollar words in years. 'We have multiple agencies monitoring it. They are not actively fighting it, though, due to concerns that there could be secondary explosions. It'll take time for the scene to be safe.'

He stopped and shoved his hands in his pockets. Two heartbeats later, the barrage started.

'How many—'

'What response time—'

'—be sure it wasn't a bomb?'

'You say Skyrocket "was" a facility.' One voice cut through the noise. 'Does that mean the whole place is gone? Is destroyed?'

'Yes.'

The starkness of that silenced the questions. He waited. For a second, the only sound was the hum of the news vans. Then a print reporter asked about casualties.

'It did occur during the middle of the work day, yes. We don't yet know, though, how many people were inside at the time. Obviously, that will be our priority once we're able to examine the scene.'

'When will that be?' asked a TV cameraman who appeared to be doing double duty as a reporter.

'I don't know. The fire is still going.' What else could he say? He thought of Bart Giacalone, who had aged right before his eyes in the two hours he'd been with him today. 'We have very experienced people who are going to judge when it's safe to get in there. Because we don't want anyone else to get hurt.'

'Does the company have a record?' This was from Jadhur Banerjee, the reporter for the local *Branson Daily Herald*. 'Any infractions or citations for safety violations? Things like that?'

Hank had no idea. He didn't think so. He would know if there were. But if he said that and it turned out to be wrong . . .

'The sheriff's department is not the agency that regulates these types of facilities. I can tell you that we've never been called out to this business on a law enforcement matter. Other citation questions are going to have to be answered by other agencies.'

That produced some grumbling. Then the print reporter who first asked about fatalities chimed in again.

'You say you don't know how many people were in the building at the time of the explosion. Can you at least tell us how many people Skyrocket employs? Or more specifically, how many are supposed to be at work at 10:32 a.m. on a Tuesday morning in June?' Silence. Hank felt the sweat rolling down his back and slicking his palms. He wanted to dodge the question. He wanted to turn around and walk away. He wanted it to be a Saturday with employees safe at home or running errands or watching a Little League game. But it wasn't, and he couldn't. He took his hands out of his pockets and wiped them on his pants.

'We don't know. But it's going to be a lot.'

All the local television stations, as well as CNN, were wall-to-wall explosion coverage. Aerial shots of the explosion site, talking head experts, graphics on how fireworks were made. And then a press conference, over the airwaves and streaming online. The sheriff, live and uninformative for fifteen solid minutes. And then they replayed it. Different snippets, over and over. To the point where his face became annoying.

The internet was even worse. It was a bomb. It was illegal immigrant terrorists. It was the wrath of God. The possibilities were endless. That last one was at least true. There were multiple avenues that might've been taken before the explosion and that could be taken now it had occurred. That was the worry.

The laptop shut with a snap. And a hand reached out and picked up the phone.

FOUR

S am gratefully accepted a cup of coffee from the Methodist minister manning the firefighter care station. Father Tony had done well – the shade tents were tucked behind a small wooded hill, out of sight of the families but plenty far away from the explosion site. Firefighters were starting to come up in pairs to grab a quick sandwich and drink, murmuring to each other as they ate. Sam sidled closer. It seemed the fire wasn't getting worse, but it wasn't showing any signs of dying out, either. They were waiting for reinforcements from bigger departments with more advanced equipment.

The state patrol officer was going to love that, having to let even more people through his perimeter. Sam felt a smug satisfaction. He'd spent fifteen minutes squabbling with the guy about access and finally won the argument. The next wave of clergy were allowed in, and now he could tell the guy to expect even more traffic through his checkpoint. That would keep him busy and hopefully quiet. He took a sip of his coffee as the latest fire duo finished up. One requested an extra coffee and a couple of waters. There was an ambulance driver parked down the way who'd asked for some.

He'd completely forgotten about Larry. And the woman. He grabbed the drinks himself and hustled around the bend, where Larry's rig sat under a white oak. The woman huddled just inside the open back door. She was shivering despite the warmth of the June day, and Larry had tucked a blanket around her. He motioned Sam toward the cab.

'She won't talk,' he whispered, taking the coffee with a nod. 'Just said, "Why didn't he wait?" one time and that's it.'

'Well, she obviously knows her way around this property. She wasn't with the rest of the families, didn't come in the way they all did. She wouldn't have gotten so close to the scene if she had. I'm hoping she can give us some information.'

He walked back and looked at her. She was thin, probably in

her fifties, with shortish dusty blonde hair that was littered with leaves and twigs. Her face was blotchy and her eyes swollen from crying. She looked up at him and then rested her head on her knees, which were drawn up to her chest. He didn't think looming over her was a good idea. He thought about what Hank would do and then slowly sat himself on the farthest edge of the back bumper, putting as much space between them as possible. He set a bottle of water at the edge of her blanket. And waited.

It took a few minutes, but she finally reached for the water. Sam continued to study the trees and the passing firefighters and pretty much anything but her.

'Can I . . . can I go home?' Her voice was hoarse and weak.

'Where's home, ma'am?'

'Out farther west on 160.'

That was a long road. Which made it a useless answer.

'Whereabouts? Close to here?'

She took a sip of water and stared at the ground. Sam tried not to fidget.

'We can get somebody to drive you there. But I need to know where it is. Who you are. That kind of thing. Because we want to help.'

The water bottle's plastic crackled in her hands and she curled into herself even more. He swore silently. He'd pushed too much. He stared at his own patch of ground for a moment. *What do you know, lady? Who are you weeping for?* He rubbed at his ear and tried to figure out what to say. Nothing came to him. So he sat. And she sat. He lost track of the minutes and still they sat. The smoke drifted past them and through the ambulance and into their clothes and their lungs. She curled even tighter. And then a squad car crept over the rise, coming from the main road.

Sam almost cried with relief as it came to a stop in front of them. He made to stand but Larry beat him to it, appearing from around the side and striding quickly over to the driver's window. He leaned down and spoke to Hank so quietly Sam couldn't hear. So he stayed put. Hank would know what to do. Larry straightened, but instead of getting out, Hank turned to the car's laptop. Sam desperately wanted to stand and move around. But he sat and watched until his boss finally finished whatever the hell he was doing and left the car.

Hank walked over and knelt in front of the woman.

'Mrs Halliday. I'm so sorry.'

She startled at the sound of her name. So did Sam. Here just five minutes and Hank had already figured out who she was. What else did his boss know? Sam waited.

Hank reached out and laid his hand next to the blanket, careful not to touch it or her. He introduced himself. And then he asked for her help. 'We need to know who was working today. We need to know what inventory you had and how much.' He tried to get her to look at him. 'Can you tell us?'

She wouldn't meet his eyes. The water bottle crinkled distressingly in her grip and started to leak. Hank gently took it away. She moved her wet hand to her face and looked anywhere but at the two men sitting with her.

'OK,' Hank said. 'We're going to get you away from the smoke, get you somewhere nice and quiet. Deputy Karnes here will drive you to—'

She jerked back, banging into ambulance equipment behind her. 'Home. I want to go home.'

'We'll certainly see about that after—'

Hank's sentence was cut short as she looked from Hank to Sam in alarm. 'Then I'm staying here.'

She stood and quickly twisted away from them. They were both on their feet immediately. Hank quickly sidestepped directly into her path and she bumped right into him. Sam knew panicked stubbornness when he saw it and was ready for her dodge away from Hank. She smacked into his chest and the blanket pooled on the ground as she gave him a good whack with her fists. He instinctively grabbed her wrists and held them. They looked at each other over the top of her head. Hank started to gesture, but stopped at a shout from behind them. Two older men in police dress uniforms and carrying fire extinguishers materialized from down the lane. More yelling brought several firefighters from the explosion site, and they all disappeared into a stand of trees that was starting to smoke alarmingly.

'See, ma'am? You can't stay here,' Hank said. 'It's not safe.'

She looked at the new smoke in the woods and gave in, walking voluntarily over to Hank's squad car. They put her in the front passenger seat and then moved a good distance away.

'How did you know her name?'

'I didn't. Larry told me you'd isolated her because she seemed to know something, so I ran the owners' names in the drivers' license database.' He pointed at the laptop in the car's center console. 'The photo matched. She owns the whole operation with her husband Lyle.' He slapped Sam on the shoulder. 'Great work on your part. I'm sorry your reward is going to be babysitting her some more.'

'That's fine. I can drive her home.'

Hank shook his head.

'No. Take her, I don't know, someplace like the library. Definitely don't take her to our office.' He gave her a long look as she sat in the car with her eyes closed. 'I don't want her to think she's being interrogated. She's not in any trouble.'

'Yet.'

The fire looked no different to Hank. But Bart seemed optimistic. If 'only maybe another day' was taken as a good thing. The fire chief surveyed his domain as a passing firefighter handed him a cup of coffee. There was already a stack of empty cups by the front tire of his SUV. He took a gulp and pointed toward the line of squad cars from Whittaker's funeral. It didn't look like a single one had left.

'Your boys on parade are doing pretty good,' he said.

They were his boys at the moment. He should check on them. He grabbed a bag full of sandwiches from the food tent and went looking. He found them dirty and smelly, with ruined uniforms and sore arms from carting around unfamiliar equipment. And enjoying themselves immensely.

'I gotta tell you, Worth, I haven't been out of the office this long in years,' a Springfield PD commander said. The man looked it. He had a belly that would do Santa proud and the pallor of a master paper-pusher. He wiped the sweat off his face with a grimy sleeve and grinned as his chief walked over.

'Heard you gave a press conference, Worth. Couldn't avoid it, huh?'

'What? You don't think it's my favorite thing to do? I'm so good at it.'

Both men chuckled. They'd seen his past performances. He

handed them sandwiches and walked down into a small hollow
where the sheriff of a farm county northeast of Springfield was
stomping out the last embers in a scorch spot. He took a sandwich
and contemplated the black earth.

'Fires are great work. You put it out, you're done, you walk
away. No evidence, no paperwork, no poor sap you got to take
to jail. No accomplices to track down.' He paused. 'You know
what I mean. This here today is horrible. But there's something
mighty satisfying about dealing with a problem and knowing it's
not coming back.'

He saluted Hank with his half-eaten sub and headed happily
in the direction of a call for more fire extinguishers. Hank envied
him the finality of his sooty boots. His dirty work on this disaster
hadn't even started yet.

The house was new, built within the last decade or so. A long
ranch style with a large detached garage, all nicely coated in brick.
Several sheds, to be expected on a ten-acre parcel in this area.
And Google Maps showed one outbuilding down in a hollow on
the west side of the property. They would get to all of those later.

There was no response to their knock, so they let themselves
in. It looked like an ordinary morning had occurred. A cereal
bowl in the sink, a hastily made bed. They didn't care. There
was an iPad on the coffee table, but that was it. They would need
to search the garage. It held just what they hoped. A home office.

'Are you sure?'

'Two computers and a bunch of filing cabinets.'

'OK, I'm coming in.'

'I really don't think that's a good idea.'

'I didn't ask you.'

'No. But you do need me.'

There was no answer to that. There was no more talking at
all until they stood together in front of the computers.

'They're locked. We'll need passwords.'

'Shit.'

Filing cabinets were opened and folders pulled. More swearing,
but little else until an invoice shook loose and fluttered to the
floor.

'Well, well,' Sheila said. 'There it is.'

FIVE

Hank's entire staff was working the explosion, except for one deputy he'd left on patrol duty. And of course the most important one, Sheila Turley. He pushed all thought of the convalescing chief deputy out of his head and logged into his squad car computer. The Google satellite image of Faye Halliday's property showed a main house, a separate garage, a few storage sheds, and something that could be a barn. There might be nothing company-related in any of them. Or there could be records relating to handling, storage and safety. Those were documents he – and the state and federal investigators about to descend on his county – very much needed to see before allowing Halliday any access to them. Hence Sam's babysitting.

He also prayed that Halliday kept employee information there. That was the most urgent. He would need it to match to the bodies. He knew it was probably in the cloud somewhere, backed up by IBM or Amazon, but getting access to those places was a pain in the ass. Getting permission to enter a local house was much easier. He pulled out his cell phone.

'Judge Sedstone, please. It's Hank Worth.'

The court clerk didn't even put him on hold, just hollered at her boss to pick up his extension.

'Good Lord, son. Are you at the scene? Is it as bad as they're saying?'

'Yes, sir. Everything's gone. Which is why I'm calling. I believe the owners might have backup records at their home. I'd like a search warrant so I can get in there and see. Mrs Halliday isn't in any shape to take us through and I'd rather have legal authority to be in there anyway, instead of just the debatable consent of a grieving widow. I especially need employee information so I can start preparing to identify the bodies.'

'Well now, I've—'

Hank put the judge on speaker and kept going while hunting-

and-pecking on his laptop. 'I'm typing up an affidavit now and I'm hoping you'll grant it for me and—'

'Hank, my boy, I already have.'

Hank's fingers froze over the keyboard. 'What?'

'I already approved a warrant for that address. About an hour ago.'

'Really?' It better have been a fast-thinking state investigator. It better not have been . . .

'Yes. Deputy Turley called and then sent over all the information. I did tell her to be extraordinarily complete with the return. Seeing as we'll have the feds mucking about in things as far as the blast investigation goes. We've got to show them we know what we're doing down here.'

Hank tried to stutter a response, but the judge kept going.

'I hadn't realized she was back at work yet. We all thought it would take a lot longer for those abdominal injuries to heal. 'Course, if anybody would survive a beating like that, it'd be her. She's quite something.'

'Yes,' Hank said through gritted teeth. 'She's something else, that's for sure.'

'You called Judge Sedstone? From home?'

'You don't think I have that man's phone number memorized? I got to, seeing as I'm the only one thinks to request these things.'

'You're not supposed to be working.'

'Uh huh,' Sheila said. 'That'd be a lot easier to do if you'd been able to keep the county from exploding while I'm gone.'

Hank didn't respond to that.

'An event, by the way, that I had to learn about from the TV news.'

'There's no way I was going to call you. Because then you'd want to work. Which the doctors have specifically said you aren't allowed to do.'

She gave him a dismissive grunt as she stood in the Hallidays' garage office.

'Sheila, please, just don't. You need to be taking it easy. We've got this.'

That ridiculousness got him a snort, which turned out to be unwise as pain shot through her belly. 'If you didn't need me, you would've thought to call Sedstone before I did. So I've heard enough of this nonsense, and I'm going to hang up.'

She ignored his protests and did just that.

'He's right, you know. You should be in bed. You don't look good.'

'Shush. I picked you because you're one who won't go all nursemaid on a person.'

'No,' said Deputy Amber Boggs, 'you picked me because I'm the only one not at the fire scene.'

'Well, that, too.'

They fell into silence, both staring at the garage office's computer. Daylight shafted through the room's one high window and across the dusty monitor screen. They would need an expert to unlock the password. And they would need someone more able-bodied to process the filing cabinets, Sheila admitted to herself as she slumped against the desk. The pain sent spokes from her middle into her pelvis and her upper chest. She'd deliberately missed her last dose of tramadol because she wanted a clear head. She was starting to realize sharp thinking wasn't doing her much good when she couldn't even stay upright.

'Am I going to have to carry you?' Boggs said.

Sheila scowled. The pain was increasing so rapidly, if she didn't leave the room and get down the four outside steps right now, then she likely wouldn't be able to on her own. And although the sturdy Boggs was quite capable of slinging Sheila over her shoulder and walking her all the way to the car, Sheila would rather die than allow that to happen. She started to shuffle toward the door. She made it five steps before her knees buckled. She flung out her arms but found herself in the no man's land between the desk and the doorway. *If I fall, I'll never get up.* Then Boggs was there, one arm around her waist and the other reaching for her hand. Sheila looked down at their fingers, hers a rich mahogany and Amber's a pale white. Hers a frail collection of bones and Amber's a solid slab of health.

The young woman helped her down the steps to the driveway where they'd parked her walker. Yes, walker. She was an old goddamn woman who couldn't even make it to the car without help. She hadn't wanted to bring the walker, but Boggs insisted. Damn her good sense. Sheila sank into the seat and congratulated herself that she'd at least gotten the one with all the luxuries – padded folding seat, hand brakes, metallic blue with racing stripe. Her goal when she ordered it was to force the county to fork over as much money as possible for her treatment. Now she was just glad to rest.

'You catch your breath while I move the car closer.'

'No. We're staying. I'm fine now that I'm sitting.'

'No, you're not.' Amber looked her up and down. 'You're still really, really bad.'

Sheila hunched over and wrapped her arms around her middle. 'Be that as it may, we're staying.'

Because Hank would be here shortly. And there was no way she was going to miss that.

Sam worked a connection and – twenty minutes later – two perfect whole milk lattes arrived. Brenna Cassidy set them down on the library table and turned to leave. Sam gestured for her to stay. Maybe having an unthreatening woman here would make Mrs Halliday feel more comfortable. And no one was less threatening than his kindhearted, beautiful girlfriend. She slid into a seat on one side of the small children's table where he and Mrs Halliday sat across from each other. Sam introduced them.

'Brenna works at Donorae's. You know, the coffee shop downtown?' He nodded at the to-go cup. 'She makes a really good latte.'

Faye Halliday poked at the lid. 'Nobody survived, did they?'

That was certainly not where he'd hoped the conversation would go. He looked for a moment at the tall cheery sculpture of oversized children's books in the middle of the room and tried to keep his face expressionless. There was no point beating around the bush. Molly said she'd chased the lady all the way to the edge of the blast zone. So the poor thing already knew the extent of the devastation. He looked her in the eye.

'No, ma'am. Probably not.'

She nodded without taking her eyes off the cup. 'Lyle couldn't drink coffee anymore. His heart. He'd been off it for a year. Lord, he missed it. He should've just kept on having it. Enjoyed the last year of his life.' She choked on the last few words and slowly lowered her head to the table. Brenna gently moved the latte out of the way.

'When did he go to work this morning?'

'Eight o'clock. Same as always.' The words, coming through the arms shielding her face, were muffled.

'Is it, um, is it a busy time of year for you?'

'A little. Starting to gear up for the Fourth of July. All the seasonal retailers need their stock.' A pause. 'This morning, that's all we were worried about. Now . . .'

Sam fought the urge to lean forward. He didn't want to seem like he was pressing her. But he was. 'Can you tell me who was working today?'

'Paula is the one who knows that. She . . . she *was* the one who knew that.' The last few words were a whisper and then the only sound they could hear was the kind of hiccup that only comes with crying. Brenna reached out and laid her hand on Mrs Halliday's arm.

'I'm sure Paula did a really good job with that,' Brenna said. 'Did she do payroll?'

'Yeah.'

'How many folks work full time?'

'Fourteen.'

'Paula, right? Who else?'

Sam quietly pulled out his notebook as Brenna coaxed name after name out of Mrs Halliday. Something about the soft voice and the warm touch elicited the answers neither he nor Hank had been able to get. He got eleven names – twelve if you counted Lyle – when she gave up. 'I can't remember. An older woman who just started and the millennial who was always calling in sick. I don't . . . I don't remember. Oh, God, that's so horrible. I'm so horrible. How can I not remember?'

There was more hiccupping and Mrs Halliday's slight form shook with sobs. Brenna reached down and pulled her purse up on to the table. She rooted around briefly with her free hand and then shoved it at Sam. She pantomimed blowing her nose at the same time Sam remembered the packet of tissues that Sheila always seemed to have during sensitive interviews. Brilliant. He dug through and found Brenna's, pulling it out quickly as the sobs increased. Brenna moved her chair closer and slid the tissue into Mrs Halliday's hand, then put her arm around the woman's shoulders.

They sat that way for a long time, Brenna silently comforting and Sam ignoring them – and feeling like an ass – as he surreptitiously typed the names into an email for Hank and then used the Google satellite map to look at both the warehouse and her home on Highway 160. Finally, the crying lessened and she lifted her head enough to be able to mop at her face with another tissue. Sam had to avert his gaze from the raw agony.

'We had a fight. I yelled at him.'

Both Sam and Brenna leaned forward to catch the bare whisper.

'I slammed the door on him and didn't go. I should have been there. I should be dead, too.'

SIX

Hank saw the squad car first. Then Deputy Boggs. And then . . . 'God dammit. What are you doing? You're not supposed to be out of bed, let alone out of the house. I thought you were there when I talked to you. You were here? What the hell are you thinking?'

She tried to wave away his protest but couldn't raise her arm enough. She had to settle for a dismissive flick of her fingers. That horrified him even more than the sight of her crumpled in the walker's seat. Her shiny black hair was neatly smoothed back like normal, but her green sweatshirt hung off her in folds and the gray tinge to her brown skin was worse than it had been in weeks.

'Tyrone is going to kill me. And I'm going to kill you.' He knew he was yelling and didn't care. 'You're getting in the damn car.'

'My husband's just fine.'

'Because he doesn't know you're out here. He's not going to be fine when he finds out.'

Another finger flick. 'I'm not going anywhere. We need to show you the office. And search the sheds and everything.'

He was so frustrated all he could do was pace up and down the driveway. He counted to ten over and over until he felt calm enough to speak without shouting. Then he took a breath and knelt in front of her. Bad move.

'Do not get at eye level with me,' she said. 'Don't you dare. I'm not an invalid or a toddler. So back the fuck off.'

Hank held her glare. She was in agony. She couldn't do her job. She couldn't run the disaster response. She couldn't coordinate the staff. The physical pain was all secondary. To her. To him, it was paramount. He wanted to help. And he knew that would be what killed her.

'Fine.' He rose to his feet and prayed Tyrone would forgive him. 'Tell me what you found in the office.'

'Unpaid invoices.'

'That people haven't paid them? Or that Skyrocket hasn't paid others?'

'Both,' Boggs said. Sheila was busy clutching her ribs.

Could be significant. Could be irrelevant. He shifted to what was unquestionably important.

'What about employee records?'

'Hiring.' It was all she could get out.

Boggs cleared her throat. 'There's lots of hiring applications and stuff. Some of it looks pretty old. There's not any kind of work schedules, though. So who knows which people were there when it blew up.'

Hank realized he was pacing again.

'Computers. Password.' Sheila gasped out the words. 'Will need to break in.'

'No, we just need to get her out here,' he said. 'Get her functioning and out here so she can get us a list of who was actually working today.'

'Her who?'

'Faye Halliday.'

Sheila's eyebrow rose. It was the first normal, healthy movement he'd seen her make.

'She survived?'

He stopped pacing. 'No. Well, yes. She wasn't there at all when the blast happened. She came to the scene. We couldn't get anything out of her. I had Sammy take her someplace quiet. Try to get her calmed down.'

Boggs stared at him quizzically. 'She just lost everything. You think a pat on the back is gonna help?'

Hank raked his hand through his hair. Boggs's interpersonal skills certainly hadn't improved in the several months she'd been with the department. He knew it was a genuine question – she wasn't being sarcastic. She just flat out didn't understand a lot of context, and wasn't shy in remarking upon it. On the other hand, she stayed cool and composed in every situation, a huge asset in a patrol officer.

'Aren't you supposed to be out on patrol?'

'Yeah. But are you capable of ignoring an order from her?' She pointed at Sheila. 'Cuz I'm not.'

She also had the irritating habit of puncturing a person's comforting self-deceptions. Like the one that he was in charge. 'No. I'm not capable of ignoring her orders, either.'

They both looked at the hunched woman who was starting to list to one side, but managed to raise her arm and point.

'Now that we've cleared that up, let's search the house, shall we?'

They were arguing over how to get down there when Hank's phone went off. 'Sam's got the names. Who was working today.'

Boggs grunted in surprise and Sheila muttered something that sounded like 'good boy'. Hank tried not to smile. He had her now.

'The house can wait. I need you to get started on that list.' Which she could do in front of her home computer, near her hot tea and her pain meds and her hovering husband. 'I want next-of-kin information. I don't know if we're going to need DNA samples or not, but I want all contact information nailed down as soon as possible.'

'I know what you're doing.'

'I don't care. It needs to be done and you'd be doing it if you were on normal duty. It's pure coincidence you can also do it safely in your living room while on sick leave.' He pointed at Boggs and then jerked his thumb in the direction of her squad car. 'So take her home.'

Hank had given an update to the TV cameras. The least he could do is give one to the families, too. So instead of taking the easy way, back to the blast site, he took the hard route past a surly state patrol officer to where the families were holding vigil. There looked to be at least fifty people huddled under shade tents in the late spring heat of the afternoon. He took a moment to gather himself and got out of the car.

Someone recognized him right away and called his name. Everyone stopped what they were doing and gathered silently around him.

'I don't have much to tell you right now, and I'm sorry about that. You all know the fire still isn't under control. Once it is, once it's out, we will get in there and we will start to get you some answers. Right now I can't say for sure who was working today, so if you do know that about your loved one, I'd like you to tell me. If you can tell me what their exact job is, I'd appreciate that, too.' He didn't know where bodies would be located within the building footprint, so knowing who did what might help narrow down ID possibilities. 'And if there's anything else you think I should know, please don't hesitate.'

'Where the hell is Faye?' This from a tall, broad man in the back, his face blotchy with panic. 'She knows all this. She knows if my son was working. My son I can't get a hold of. Where is she?'

There were angry murmurs. 'They swooped in and took her away,' said a lady standing off to the side. 'What did she do?'

'Oh, my God, that was the owner? The one who snuck off in the ambulance?'

The murmurs were graduating to shouts from all sides.

'Did you arrest her?'

'Where's her husband?'

'Yeah, where the hell is Lyle? It's her and him that run it. Both together.'

'Well, if we haven't seen him,' said the woman off to the side, 'then think about it. He's dead, too.'

'Or ran off,' the tall man said. He crossed his arms and glowered at Hank. 'Maybe he got the hell out of Dodge.'

Hank held up his hands. 'Folks. Hold on. We have no information that Lyle Halliday went anywhere. And we also don't know what caused the explosion. At all. I promise you we'll be investigating it, along with the state fire marshal's office and the ATF. But right now, I need to please ask for your patience.' He paused as everyone registered that the federal Bureau of Alcohol, Tobacco, Firearms and Explosives would be coming to town. That only amplified the glares and angry mutters. He'd take the emotional assault if it made them feel better. He stood silently until the hostility ebbed a little and then started taking people aside, one by one.

He already had the employee list from Sam. But he hoped that allowing these families to tell him directly – to say their loved ones' names aloud to someone in authority – would validate their pain. At the moment, it was the best he could do.

*   *   *

'What are you doing?'

Sheila looked up at her husband. 'You're home early.'

'Of course I'm home early. I heard about the explosion.'

'Everybody's heard about the explosion. It don't mean they take off work.'

'Everybody don't have a wife who's going to use it as an excuse to do things she shouldn't be doing. Like working.'

Her response to that was to resume typing. Her laptop sat on a pillow balanced on her lap. The one concession she'd made was to sit in the recliner instead of at the dining table. She told herself it was just so she could easily see the TV and its continuous explosion coverage. Tyrone took the remote off her side table and muted it. She sighed and stopped typing.

'Why are you doing this? They can handle this without you.'

'No. They quite literally cannot handle this without me. You know we're short-staffed as it is. And right now everyone is needed out at the scene. So I'm doing this. It's just research.'

Tyrone squinted at her computer screen. 'These are the dead people? Compiling a list of dead people is not "just research". It's horrible and stressful and exactly what you're *not* supposed to be doing.'

'It's horrible and I'm stressed if I'm *not* doing it,' she said, accentuating the negative just as much as he had. 'We're going to need to know proper next of kin for these people. Especially since the medical examiner's office is in God-knows-what kind of disarray, what with Whittaker dying.'

'I don't give a good Goddamn about Whittaker dying. I care about you dying. Which you almost did. And you're not out of the woods yet. So give me the damn laptop.'

She knew he was only doing this because he loved her. Because he was the only person on earth who could talk to her like this. Because he was the only one she might listen to.

But not today. She just couldn't.

'I'm going crazy, baby. I sit around all day with nothing to do. I see things going undone and . . .' She swallowed and stared out the window for a moment. 'And I could live with it. Until today. This can't be put off. This won't wait 'til I'm "healed". Whatever that is.' She looked up at him, the sharp cheekbones and warm brown eyes. She wanted to take away his worried look.

'It's more stressful for me to do nothing. I know you understand that.'

He looked at her long and hard and finally sighed. He leaned down and stroked her hair back from her forehead and then kissed her gently. 'I'll make you some tea.'

She sagged into the recliner with a relieved sigh as he headed toward the kitchen. Everything was good. Until he walked past the foyer and saw her walker.

'Wait a minute, why is this dusty?' He stomped back into the room. 'Have you been out of the house?' His voice rose and echoed through the small room. 'What the hell are you thinking?'

SEVEN

Fireworks Distribution Building Explodes, Kills Fourteen
By Jadhur Banerjee

Branson Daily Herald

BRANSON – A warehouse storing an unknown amount of fireworks exploded yesterday, killing at least a dozen employees and the owner with a blast that was felt many miles away. The resulting fire has burned throughout the night.

Skyrocket Distribution Company, located just west of Highway 65 about eight miles north of the city limits, exploded just after 10:30 a.m. yesterday. Emergency responders closed down the highway – the major route between Branson and the metropolitan Springfield area – for much of the day. It reopened just before midnight, but motorists should still expect delays today.

'We hope to have the fire out by mid-morning tomorrow,' said Bart Giacalone, chief of the Western County Fire District, when interviewed at the scene yesterday evening. 'We are being very careful. There are still hot spots and I don't want any emergency personnel injured.'

The blast destroyed the entire structure and was so devastating that no one inside at the time could have survived, said Sheriff Hank Worth.

'We will be figuring out which employees were at work and making identifications as quickly as we can,' Worth said. 'We understand that people want information, but we also need to be as thorough as possible.'

Families of employees are already demanding an investigation.

'They were supposed to have procedures, safeguards, whatever you want to call them,' said Jerry Ustus, whose

son Pete has worked at Skyrocket for two years. 'It wasn't supposed to be a dangerous place to work.'

Skyrocket Distributing has been in business since 1995. Owners Lyle and Faye Halliday built it from a small seasonal storage facility into a year-round distribution hub for fireworks retailers throughout the central Midwest. It employs more than twenty people and is a notable business presence in the area, regularly contributing to local causes and sponsoring community youth sports leagues.

'And where are Lyle and Faye?' asked Brooke Timmons. She said her sister Paula has been with Skyrocket since its first day in business. 'They aren't out here with us. Aren't giving us any information. I'm really upset.'

According to a law enforcement source, Lyle Halliday is believed to have been in the warehouse when the blast occurred. Faye Halliday could not be reached for comment.

Timmons and Ustus were among the dozens of relatives who gathered as close to the scene as possible yesterday, hoping for word on their loved ones. Many continued to stay at the makeshift relief center into the night.

'This is just agonizing for them,' said Douglas Lancaster, pastor of Lake Baptist Church in Forsyth, one of many local clergy who are providing food and comfort to those waiting for word. 'We're trying to help in any way we can. We'll be out here as long as they need us.'

Both the volunteers and the families were preparing for a long wait for any definitive answers.

'I think he went to work this morning,' said Linda Dowder, whose son Ron started at Skyrocket six months ago. 'And now I can't get a hold of him. He isn't answering his phone. So there's no other conclusion to draw, is there?'

Duncan McCleary tossed the newspaper on the kitchen table. 'Wow. That quote is drier than a bone. Couldn't you have sounded a little bit more like a human being?'

'I did. I said something about owing it to the families to be careful. They just didn't put that part in the article.'

It was so early in the morning, not even the kids were up. Just Hank and his father-in-law in the pre-dawn gloom and the weak light of the bulb over the stove. Hank had hoped the old man would still be asleep in his basement bedroom, but no such luck.

'You'll be able to get in there today, it sounds like,' Dunc said.

Hank topped off his coffee. 'Somebody'll get in there. Me, the ATF, the special forensic people, some state fire marshal folks – there'll be a damn line.'

'That mean you'll have a turf war?'

He pinched the bridge of his nose. 'I hope not. I just need the identifications sorted out. Then everybody else can take all the time they need to figure out why the damn thing exploded in the first place.'

'You have any ideas why it combusted like that?'

'I got no clue. They were up to date on all their safety inspections and Sheila's checking on the most recent reports.'

'Wait, she's back at work?'

'No. She is not back at work. She is back to being a pain in my ass, though. She's insisting on helping, even though her doctors are still telling her it'll be weeks before she can come back.'

'Good for her. Doctors are full of shit. Most doctors anyway.'

He glared at Dunc over the top of his mug. 'No they're not. She had massive internal injuries. You don't get attacked with a tree branch by a delinquent like Eddie Fizzel and just come skipping back to work the next week.'

'It's been four weeks.'

'And that's not long enough.'

Dunc waved his hand dismissively. 'It's not like she's out on the scene traipsing around or anything.' The look on Hank's face stopped his next sentence before it started. 'Oh, she was? Ha, I'd have loved to see you try to handle that. No wonder you look all tired and raggedy. She probably ate you for lunch.'

Hank ignored him and turned to root through the cabinet for a travel mug.

'You should eat something. Make yourself some eggs. Hell, I'll make you some eggs.'

'No, thanks.'

'You're going to be out there all day and night again. You need to eat.'

He really wished Dunc wasn't an early riser. He didn't want

to talk right now. And he really didn't want to put this next bit into words.

'I don't want to have any food in my stomach,' he said. 'Not with what I'm going to see.'

Bart Giacalone stood and surveyed the smoking wasteland he hadn't left in twenty hours. His people were in the last stages of mopping up around the edges of the building that no longer existed.

'Then I'm sending 'em home. A couple crews from Springfield are coming down. They'll be here to help when y'all make your way into . . . whatever the hell that is.' He gestured wearily at the hole in the ground. 'Rubble? Char and ashes? Dreams? Death? I don't know. I just want it to be over.'

Hank silently handed him the extra cup of coffee he'd brought from the house. The fire chief sipped and watched as the oxygen-masked, soot-coated fighters seemed to float through the smoke, skirting debris and blackened ground holes with tired grace. Hank could hear Bart's breath rattle in his throat. He shifted his weight from foot to foot and rubbed at his cheek. The man wanted to ask something. Hank stayed quiet.

'You got a list yet?'

'Yeah. Not definitive, but almost. Fourteen. Including Lyle Halliday. Sam Karnes tracked down that kid who enlisted in the Marines. He was able to give us a layout of the building and who generally worked where. So we've got places to start.'

Bart nodded. 'Good. That'll be better with the state fire marshal folks. Now that the fire's out, they'll send their investigators. The feds are already here.'

Hank looked around. He hadn't seen anyone.

'ATF showed up about two a.m. Took a look and said they'd be back.' Bart waved half-heartedly toward a stand of trees. 'Left the pimply kid over by that sedan to keep an eye on us. I don't know what he's gonna do, we start screwing things up. Wag a finger at us?' He finished off the coffee in one final gulp. 'They seemed determined. All keyed up.'

That wasn't good. He glanced over at the young man, pretending to be engrossed in his phone but clearly listening to their every word. He turned slightly so he faced away from the kid. 'So's there anything you want to tell me before they come back?'

Bart smoothed his mustache, which did nothing but smear black residue across his cheek. 'Walk with me.'

They slowly sauntered away from the ATF rookie. They kept to the edge of things, where the black char gave way to just dead vegetation. It had been a wide grassy field on one side, with the adjoining property home to a contented herd of cows. Well, previously contented.

They continued skirting the zone. The other side of the warehouse backed up to thin woods. The nearest trees had become instant kindling and ignited ones farther out. Those were the spot fires that the funeral attendees helped extinguish. Hank kicked at a burned branch lying in front of him and it crumbled under his boot. 'How the hell are we going to recover anything out of this mess?'

'I don't know,' Bart said. 'But y'all going to need equipment. You can't get closer without protection. Hell, even this far away, we should have respirators on.'

Hank thought about Maggie. She'd kill him if she knew. No one was bigger on safety than his doctor wife. Bart read his mind.

'I only had to send one guy over to your wife at Branson Valley General. And that was because he tripped over a beam. Twisted something. So I'm pretty pleased, considering.'

Hank let out a half-laugh, half-sigh. 'And I was hoping – as I drove down here, before I saw this – that she would do a brisk business. That there would be survivors.'

He stopped and contemplated the wreckage. They were just about to the front entrance. He could see the concrete walkway leading to what now was nothing but one lonely beam tilting diagonally toward the sunrise. A firefighter materialized out of the haze behind it and bent over with his hands on his knees. After a moment, he pulled himself upright and carefully walked toward them. He nodded at his boss and turned to Hank.

'We haven't gone in very deep to see everything,' he garbled at Hank through his mask. 'But this here might be where you want to start.'

All Hank could see of him through the mask were his eyes.

They were red and weepy. Hank didn't think it was due to the smoke. 'How many?'

'Three right inside. They . . .' he trailed off and just stood there, slumped against the smoke like it was holding him up.

'You can head on home, Jim,' Bart said. 'Springfield FD will be here any minute. They'll assist all the law enforcement.'

Jim gave an exhausted nod and shuffled away. Bart rubbed at his mustache again, this time getting black on his chin. 'From what I saw the times I went closer, and what my guys have told me, we don't know exactly where it started. But we haven't gotten into the thick of it, not truly. That'll be today. And you'll have experts.'

Hank scoffed. 'Yeah, lucky me.' He turned toward the sound of large vehicles arriving in the staging area. He hoped it was Springfield fire trucks and not the ATF. Either way, it was time to face them. He slapped Bart on the shoulder. 'You and your people go get some rest.'

The fire chief didn't move. 'My crews, yeah. Not me. My county, my fire scene. I'm not going anywhere.'

Hank looked at him. He was thinking the same thing. Even with all the specialists, this was his responsibility. His county. His disaster.

EIGHT

'Well, somebody sure fucked up.'

The ATF agent stood there, hands on her hips and windbreaker bunched around her waist. Hank hoped she wasn't referring to Bart.

'Warehouses don't just explode.'

'Not usually, no,' Hank said.

She gave him the side-eye and pulled her baseball cap lower on her head. 'You have the site secured all night?'

No, we thought we'd give tours. 'Yes.'

'How many inside?'

'Fourteen. That's how many have been reported missing.'

Her gaze swept over the scene with its jutting building scraps and smoking crater. She pointed past the incinerated cars in the parking lot to the hulk of a semi-truck. 'That the loading dock?'

Hank pulled out the building layout that the Marine kid had sketched out for Sam. 'Yes.'

'Where are the rest of the trucks?'

He had no idea how many trucks they even had. When he told her that, she pulled her phone out of her back pocket and started typing.

'Look, Faye Halliday – the owner – is in pretty bad shape,' he said. 'We've been trying to get her calmed down.'

She looked up at Hank. She was medium height and came up just below his shoulder. With the cap pulled so low, it was the first time he was able to see her full face. She had high cheekbones and a recent sunburn that hadn't completely faded from her olive skin. Her eyes were brown and narrowed in annoyance.

'I don't care. Find out how many they have total. She should know that off the top of her head. This isn't that big an operation. Then try to find out where they are. What are the delivery routes? I want to get my hands on a truck. At least one. Preferably all of them. And absolutely before they make their deliveries.'

Hank stared at her in horror. 'You think there's something

wrong with the fireworks themselves? Like the packaged ones out for delivery to retail stores?'

'I don't know what I think yet. All I do know is that I want those fireworks. They're all that's left of this damn business. So I want to talk to that owner immediately. And anybody else who would have that information.'

'She's it.' Hank gestured at the remains of the warehouse. 'Everyone else is in there.'

'All right. You've got my team. They'll start on the forensics, help you with accessing areas you need.' She pivoted toward a black SUV. 'Tell your man I'm coming, and that then he can leave.' She paused and a flash of something like sympathy crossed her sunburned face. 'The owner is mine. The dead are yours.'

The dead were a problem. They could be found, extracted and transported, but then the process came to an abrupt halt – right at the door of a vacant pathologist's office. Damn that Whittaker. He was proving to be as irritating in death as he had been in life. Sheila drummed her fingers on the arm of her recliner and stared at the wall.

She knew no one was rushing to replace him. The private company that employed him was headquartered out of state and could barely staff the office with medical assistants and secretaries, let alone find another doctor specializing in forensic pathology at a moment's notice. So where could she find one? One willing to come when she used phrases like 'limited resources and facilities' and 'massive explosion' and 'fourteen'.

Her fingers stopped their tapping and drifted over to the laptop keyboard. She typed and clicked and clicked some more, and then picked up the phone. She hated and usually refused to plead for anything. But since the situation was so urgent, and there was no one around to witness her doing it, she decided she'd completely prostrate herself if she had to.

She dialed the 573 area code number.

'Oh,' said the young man who answered after she punched through several phone menus and identified herself as Branson County's chief deputy sheriff. 'Oh, hot damn. We were hoping you'd need us.'

Well. She hadn't even said what she wanted. Now she was

speechless with surprise. And the excited kid on the other end of the line was hollering at someone in the background. 'Uh, sorry. Yes, ma'am. We, um, stand ready to assist. We heard, 'course, about the explosion yesterday.' The background noise was getting louder. 'My professor would like to talk to you. Ma'am. Is that OK? With you, ma'am?'

This was a young person she could grow to tolerate. She answered in the affirmative and a deeper, obviously not-twenty-something voice came on the line.

Ten minutes later, she had a new colleague in Professor Tom Watanabe, MD, half a dozen medical interns and residents ready to drive to the blast site, and the resources of the entire University of Missouri, Columbia Department of Pathology (forensic subspecialty) at her disposal. She almost wept. Instead she just said thank you.

'And I'll tell the officers out at the scene to expect your people in about four or five hours,' she said.

'I'm also going to call a friend of mine over in the anthropology department,' Watanabe said. 'He's a professor emeritus in forensic anthropology. They're the best ones to work with burned remains. My students can assist. This'll be great experience for them to see a case all the way from transport to autopsy. And to work under conditions that aren't . . . well, aren't as fully funded as we are here at the university hospital.'

'Oh, you can say it. We are definitely a shoestring operation down here.'

'On that front, I should ask – how many autopsy tables are at Whittaker's facility?'

'Two.'

Watanabe's sigh was a blend of despair and irritation. 'The resources that rural counties don't get. I'm always infuriated.'

'You and me both.'

He chuckled. 'I'll go directly to your morgue. I'd like all the deceased taken there, and then we can decide if we need to transport some of them up here to Columbia.'

'However you'd like to do it.' Sheila tried to keep the relief out of her voice. Now Hank wouldn't be out there collecting bodies without someone to receive them. She tried to picture him at the scene but her mind's eye could see only the smoking crater footage shown by the news helicopters. The painkillers made thinking so difficult. She forced her foggy brain back to the conversation as she realized Dr Watanabe had a question.

'I was just asking if I'd see you there? At Whittaker's facility?'

She looked around her claustrophobic living room. Tyrone was at work. Her walker was dusty and poised for action by the front door. Her car keys were in her purse. She gritted her teeth and lifted herself out of the recliner.

'Yes. Yes, you will. I'll meet you there.'

All that work calming Faye Halliday down evaporated within five minutes of the ATF agent walking in the door. Sam sat next to the poor woman on her cousin's plaid sofa and swore to himself.

'The delivery schedules, ma'am. Or your company computer log-in. I'll take either one, but I want it right now.'

The lady had introduced herself as Angela Alvarado and immediately invited Sam to leave. Hank's orders still ringing in his ears, he politely declined. 'Don't you dare go anywhere,' Hank had said. 'She'll do her questioning however she wants, you can't stop that. But don't leave Faye alone. And let me know what they both say as soon as you can.'

Sam shifted awkwardly and handed Mrs Halliday a tissue. Molly March had thoughtfully brought two boxes when she came to stay overnight. Mrs Halliday had her elderly cousin to keep her company, but Hank didn't necessarily trust that the old lady would prevent her from running if she decided to make a break for it.

'She's not a suspect. But she's not *not* a suspect, either. We don't know yet if she cut safety corners,' Hank had said. So Molly took the overnight shift and now Sam was back, and he was now not *not* really irritated.

'Maybe we should slow down here.' He frowned at Agent Alvarado as Mrs Halliday sobbed beside him. 'Let everybody catch their breath.'

'Only one person needs to do that.' Agent Alvarado pinned Mrs Halliday with an exasperated stare. 'And by all accounts, that person is lucky to still be breathing at all. So maybe she owes it to the ones who aren't breathing anymore to help us out with some critical information.'

Damn. That was cold. And it acted like a slap. Mrs Halliday dropped her tissued hands to her lap and glared right back at Alvarado. Sam inched away from them both.

'My husband is dead. My friends and employees are dead.'

'Yeah, I know. And I want to make sure no one else dies. Don't you?'

Sam increased his distance.

'You think we did something wrong. With our safety procedures.'

'I don't know what the hell happened,' Alvarado said. 'I don't know if it was you. I don't know if it was bad fireworks that you stored and possibly also have already distributed all over the place. I don't know anything yet. Which is why you're going to cooperate.' The last bit was accompanied by a finger jab. Sam had now reached the edge of the sofa and could go no farther. Mrs Halliday tossed the crumpled tissue at the coffee table – or at Alvarado, if you took the less charitable view – and rose to her feet.

'Tuesdays are northern Missouri. Wednesdays are the St Louis area. And yeah, we were gearing up for the Fourth, so we had more inventory than normal, but the standard amount for this time of year.'

'Vehicle records show you have four semi-trucks registered to your company. Is that correct?'

'Yes.'

'Do you know which one was still at the warehouse?'

Mrs Halliday sank back on to the sofa. 'One was still there? Oh, no.'

'We need to know which one. That'll narrow down which license plate numbers we're putting alerts out for. And help us identify the driver when it comes time for that.'

Mrs Halliday let out a wail. Sam glared at Ms Alvarado as the cousin rushed into the room. The agent sighed and leaned back in her chair. 'I also need those living drivers' cell phone numbers,' she told him.

Sam looked pointedly at Mrs Halliday, huddled and inconsolable in her cousin's arms. Then he swung his gaze back to Alvarado and tried to keep the reprimand out of his tone. 'Well, ma'am, then you might want to make yourself comfortable, 'cause it's going to be a while.'

NINE

The first one was Paula Timmons. She lay a dozen yards from what had been the building entrance. She'd been thrown by the force of the explosion, landing against a retaining wall that had battered her beyond recognition. Except her hair. The silver-gray bob shown in family photos on last night's news was in a still somewhat recognizable state. He knelt down. Nothing had fallen on her that would impede an easy extraction once the fire marshal investigator with him was done.

Now he stood and took a step away. He told himself that his breathing was ragged only because of the tight respirator over his face. He turned away from Paula and saw two others in what had been the little lobby leading into the warehouse interior. They would be more difficult to get to. Rubble covered the top half of the nearer body. The other one had a beam tilted precariously across the legs. That would all need to be photographed, sketched, probably swabbed, definitely tagged, and then removed before they could get to the bodies. He stared at the shriveled left arm of the second person, locked in a bicep curl position with the hand frozen into a contorted claw. He couldn't see enough of the skull to get a look at any hair.

He carefully walked out to the perimeter before pulling out his phone and calling Sheila. When she didn't answer, he left a message asking her to pull the driver's license photos of all the probable victims. Having possible hairdos could help speed up identifications. He didn't go back to Paula. State and now ATF investigators were everywhere, and he knew if he got closer he'd just be in the way. So he started to circle the site, a ghoul looking for ghosts. He made loop after loop and slowly another flag would appear, marking possible remains. He pulled out his copy of Sam's warehouse floor plan and made his own pencil marks where he thought the bodies lay. And he counted.

When the flags reached fourteen, he took a deep breath and stopped his circling. Then number fifteen went up. Sixteen, seventeen, eighteen in quick succession, blooming from a spot near the worst of the damage. And he kicked himself. With all the different agencies and authorities competing for his attention, he'd been able to avoid thinking it through. *Find fourteen bodies and we're done.* But an explosion blew things apart. There were going to be pieces. Nineteen, twenty. He watched another bloom rise on the other side of the site and had to turn away.

He walked into the surviving trees and wandered around for a moment. An excited hubbub of conversation penetrated his thoughts and he emerged to find the pathology students from Mizzou crowding the staging area. He headed over to greet them, pulling off his respirator and taking several gulping breaths as he walked. It helped ease the tightness in his chest, if not the heaviness in his heart. He reached the group and said hello. They all looked like kids, except a woman who had to be their chief resident. She was older – although still young – and had an air of authority as she stood talking to the paramedic, Larry Alcoate. Larry waved Bart Giacalone over as Hank approached. The two men launched into a debate about additional transportation resources as Hank introduced himself to the resident, a woman with medium brown skin and close-cut hair named Ngozi Aguta.

'We're glad to help.' She looked out over the site. 'It's going to be really good training for us. We're just waiting for . . . ah, here he is.'

An older white man approached, paying no attention to the little group. He only had eyes for the wreckage. He stood and stared for several minutes before turning. 'Doug Nielsen. I'm your forensic anthropologist. And it looks like I'm going to be here a while.'

He'd been tall once but now was settled into a gentle stoop, likely the result of a lifetime bending toward the ground and the bones it held. He had a tufty ring of hair around his otherwise bald head and an analytical gaze. He didn't bother shaking Hank's hand. He looked at Aguta. 'You the pathologist?'

She nodded.

'Wish we had anthropologists instead. We might need to call more in.' He waved at the multiplying flags. 'But you're better than nothing, I suppose.'

She smirked at Hank behind his back and then followed as he

walked over to her cluster of medical students. Hank turned back to the rubble, his respirator dangling from his hand, and couldn't keep himself from counting again.

They were up to thirty-one.

Professor Tom Watanabe was in full charge of his borrowed morgue by the time Sheila arrived. He had Whittaker's assistant getting things ready for the impending arrivals and was patiently telling the front desk worker what she would need to do with the paperwork. Neither woman had the edginess Sheila was used to seeing from them. They moved calmly and spoke quietly. Even the room felt different. Hushed and waiting – but in a serene way, not a nervous one. That hadn't been the way before, with Whittaker bouncing around, chortling and waving his pudgy hands in the air. Instead, a tall thin man with a slight stoop and black hair streaked with gray looked up from the autopsy table and started to smile a greeting. It froze on his face as he got a look at her.

She wanted to say it was due to her wearing a sweat suit in a professional setting. But he likely hadn't even noticed that, what with the wheelchair and all. And the impertinent off-duty deputy pushing it.

'I'm so sorry.' Watanabe looked aghast. 'I didn't know you were ill. I wouldn't have asked you to come.'

Sheila waved off the comment, then wrapped her arms around her middle in an effort to contain the pain. 'It's fine. I'm fine. I needed to get out of the house anyway.'

Behind her, Austin Lorentzen snorted in disagreement. She ignored him. They'd gotten into it when the rookie deputy insisted she take the wheelchair instead of the walker. Said if she didn't, he would refuse to drive her. So he won that one. She wasn't going to give him the satisfaction of winning anything else. She tried to sit up straight and smile at the pathologist.

'So have your students given you any updates from the scene?' She hoped it sounded like she was curious about their education instead of fishing for information because she was out of the loop.

'They should be here any minute with the first two,' Watanabe said. 'I gather these ones were the most easily removed from the wreckage. Your man at the scene gave Dr Aguta a likely ID on one, so that'll be helpful.'

Her man at the scene. She almost chuckled but winced and stopped herself just in time. Laughter was not her best medicine right now. She gestured to Lorentzen, who sighed and unhooked her purse from the back of the wheelchair. He pulled out a sheaf of papers and handed it to the doctor.

'These are the driver's license photos of the fourteen people we're fairly certain were in the warehouse,' Sheila said. 'Hank said the hair was intact on at least one body, so we thought the pictures might help if other ones are in the same state. But in case things turn more difficult and you need to do DNA, I also have next-of-kin information. They are all ready and willing to be swabbed.'

'Wonderful. Thank you. I hope it won't come to that, but—'

The doors slid open and everyone turned except Sheila, who couldn't twist her torso if her life depended on it. She sat staring at the far wall until Lorentzen noticed and spun her chair around so she could see. Two young men in the same twenty-something age range as her deputy rolled a pair of gurneys over and slid the body bags on to the cold metal tables. Watanabe donned nitrile surgical gloves in one smooth motion and bent toward the first bag. He held out his hand and one of the kids gave him a clipboard. He compared the number on the paperwork with the number on the bag then straightened.

'So, based on this, we know nothing. Not ID, not gender, not approximate weight or height, not race or ethnicity. No clothing, no surviving identifying marks.' He eyed the clipboard and then his junior doctors and spoke again in the same even cadence and kind tone. 'So what *do* you know?'

'This one – uh, this deceased – was found near the front door of the warehouse,' the shorter one said. 'Aside from the burns, there are no other obvious signs of trauma. Gray scalp hair remains somewhat intact and appears to be a woman's style. But that's not a fact, just an observation.'

Watanabe nodded. 'Good. Now let's see what else we can learn.'

He stepped away and pointed at the shorter junior, who carefully unzipped the body bag. The hair almost glowed under the bright morgue lights and made the shriveled brown and black of the body even more horrifying.

Sheila glanced up at Lorentzen and saw what little color there was in his handsome white face drain right out. If she were white, she might've gone pale, too. As it was, she swallowed hard and tried to focus on Watanabe and not the corpse. The taller junior moved over to the second body bag. Behind her, Lorentzen shuddered. She didn't blame him. It was a brutal way to see what were likely his first dead bodies. And he wasn't even on duty. She'd pulled him in after a long shift directing snarled traffic near the blast site. He was one of the only deputies available and, as luck would have it, the least likely to rat her out to Hank.

Watanabe stopped the shorter one and had them put the probable Paula Timmons in the cooler first. He ticked off space on his fingers. 'Do we know how many deceased are intact?'

'At least three. We don't know about the rest. Although we do know for sure that some definitely aren't.'

'To be expected,' Watanabe said. 'We'll need to get all of those up to Columbia. We'll have to run them through the CT. Even the intact ones, so we can get a start on the actual causes of death.'

Behind her, Lorentzen made a puzzled noise. Watanabe smiled. 'Burns, right? That's what you're thinking. Pretty darn obvious. But . . .'

The two students grinned at each other. The one closer to Sheila leaned toward her with a stage whisper. 'You're in for it now.'

'There are multiple possibilities in an explosion like this,' Watanabe said. 'Blunt force trauma – falling debris – could kill someone before the body burns. Or high-velocity projectiles sent flying by the explosion can be the cause of death. Sometimes with fires, it's smoke and toxin inhalation. But here, the explosion was likely too severe for anyone to have lived long enough to inhale enough for that to be the cause of death. And if it's a high-order explosion, you get pulmonary barotrauma and abdominal hemorrhage because there's a supersonic blast wave.'

Lorentzen groaned. The taller junior eyed him and started to say something when his phone buzzed. 'They're almost here with the third one.'

Sheila breathed a sigh of relief. Like the young Lorentzen, she had no desire to learn more. She let him roll her out of the way as the doors swung open and the next fatality arrived.

TEN

'Did they tell you I've got one of your deputies in my ER?'

Hank stopped cold with his phone pressed to his ear. He was halfway down the dirt track leading to all the parked emergency vehicles as his wife repeated the question.

'No,' he finally responded. Dread uncoiled in his stomach. 'I haven't heard anything. What the hell happened? Who is it?'

'Derek Orvan.'

'What the hell happened, Maggie?' He knew his voice was rising in pitch but he couldn't stop it. He couldn't count to fifteen. Please, no.

'Hank, honey. He'll be OK. I'm keeping him for a while, though. Apparently he got hit by a car. Broken leg. He's getting X-rayed right now. There might be hip damage, too.'

Orvan had been on traffic duty. 'Did he tell you how it happened?'

'The driver was looking the other way, to merge I guess, and just smacked into him as he stood there. Knocked him several feet and did a number on his leg.'

He had too few deputies as it was, especially with Sheila on leave. Now to have Orvan – one of the few who was both competent and helpful – out as well was a brutal blow. Thank God his injuries weren't worse.

'Can you let me know when you release him?' he said.

'Sure.' She paused. 'And now I want to know how you're doing.'

He didn't want to tell her. He started to walk again, a slow trudge that left scrape marks in the sooty dirt.

'What time do you get off?' Her shifts as the hospital's attending emergency room physician could be as unexpectedly long as his own. 'Your dad will feed the kids frozen pizza and French fries for dinner again unless somebody stops him.'

'Supposedly at four o'clock. I could hit the grocery store on

the way home. Make something for tonight that doesn't involve
massive amounts of cheese.'

He reached his squad car and was opening the door when he
heard Maggie's pager go off.

'That's me. I gotta go.' She inserted a pause that said what
words couldn't. Then: 'I love you. Don't tear yourself apart,
OK?'

It was too late for that.

He really needed to stop answering his phone.

'There's a whole mess of them at the bottom of the driveway.
Crying and yelling. Wanting to know where Faye Halliday is.'

'Did you tell them she isn't there?'

'Heck, yeah. Repeatedly. They don't believe us. "You're not
officers, what the hell do you know?" is what they're saying.'
Alice Randall sighed. 'It sure would be nice to have a deputy
out here to help us out.'

Despite everything, Hank smiled. He could picture the petite
evidence technician standing there in her crime scene coveralls
and attempting to placate an emotional crowd with rational argu-
ments. If anyone could do it, she could. But he felt horrible that
she was having to try.

'I'm sorry I don't have anybody to spare,' he said.

'Oh, good heavens. I know you all got your hands full. I just
wanted to let you know what was going on.'

'Have you been able to process the house at all?'

'Kurt's getting a lot done inside. Bastard won the coin toss.
That's why I'm the one stuck out here watching this herd of cats.
I'm supposed to be searching the garage.'

Despite the name-calling, he knew she and Kurt Gatz were
great professional partners and good friends. And highly skilled
sheriff's department technicians, able to collect and process
evidence from almost any scene. Any scene but a huge explosion,
which was why they were available to go through the Halliday
house looking for anything related to negligence, malfeasance, or
whatever else might have played a part in the warehouse disaster.

'Eeep.' An indignant squeak. 'There's another one trying to
sneak through the bushes again.' She moved the phone away and
yelled at someone for a good thirty seconds, then came back

with a sigh. 'We don't have guns, so they know they can ignore us and keep coming back.'

Grief deserved a lot of leeway, but not that much. Hank reached down to his belt and the holster attached to it. He could look at Sheila's next-of-kin list later. 'Hang tight. I'll be there in ten minutes.'

There were only about a dozen of them but they were definitely, to use Alice's words, making 'an all-fire ruckus'. Yelling and milling around at the end of the Halliday driveway. Hank could see the house down at the end and the crime scene van parked out front. He watched for a moment and then walked straight through the group and turned to face them. Everyone fell quiet. A guilty, teacher-returns-to-the-classroom quiet. Some shifted from foot to foot and others stared uncomfortably at their shoes. Only beet-faced Jerry Ustus stood his ground, glaring at Hank with his hands on his hips.

'I know that you want answers. But this isn't the way to do it. You can't be out here. You definitely can't be trespassing.'

'We want to talk to Faye,' Ustus said. Mutters of agreement came from several others.

No, you want to yell at Faye. 'Faye's not here. She won't be here. So there's no point in you all waiting around.'

'What'd she do, run away?'

'No. Not at all. She's cooperating fully.' That generated mutters of disagreement and one coughed 'bullshit'.

Hank stifled a sigh. 'Look, she really is busy helping us.'

That was a stretch, but Sam and ATF Alvarado had at least finally gotten delivery schedules and driver phone numbers out of her. Not much else, though.

'We're one big family,' Ustus said in a snide singsong voice. 'That's what they always told my son. And everybody else. And now she's abandoned everyone.'

Another swell of muttering. Hank nodded in sympathy and waited for it to die down. If they left feeling like they'd been listened to, maybe they wouldn't come back. And they would be leaving. That was for damn sure. Because he didn't have time for this. So he needed to lead them where he wanted them to go.

'Do you want my department investigating what happened?'
Emphatic agreement.

'The Missouri Division of Fire Safety – the state fire marshals
– and the ATF, they're here too, with all their resources. Do you
want them working on this?'

'Well, maybe not the feds,' a lady in the back grumbled. Hank
bit back a smile.

'My point is that all of us are putting everything into this.
Because we know how important it is to you. To the whole community. But you being here takes away from that. It takes away from
me investigating and,' he paused and swung his arm toward the
house, 'it takes away from the department evidence team doing
their job. If she's busy stopping you from sneaking through the
bushes, then she can't be looking for answers, can she?'

Even Ustus had the grace to look sheepish at that.

'That's what they're doing up there?' said a rotund man
standing off to the side.

'Yeah.'

'So you are thinking Faye did something wrong?'

Hank put his hands up in a 'stop' motion. 'Nope. Not at all.'
Maybe. Possibly. Not going to tell you that. 'You know everything
was destroyed. Records, paperwork. We're just looking to see if
there are copies here. That's it.'

'Can't you get that stuff from the computer cloud?'

'We are. But again, we are doing everything possible. Every
single avenue will be looked at. For you and your families.'

He punctuated that by crossing his arms and looking expect-
antly at the group. They slowly began to shuffle back to their
cars, mumbling to one another and throwing glances back at
Hank. Eventually, Ustus was the only one left.

'Look, Jerry. I will keep you updated.' He paused. He'd learned
long ago not to tell a grieving relative that he 'knew' how they
felt. 'I can only imagine how hard this is for you. We will do
everything we can.'

Ustus stared at him, and the house, the trees, the sky. A father
lost in the wilderness.

'I don't know what to do.' This time his voice was small,
broken. 'It's just me and him. Was just me and him. This was
his first real grown-up job. Full time, benefits. He was so proud

of himself. He . . .' The poor man broke down. Hank stayed with him for the ten minutes it took for him to recover enough to walk to his car. Then he turned and made his way up to the house, where Kurt stood on the steps with an evidence bag in his hands and a frown on his face.

They needed a representative at the morgue. And Sam was the only one available. So now he sat in the building's parking lot as day slipped into night and apprehension slid into dread. He did not want to go through those doors. He did not want to see what was inside. So many. So burned.

Hank said he didn't need to stay for autopsies. Just track which numbered bodies went up to Columbia and which stayed here. Be available if anyone had questions. Or needed department resources.

Maybe he could do all that from the lobby. He eyed the front door. Then slouched down until his forehead rested on the steering wheel. He was being ridiculous. He'd seen dead bodies before. Hell, he'd been the one to find dead bodies. That one out in the woods. And that other one, in the crevice in the woods. Now that he thought about it, he kind of had a niche. Ha, ha. So why was he freaking out now? He clunked his head against the wheel and thought about it.

Those had been sudden discoveries. No time to obsess. No opportunity to spin himself into a ball of worry. Also, a lot fewer bodies.

He made himself raise his head and look again at the entrance doors. It was only going to get worse the longer he sat here. Before he could change his mind, he swung open the squad car door and got out. He straightened his uniform shirt, grabbed his file folder, and marched into the building. Purposefully not giving himself time to think, he walked straight past the reception desk into the morgue itself. And stopped in horror.

'What the hell?'

Sheila looked up at him and sighed. 'You shouldn't have come all this way. You could be working other aspects.'

Sam spluttered then jabbed a finger at her. 'We didn't know you were here. Hank sure as hell doesn't know you're here. He's going to be so pissed off.'

She unwound one arm and flicked a few fingers at him. It was a pale imitation of her typical dismissive wave. 'He already yelled at me yesterday.'

'You should've listened.' All of his morgue fears came pouring out. 'You should be home. You should definitely not be sitting in a cold morgue in your pajamas when you aren't even well enough to walk.'

She raised a defiant eyebrow at him. It appeared to be the only thing she could move properly. She sat slumped in the wheelchair with her arms wrapped around her middle. Her legs had to be supported by the chair's footplates and she was wearing Crocs, for God's sake.

'This is a sweat suit, not pajamas. And the wheelchair is faster, that's all.'

Just in time, Sam stopped himself from saying 'bullshit' right to her face. He straightened to his full gawky height and dragged his eyes away from her wretched form. He glanced right past Austin Lorentzen, who was standing in the corner, and focused on the bodies for the first time. Two of them, on the tables. Burned to a crisp like he'd imagined. Three doctors stood around them, all staring at him with gloved hands suspended mid-air. He felt his face go red hot.

'This is Deputy Sam Karnes.' Sheila's voice was calm and measured. 'He might have some additional information from the scene.'

He wanted to glare at her but refrained. He didn't need to look more unhinged than he already did. He cleared his throat and pulled out his paperwork.

'I'm supposed to let you know that we've narrowed down which delivery driver was in the building. Three of the four have been accounted for. Ned Wickham is the one who's missing. His wife says she hasn't heard from him since he left for work early Tuesday.'

'Excellent,' the oldest doctor, a tall Asian man with salt-and-pepper hair, said in a warm tone that inexplicably made Sam feel better. 'We have a list. Perhaps you could . . .?' He pointed at a small shelf in the corner.

'I brought you an updated one,' Sam said. He was starting to feel on firmer footing. Like a professional again. As long as he didn't look at Sheila. He focused on the doctor. 'I also have a layout of the building for you.'

The sheriff's department records clerk had worked with the county planning people to pull the Skyrocket blueprints and distribute copies to all the involved agencies. He pulled it out of the file and unfolded it for the first time. It was bigger than he'd expected, probably three feet by four. He looked around for a place to put it.

'I'll find some tape. Then we can hang it.' Austin detached himself from the corner wall he was leaning against and left the room. Sam thought for a second and followed him.

'You must be who drove her up here, right?' Sam said once they were in the otherwise deserted lobby. Austin responded with an exaggeratedly helpless look.

'Bro, you know I couldn't tell her no. That is not how that lady works.'

'Oh, I know.'

'I at least was able to get her in the wheelchair. She wanted to take the walker.'

'Jesus. She can't even stand up.'

'I know. But now that you're here, maybe she'll let me take her home.'

They both had a good laugh at that. Then Sam grew serious. 'How you doing?' he asked the rookie deputy. 'With the bodies and all?'

Austin rooted around in the receptionist's desk for a minute before answering. 'It's not what I wanted to be doing during my twelve hours off, that's for sure. They . . . it . . . well, I don't think I'm going to sleep good for a while. Let's just say that.'

He plucked a roll of tape out of a drawer and waved it. They returned to the morgue and attached it to the wall with the best visibility. Austin returned to his corner, carefully avoiding any glance at the tables. Sam took a step back to take the blueprint in more fully. Something was off. He rubbed at his ear and stared at it.

'What do you see, Sammy?' Sheila said quietly. She'd somehow rolled up behind him.

He reached into his back pocket and pulled out a creased and smudged paper. He slowly unfolded it but didn't look at it. He knew what it showed. 'This is what the former employee drew for me, the one who just quit to enlist in the Marines.' He held it so Sheila could see.

'It's not the same.'

'No,' Sam said, pointing to a room that wasn't on the county plans. 'It most definitely is not.'

Hank looked down at the Skyrocket invoices spread across the dining-room table. It was past midnight and everyone was asleep. His only company was Guapo, gnawing on a bone under his chair. He shuffled some of the papers and added more numbers to his notes. His first conclusion was that the investigation needed a forensic accountant. His second was that at least he was capable of basic addition. He circled two dollar amounts and sat back.

'Don't tell me you're balancing your checkbook at this time of night.'

Duncan stood in the archway between the dining and living rooms, his arthritic body wrapped in a robe even though the June night was plenty warm.

'No. I'm trying to figure out how much debt Skyrocket is in.'

Dunc shuffled closer. 'Why does it matter? It's not like they blew up their warehouse for an insurance payout. The owner was inside, for heaven's sake.'

'One of the owners was inside,' Hank corrected. 'But yes, you're right. We don't suspect insurance fraud. It's more the question of what were they doing to get out of that debt? Were they storing too many fireworks? Were they storing them improperly? So if I know how much they owe, maybe it's a place to start.' He shrugged. 'Plus, I couldn't sleep.'

'Ah. Well, you're in good company there. I couldn't either.' He turned toward the kitchen. 'I'm going to make a cup of tea. You want one?'

Hank looked at him in surprise. 'Sure. Thanks.'

'You gotta come with me. I don't deliver.'

Of course not. Hank smiled to himself as he followed his father-in-law. Soon they were sitting at the kitchen table with hot camomile. Dunc updated him on the kids' latest trip to the park and complained about Mrs Crawford and the stinky new shrubs she planted next to their shared property line.

'Is that where that smell is coming from?' Hank said. 'I'd been wondering about that.'

'I've half a mind to take your electric hedge clippers and have a go at them.'

Hank put down his mug. 'Don't you dare. They're on her property.'

Dunc gave a dismissive wave. 'I'm old. I get confused easily. I might not know where the property line is.'

'You're only seventy-three.'

'Well, thank you.'

'It wasn't supposed to be a compliment. I was just pointing out that you can't pull the doddering old man bit on people. Everybody knows better.'

Dunc grinned. 'Eh, you don't have enough faith in me. Every once in a while I can pull something over on somebody.' He stood and put his mug in the sink. 'So a good night to you, boy-o. I'll see you in the morning.'

He left Hank alone with his cooling tea and the sneaking suspicion that one of those times had just happened. His thoughts had been artfully tugged away from the investigation. Sometimes the old man really was good company.

ELEVEN

Smoke continued to rise from the crater, weary tendrils curling skyward. Better than yesterday's angry plumes, Hank thought as he once again stood in the early morning gloom. It looked more like a graveyard now than it had under last night's spotlights – even though the bodies were gone. Ghost-suited evidence techs flitted through the rubble in eerie silence. Concrete chunks jutted up like headstones, and one brave crow had laid claim to the top of a tall beam, where he watched but didn't comment.

Gravel crunched behind him and he turned to see Larry Alcoate approach. He raised a questioning eyebrow and his friend shrugged.

'They want an ambulance on standby. Just in case.' He looked around. 'There are a lot more people here than I expected.'

Hank took a sip of his coffee. 'That's what you get with a fully funded federal agency. And a decently funded state fire marshal.'

Larry stuffed his hands in his pockets. 'So basically anybody who isn't reliant on our miserly county commission, that what you're saying?'

Hank snorted and took another drink. Larry looked around.

'Bart finally go home?'

'Yeah. Last night about midnight. He could barely stand up. I had Deputy Gabler take him home. I didn't trust him to drive.'

Larry eyeballed him. 'You can't be much better, dude.'

'Eh. I've at least slept. Got about four hours last night.'

Now it was Larry's turn to snort. He started to follow it with a wise-ass remark but was cut off.

'Worth. We need to talk.'

Both men startled and turned. ATF Agent Alvarado had somehow approached without sound and stood directly behind them.

Hank tried to ignore the hot coffee now dripping down his

hand. 'Good morning. Nice to see you. What can I help you with?'

'You can tell me why the hell I got a middle-of-the-night email from you with what looks like a child's drawing of a floorplan. And why the hell it doesn't appear to match your county's official records.'

Sammy's sketch hadn't been that bad.

'I sent it because I thought you'd be interested. And I have no idea why the hell it doesn't match the county plans.'

'Your source for it – did he know what the room was for?'

'The former employee? No, he didn't know. Which in itself is pretty odd.'

She frowned. 'Considering that it wasn't otherwise that complicated of a building and there weren't that many employees, yeah, I'd have to agree with you. He, and everybody, should've known something about it just by virtue of working there. So what was stored there and how was it stored?'

'I think those questions are better directed at Faye Halliday,' he said.

'No kidding,' she said. 'That's why I'm talking to you. I want to borrow your interrogation room.'

'Most people just ask for a cup of sugar,' Larry muttered.

Her head swiveled toward Larry and Hank took a step back. But she just chuckled. 'That's because most people bake cookies. I bake suspects.' She turned back to Hank. 'And that's what Ms Halliday is turning in to.' The look on her face dared Hank to contradict her.

He nodded instead. 'Absolutely. She isn't exactly being forthcoming. I heard you and Sam Karnes tried for hours yesterday.'

'Yeah. I gave her a chance to do it in the comfort of a nice living room with her cousin holding her hand. Now . . .'

'Now you want my Formica table and hard plastic chairs?'

'Exactly.'

'It's all yours. On one condition.'

'What's that?'

'I get to be there.'

She laughed. 'You play hardball. Fine. Can your deputy bring her in?'

Molly March was the one babysitting her at the moment. Hank

nodded. They arranged a time later in the day and she walked away as her phone started to buzz.

'So she's the price you're paying for all this crime scene help?' Larry asked.

Hank wiped his coffeed hand on his jeans. 'Yep.'

Larry pondered her retreating figure and then looked at Hank with a glint in his eye. 'Totally, totally worth it.'

Hank stared at his friend in surprise. He was about to say something when a technician with a cut finger approached and Larry left to get the first-aid supplies. Hank watched them go and then circled the site. He didn't know why he was here. There was nothing he could do. He didn't have the specialized forensic skills needed to process the scene. So he was pretty much just in the way. He scolded himself. He really had grown used to being in charge in the year and a half since he became sheriff. So much so, he was enviously haunting an incident scene that rightly wasn't his.

He forced more energy into his step and headed back to his car. He could get other things done until it came time to interview Faye Halliday. None of the technicians paid him any attention. It served him right that only the crow noticed him leave.

Sheila was silent on the ride to the morgue, thinking about the case. Sam was silent, fuming about having to chauffeur her. At least that's what she assumed from the look on his face. When they got there, he wrenched her wheelchair out of the back of his Bronco and unfolded it with more force than the manufacturer probably recommended.

'There. Get in.'

She raised a reprimanding eyebrow and was met by a finger jab in the air. She drew back in surprise.

'Don't. You. Even.' He scowled and jabbed again. 'You're the one in the wrong here. Not me. You're putting back your healing by . . . I don't know . . . weeks.'

She settled herself in the chair and started to roll herself toward the building. Damn, it was difficult. Her arms hurt after four swipes at the wheels and every movement shot pain through her middle. She was on a fifth agonizing rotation when Sam grabbed the handles and pushed her quickly through the doors, past the reception desk and straight into the morgue. He wheeled her over and stuck her in the corner Austin had occupied yesterday. She wanted to be over by the wall with the building blueprint and better view of the tables. But she looked at his expression and held her tongue. No need for impressionable young doctors to see a law enforcement officer lose his shit over a wheelchair parking spot.

'Thank you for the ride,' she said. 'I'll give you a call when I'm ready to be picked up.'

'I don't know,' he said with razor-sharp politeness. 'Maybe I'll be too busy. Maybe I'll send Tyrone. Or Dr McCleary.'

Tyrone didn't know she was here, and her husband didn't know she'd come yesterday, either. Neither did Hank's wife, the doctor who'd told her to stay in bed. That was because Austin Lorentzen hadn't ratted her out and she knew Sammy wouldn't either. Although the glare he gave her on the way out made her nervous. Both her husband and Hank's wife would kill her if they found out. She pushed the worry out of her mind and turned to Dr Watanabe. He smiled and told his students they could take a quick coffee break. The three rushed for the door before he could change his mind. He grinned at Sheila.

'We're going to be here a while. They always work better properly fueled.' He came around the autopsy table, rolled a stool over and sat down in front of Sheila. 'Plus, I wanted to talk to you.'

She looked at him suspiciously. This didn't have a let's-discuss-disaster-victims vibe. This had a concerned-grandfather vibe. Or, oh God, a doctor–patient vibe. She braced herself.

'It's very nice to see you,' he said slowly, 'but I worry that perhaps you might be overextending yourself. You're not normally in a wheelchair, yes?'

'Correct.'

He looked at her and seemed to make a decision.

'Sometimes the movements needed to use the chair can make things worse. Just because they're typically not ones that people normally do. I've seen many healthy people have trouble.' He pantomimed rolling a manual wheelchair. 'So I – or any of us – would be happy to move you around to where you want to be. Just let me know.'

He paused. She curled her hands into fists and dug her finger-nails into her palms. He was reading her like a book and it made her want to cry and punch the wall at the same time. She just nodded instead. He scooted his stool away a bit and changed the subject. They talked about the widespread road construction and then traded local restaurant recommendations until the residents returned. One of them kindly pushed her over to the blueprint wall and lowered the paper down to her level so she could mark which numbered body parts had been found in which spots. Thank God she hadn't been taken off the email chain, otherwise she wouldn't even have that information.

The decision had been made to charter a refrigerated truck to take all the bodies to Columbia, where they could be given CT scans and autopsied in a facility big enough to house them all. That left Whittaker's morgue and the two sad corpses he hadn't finished with before his death. They lay waiting in the cooler. That smart young chief resident, Ngozi Aguta, was in there right now. Ten minutes later, she came out with a stack of paperwork and shivering hands.

'I'd roll them out here, but there's no room,' she told Sheila with a smile as she stopped next to her wheelchair. She was tall, with skin only a shade lighter than Sheila's own. She smiled back. She always loved to see a Black female doctor. And one who would be a medical examiner, well, that was even more rare and so even more special.

'And I can't do the autopsies yet, anyway,' Aguta said. 'I still need permission. Hey, actually, maybe you can help me. I can't get a hold of the Lawrence County sheriff. One of the deceased is from his jurisdiction and I'm going to need him to sign off on me being the one to do it.'

'Oh, I've got his cell number,' Sheila said. She looked it up on her phone and read it off. 'Are you going to stay until they hire a new pathologist for this office?'

'Oh, no. I'm not done with my residency at MU. This is just because there's pending stuff because Dr Whittaker died so suddenly. Such a shame.'

The nicest response Sheila could manage to that was a noncom-mittal grunt. Which sent a curl of pain through her abdomen. She focused on Aguta's stack of papers until it passed. The young woman eyed her worriedly. Dammit, was Watanabe teaching them his penetrating doctor spidey-sense along with his forensic skills? She smiled weakly and turned back to the blueprint. Aguta laid a gentle hand on her shoulder and left the room. Sheila looked at the wall and the suddenly blurry blueprint. She would just blink until her eyes stopped watering. It took a long time.

TWELVE

M any in dire circumstances had ended up in that chair and none looked quite so wretched as Faye Halliday. Hank leaned against the wall of the interrogation room and kept quiet as Agent Alvarado turned the screws. She'd picked apart the business's licensing and permits and was starting in on the fireworks inventory.

'We've been able to pull records off the cloud and are going through them,' she said. Faye blinked in surprise. 'Oh, we've got a search warrant, don't worry. But we wouldn't have needed one if you'd just helped us out from the beginning.'

She pulled two items out of her satchel and slowly unfolded one of them. It was the county blueprint.

'Pretty, isn't it? Nice and tidy. Official.' She smoothed out the folds. 'But . . .'

She unfolded the second item. Someone had straightened the freehand lines of the sketch done by the Marine, Lamont Rydell, and enlarged it to almost the size of the county plan. She laid it on top of the official one and swept a hand over it. 'But this one. Let's take a look at it, shall we? Doesn't look quite the same. Which is interesting to us.' She gestured at Hank. 'It was an alert sheriff's department that thought to go talk to the *one surviving employee.*'

Faye curled into herself, shrinking in the hard plastic chair until her head was almost on the table. Alvarado didn't stop.

'Well, technically a former employee. But he was in the building only a week ago, right? So I'm going to consider his layout to be the fresh one. Up-to-date. And what we're going to use as you tell me what inventory went where.' A finger jabbed down in the main warehouse area. And then again as Faye stayed silent.

'I don't know,' she finally said. 'That was Lyle's thing. He dealt with all that.'

No, they didn't store or transport anything other than fireworks.

Yes, everything was already packaged for retail. They didn't manufacture anything themselves. All they did was forecast what kinds would be popular and place orders with either domestic manufacturers or the importers who brought the stuff in from overseas. Then they shipped it out to permanent retailers. Before the Fourth of July, they also dealt with folks who ran temporary stores. So yeah, there was more inventory in the warehouse on Tuesday than there would be at any other time of year. But how much?

'You'll have to get that off our cloud server,' she mumbled.

'Since you don't know the inventory, what exactly did you do for the business, Ms Halliday?' Alvarado said.

'The bookkeeping.'

'The bookkeeping? And yet you say you don't know your inventory?'

Faye had stared at the tabletop the entire time, but now uncurled herself enough to glare at Alvarado.

'How would I know that off the top of my head?'

They stared at each other. Hank waited for Faye to blink, because he knew it wouldn't be the ATF agent who looked away first. It took about thirty seconds and then, with a sniffle, Faye returned to looking at the table.

'You do anything else besides the books? Know about any other aspects of this business that has your name on it?'

Another sniffle. From his vantage point off to the side, Hank could see Faye clench her fists under the table.

'Lyle managed the employees. I made sure stuff like truck maintenance gets done. Building upkeep, things like that.'

'Building upkeep, huh? Well then, you should be able to tell us about this new room right here. When was it added? And what was it for? What was in it?'

Alvarado's finger slid across the paper and tapped at a square in one corner.

'I don't know.'

'What do you mean you don't know? You 'kept up' the building.' Alvarado jabbed the air quotes into the space between them.

'Yeah, I mean I made sure the air conditioning got fixed, and that the plumber came for the clogged sink in the bathroom. That kind of thing. I didn't change the layout. Lyle was in charge of the inventory and so Lyle was in charge of that.'

'Did you ever go in that room?'

'No.'

'Why not?'

'Why would I? I don't work with the inventory.'

'Well, this kid who quit to join the Marines, Lamont Rydell, he says he never went inside it. Which is kind of odd, don't you think? That an employee whose job it is to sort and load inventory was never allowed to go into this room?'

'Lyle did the—'

'Yeah, yeah, Lyle managed the inventory. Got it. Even though you never bothered to go into the room, do you happen to know what inventory was in there?'

'No.'

'You say that like it doesn't matter.'

'We had inventory everywhere. I don't see how what was specifically in what place matters.'

'You had a thirty thousand square foot building packed with pyrotechnics. It Goddamn well does matter what you stored where. Because this room right here was the center of the explosion. And I want to know why.'

Faye just stared at Alvarado. Not blankly, but with an exhaustion that bordered on impassive. The ATF agent leaned back in her chair for a moment. Then, without taking her eyes off the hunched woman, she lifted a file folder from her stack and handed it over to Hank as he stood against the wall. He knew what it was. The invoices Kurt found in the Halliday house yesterday. He opened the file and flipped through. The only sound in the room was the rustle of paper and the hum of the air conditioning. He finished and took Alvarado's continued silence as an invitation.

'So let's talk about your bookkeeping.'

Faye swung her gaze over to him.

'There were invoices in your house that we haven't been able to find in your computer records. Invoices that are past due. You seem to owe an awful lot of money.'

'Yeah? Did you see that we're also *owed* an awful lot of money? That people aren't paying us? That's why we're behind on our bills.'

Hank nodded. 'I do understand that cause and effect, ma'am. What I don't understand is why it isn't recorded with all the rest of your business finances, on your normal bookkeeping software.'

She wrapped her arms around her middle and sat there, staring at a spot above Hank's head. The air conditioner hum seemed louder.

'It makes me think you didn't want this known. That you were worried people would find out your business was in trouble. That it led you to make some unwise decisions about what stock you kept in the warehouse.'

Her attention snapped back to him. 'No. That's not true. We weren't in trouble. We just hit a rough patch we needed to get through. Get those customers to pay us what we're due and then we can pay the folks we owe. That's all. It didn't need to go in the computer, didn't need to be "official".'

'What you're saying sounds nice and tidy, Ms Halliday. Like it all balances out.' He pulled out his scratch paper of calculations and turned it so she could see. 'As far as I can tell, people owe you about two-point-four million. But you . . . you owe vendors more than ten million. That's not exactly a one-for-one type of thing, is it?'

Faye's lip started to tremble. Hank straightened out of his wall-lean posture and took a step toward the table. 'How exactly were you going to find that kind of money?'

'Lyle told me not to worry. He said, after the Fourth, we'd be able to pay everything we owed.'

'How?'

'I don't know. He just said not to worry and it would all work itself out.'

Alvarado scoffed.

'It seems like your husband kept you in the dark about a lot.'

'I'm starting to realize that.'

She looked from Hank to Alvarado and back to Hank. And clearly knew that neither one believed her.

THIRTEEN

Hank hadn't made it up to the morgue before all the victims were transported from there to the university facilities in Columbia. He'd been busy with the ATF and the state fire marshal investigators, with the potential involvement of the federal Chemical Safety Board, with blunt Dr Nielsen the anthropologist, with paperwork, and with God-awful press conferences. It was now four days after the explosion and there looked to be no end in sight to the bureaucratic wrangling and lack of progress in the investigation. So when he got the call from the chief resident he'd met at the scene, he leapt at the chance to escape and gladly drove up to where she was busy taking over Whittaker's domain.

The receptionist greeted him with a smile as he walked in. That was new. She waved him back and he entered the morgue room to find the assistant cheerfully humming as he cleaned an autopsy table. Also new. He'd always found both employees dour and cranky. He cautiously said hello.

'Nice to see you, Sheriff. Dr Aguta should be back in a minute. You've met her, right? I wish she could stay permanently.' He gave the table one final swipe with the cleaning agent and looked around. 'I never realized how it was . . .' He trailed off just as Aguta came in. She said hello and told the assistant he could take off this last hour before closing.

'You won't tell on me that taxpayers aren't getting their full eight hours out of him today, will you?' She grinned at him. It transformed her face from chiseled cheekbone solemnity to radiant playfulness and triggered a responding smile before he could even think about it.

'Oh, I imagine they've gotten their money's worth over the years.' He shook her hand. 'And I have to admit. You have me curious. What do you want to show me?'

She walked over to the walk-in cooler and rested her hand on the latch. 'I know that neither one of these bodies is yours, but you're the one sheriff I've met, so I thought I'd ask your opinion before I go any further.'

She'd had his full attention before, but now she had his full, *interested* attention. She swung open the door. 'These both were here when Whittaker died. This one,' she pointed to the body on the right, 'I did from start to finish. Pretty standard. Blunt force trauma secondary to motor vehicle accident.' Then they both shifted to look at the body on the left. 'But this one I didn't. Whittaker started this one.'

Actually, that wasn't accurate. Whittaker finished this one, according to his notes. He just hadn't signed it. So she was going to have to, and if she was going to attest to something, she was damn well going to review it first. And there were problems. Errors. Sloppy work. Lazy assumptions.

'You don't look surprised.'

'Um.' Hank rubbed at the back of his neck and decided that speaking well of the dead was just going to waste both of their time. 'Whittaker was odd. He had a weird personality. It's hard to explain. He was always a little bit too friendly, too chipper for the circumstances. Jovial almost. He made people ill at ease, I guess you could say. But I didn't know that extended to the quality of his work.'

'You never had cause to question how he ruled the cause of death in your cases?'

That forced Hank to admit that most of his cases had been homicides with obvious causes of death – like the poor strangled college student on the showboat, the stabbed teen in a Branson apartment, the bludgeoned pensioner found by Tyrone's postal service colleague. If not cases with easily identifiable killers, they at least had easily determined causes of death.

'So what's up with the guy on the left?'

'Sixty-two-year-old male found at home. No signs of foul play. Just dead in bed. Lived alone, so no witnesses to any medical emergency.'

'OK. Pretty standard.'

'Exactly. Except.' She walked over and pulled back the sheet covering the body. The stitched Y incision down his torso stood out against the white skin. 'I did this. Whittaker didn't. Didn't do anything, as far as I can tell. Just called it cardiac arrest and walked away.'

Hank crossed his arms and pondered the dead man. 'And it wasn't.'

'Not entirely. There were signs of gastrointestinal involvement. Renal dysfunction. Edema.' She looked at his confused face. 'Bear with me. I looked at his medical records. He was on a digitalis-class drug.'

Hank nodded. Even he knew that was a heart medication. If it's taken correctly, Aguta continued, it controls irregular heart-beats and helps treat congestive heart failure. If you take too much, you get what the incised gentleman on the slab had. GI issues. Kidney damage. Swelling. And fatal cardiac arrest.

'So that means the cause of death should be something like cardiac arrest as a result of digitalis overdose?'

'Digoxin toxicity, yes,' she said with a hard edge to her voice. 'And that means his doctor should be notified, public health statistics will be different, police should check for signs of suicidal ideation.' She flipped the sheet back over the poor man. 'And it damn sure means you always do more than just fill out the paperwork.'

She led him out of the cooler into the relatively warmer main room and over to the corner where a computer sat on a small desk. She poked the keyboard and the monitor popped on.

'So you've started looking at his other paperwork.'

'Oh, yeah. And it's bad.'

She pulled every morgue case in the last five years with heart attack or cardiac arrest listed as the cause of death. In the multi-county area, there were forty-six. In a third of those, Whittaker had confirmed his conclusion with a self-initiated full autopsy. In six others, law enforcement had opened investigations, so he was forced to do full autopsies. That left twenty-five deaths where he did partial exams or none at all. Four of those were fine, because medical records such as emergency room reports backed up the heart attack diagnosis.

Hank didn't want to know the answer to what he knew he had to ask. 'And the other twenty-one?'

'I don't have answers yet. I'm still going through them. I think he missed at least a few accidental toxicity deaths.' She pointed at the computer. 'You should never list just "cardiac arrest" as the cause of death. There's always an underlying cause that should be noted.' She sounded not only outraged, but overwhelmed. 'There are cut corners everywhere. It's like some horrific cocktail of incompetence and unprofessionalism and laziness.'

Hank reminded himself that she was still a resident. 'We're going to need to bring in state regulators. Do you want me to call them?'

She didn't hear him. 'Then there're ones like this case, from your county. Sixty-four-year-old female that Whittaker labeled a cardiac arrest death. She was brought in after dying in the emergency department. Not on any heart medication, no prior heart problems. No major health problems at all, according to her medical records. Until this ECG they did in the ER. Which showed an irregular heartbeat. But not the right kind of irregular heartbeat.' She jabbed a finger at the closed cooler door. 'It showed that guy's kind of irregular heartbeat, one that's found with acute digoxin toxicity, but not with other conditions. Her ECG looked exactly as his would've if he'd had one right before he died.'

Hank's head started to hurt. 'You're telling me she got a fatal dose of somebody else's heart medication?'

'Medication or horticultural. There are plants that produce those poisons.'

'Shit.'

'Yeah. Sorry. I know you don't need more stuff on your plate right now, but I didn't know what else to do. You seemed like somebody who would want to know.'

He certainly was. He stepped away from the desk and paced back and forth a few times. Then he forced himself to stand still. 'OK. How long ago was this?'

'That's the good thing, I guess. It was a little more than two years ago. So it's not like there's a hurry or anything.'

Her last few words sounded like they were spoken through a tube, faint and hollow. Sixty-four years old. Two years ago. 'What's the name?'

She looked at her notes.

'Marian McCleary.'

FOURTEEN

The room started to tilt. His whole horizon turned vertical and his head split with dizziness. He reached out and grabbed blindly, his hand finally hitting a filing cabinet. He seized it and held on. Aguta said something but the static in his ears wouldn't let him hear. He pushed away from the cabinet and headed toward the exit. He had to get out.

Somehow he made it to the parking lot. He sat down on the curb underneath a dogwood tree and tried to breathe. The air was muggy and thick and wouldn't cooperate.

What the hell was he going to do? Marian. Dear, dear Marian. Who learned Spanish phrases so she could talk to his *abuelita* at the wedding. Who kept her crusty husband in check with a wry smile and razor-sharp wit. Who became a doting grandmother better at snuggling than discipline. Who raised the woman he loved more than life itself.

Who hadn't died of natural causes.

He sat with his head in his hands and stared at the ground. This was going to kill Maggie. And Duncan. What could he even say? Where would he start? They didn't really know. Not definitively that it was a homicide. He rubbed at his temples. His brain was a kaleidoscope of thoughts fracturing in every direction, none of them staying still.

He didn't know how long he sat there before a pair of sturdy Dansko clogs and brown ankles appeared in his field of vision. She lowered herself to the curb beside him.

'Can I do anything?'

Make this go away. 'No. Thank you.'

'This person, she's more to you? You knew her?'

He ran his hands through his hair and raised his head. 'Yeah. You could definitely say that.'

'I'm sorry. I had no idea. I wouldn't have . . . I shouldn't have been so blunt.'

'It's . . . how would you know? What possible odds . . . I can't even.'

He fought the urge to again bury his head in his hands. In the sand. Hide.

He didn't know how long they sat there before he was able to speak. 'Are there other suspicious ones from my county?'

She shook her head. 'Not so far. And it's sloppy. That doesn't mean there's not an explanation for it. Maybe I was too definitive. There could be things in her medical history that I don't know. Things that would explain the ER tests.' Out of the corner of his eye, he could see her wringing her hands. She was clearly regretting her decision to involve him at all. 'You don't have to dig into it. I know you have so much else to do. I'll request her complete medical records. And handle the state regulators. And then I'll notify the next of kin. It's a medical examiner duty anyway.'

He turned to face her. 'I am next of kin.'

She let out a little groan.

'Well, my wife is. She's Marian's daughter. And her husband – her widower – lives with us.'

He made himself keep looking at her. Focusing on her. She obviously felt terrible. She was just a kid, not even done with her residency and doing a better job than most experienced doctors would. He needed to stop making her feel bad. There were enough others he'd have to make suffer. She didn't need to be one of them.

'None of this is your fault,' he said. 'You're doing your job. You're doing Whittaker's job. Fucking Whittaker. If he had caught this . . .'

'Then you could've investigated it at the time?'

'Then I wouldn't have had to. We didn't move down to Branson until after she died.' It would've been Branson city PD detectives knocking on Duncan's door, turning what was already agonizing mourning into downright horror. A suspicious death, possibly homicide. *Thought you'd like to know, now go bury your wife.*

Now it would be him. *I'm going to tear off that grief scab, Dunc, and make you bleed again – worse than before.* He couldn't do it. He was sick even at the thought of it.

'If it . . . if it was somehow accidental . . . if we can determine that . . .' he said. The hope in his voice sounded pitiful.

Her hands grew still. She took a deep breath. 'Unless there are meds I don't know about, or she was in the habit of making home-made tea out of dangerous plants, then . . .' She curled her long fingers into fists. 'I'm sorry. I just want to be honest with you.'

He nodded. 'I appreciate that.' His thoughts started to prism again, spinning through his head. Getting ahead of him. Dragging him along. 'And now I need to ask you a favor.'

'Of course. Good heavens, of course.'

'I need you to not say anything.'

Her eyebrows shot up.

'Don't report anything. Not yet.'

'Oookay . . .'

He rose to his feet. 'I need time. Before anyone knows what you've found.' He pushed down the nausea. 'I need to start poking around. If people know Whittaker's work is in question, someone might start hiding things. If I can get ahead of that, start asking around before word gets out, then I'm going to be in a much better position.'

'To find who did it?'

'Yeah. So even the state regulators. Can you wait?'

She stood up and rubbed her palms on her scrub pants. 'I'm only supposed to be here for another couple of days.'

'What if we asked to keep you longer? Even just another week or two.'

'If you can get me permission, then yeah, I'll stay.' She shrugged. 'And maybe my analysis of Whittaker's files will take me that long to complete. You think?'

He hadn't realized he was holding his breath. He let it out with a whoosh and a thank you. They exchanged cell phone numbers and she went back inside. He headed for his car, his stride lengthening with every step into an uncertain future. He didn't want to do this. Things were fine. They all had settled into living together, having Dunc around, having Marian not. This would rip it all apart.

Do you unbury the dead? Should you?

What kind of cop would he be if he didn't?

What kind of husband would he be if he did?

FIFTEEN

The whiteboard took up half the wall opposite the TV. Sam made a final adjustment to straighten it and stepped back. 'Happy?'

'Yes, thank you.'

'We can't exactly have a briefing in here, you know.'

'I'm aware of that.' Sheila shifted in her recliner. 'But I can participate in briefings by phone now. As long as I got this.' She flicked her fingers at the board.

'It's how you think. I know.' He sighed and uncapped a dry-erase marker. At least she wasn't trying to get up and snatch it from him. She might've wanted to, but she looked like she could barely sit up. She'd done too much the last few days. Spending all that time up at the morgue. The search warrant requests. The online research. She was supposed to be watching game shows and reading silly romance novels. He knew that because he'd been there when Dr McCleary gave her those exact orders. 'And don't think I haven't realized you asked me to do this on a day when Mr Turley's at work.'

'I don't know what you're talking about.'

'My ass.'

That got him a sharply cocked eyebrow. He shrugged at her. 'Glare all you want. I know I can't stop you from doing anything, but I don't have to like it. And I'm not going to be nice about it. 'Cause I'm worried. You're not letting yourself heal. Which means it's going to take you longer to get back to work. Didya ever think of that?'

The eyebrow snapped down. 'Disasters don't exactly follow doctor's prescriptions. Besides, who else is going to do this?'

'Uh, Hank?'

Another flick of the fingers. 'Where is he? You said you haven't been able to get a hold of him today.'

'Yeah, but—'

'And where is everyone else on this fine Saturday who's not

out on patrol? Doing security at the scene or off because they've
hit their overtime limit. Or convalescing like that fool Orvan who
let himself get hit by a car.'

'Oh, how terrible, that someone's convalescing like he's
supposed to.'

He put his hands on his hips and glared. She folded her hands
in her lap and waited.

'You. Are. Impossible,' he finally said through gritted teeth
and turned to the board. Fifteen minutes later they had a list of
all the warehouse employees and the current status of their
remains. Because Dr Watanabe was in near-constant contact with
Sheila. Because he was under the mistaken impression she was
the authorized county liaison.

'So we're now up to four people positively identified. Paula
Timmons, Ron Dowder, Randy Foulk and Ned Wickham, the
delivery driver.'

'Yep. And that's because they're farthest from the center of
the warehouse, so their bodies were relatively intact. The first
three near the lobby and Wickham by the loading dock.'

Sam added a column to the chart and wrote in those locations.
'And we think Mr Halliday might be around this office area here.'

He pointed at what everyone was now calling the Marine Map,
the enlarged drawing from Lamont Rydell, which Sheila already
had taped to the wall. She somehow had managed to put stickers
in each spot where partial remains were found. There was a
cluster in that area.

'Yeah. So Watanabe is testing those against Lyle's toothbrush,'
she said. 'If it doesn't match, he'll start with other DNA profiles,
obviously. The lab up there is running the known samples so
they can have those ready when the samples from the site are
sequenced. Then the comparisons can hopefully go quickly.' She
paused. 'I know Lamont told you where he thought the others
might have been, but it was really vague. Is there anything else
he can give us?'

'He said there wasn't really any strict division of jobs. If a
truck needed loading, you loaded it. If you were busy sorting
out different orders at the time, you stayed doing that. It wasn't
like there were a hundred employees and things were chaotic.
Everybody just kind of ebbed and flowed, he said. So workers

were all over everywhere, all the time. Any of these,' Sam said, sweeping his hand over the stickers, 'could be anybody.'

They both pondered the wall. Sam tried not to think about the families, getting their loved ones back in pieces. Their lives blown apart, too. He gave a start as he realized Sheila was talking to him.

'Hello? You there, Sammy?'

He rubbed at his ear and turned to her. 'Sorry.'

She considered him. Some of the starch seemed to go out of her and she reached a hand toward him. 'No reason to be. You're the one who's been out at the scene, the one who's met the families. Not me. You want to talk about it?'

He shook his head. He didn't know what he would say. How could he put it in words? And how could he dump it on Sheila? She had too many burdens right now as it was. He shifted on his feet as she eyed him for what felt like forever. Finally, 'OK then,' in a tone that meant she'd be watching him whether he wanted her to or not.

Start at the beginning.

Which meant starting at the end. Marian died on a sunny spring morning after collapsing at work. They rushed her to the Branson Valley General emergency room, where they barely had time to run tests before she died. 'Went on to greater rewards' was how the doctor put it when he called. Hank had wanted to punch him. Maggie just sat there on the couch in their Kansas City condo, not saying a word. Duncan, given the phone by the emergency department doctor, couldn't even speak.

It was cardiac arrest. 'Sudden cardiac death.' It was not uncommon in post-menopausal women, the doctor tried to explain after taking the phone back from Duncan. Marian did have a history of hypertension. Maggie nodded numbly from her spot on the sofa. Since it had been so sudden, however, he would ask the medical examiner to take a look. That often helped make families feel better. It had barely registered with either Hank or Maggie. He was already throwing clothes in a suitcase, arranging to pick up the kids from day care and wondering if there was enough gas in the car to make it the more than two hundred miles down to Branson. She didn't say anything the entire way.

They arrived at the house she'd grown up in to find Duncan in the same wordless state. Marian's friend Linda Ghazarian, who worked with her at Branson Valley High School, had driven him home from the hospital and was busy making tea. She took one look at Hank and poured him a bourbon instead. Then she sat Maggie down with her dad and took the kids in the backyard to play.

They wouldn't have survived those first days without Linda and Marian's other friends. And so that was where Hank decided to go first. To ask who possibly could've had a grudge against his mother-in-law, the well-liked principal of the town's only high school. He scoffed at himself. He of all people knew that even well-liked individuals weren't universally liked. Weren't safe from jealousy or hatred or fear. And it seemed Marian hadn't been, either.

He contemplated his office ceiling. The building was almost empty this late on a Saturday. The document he'd opened on his computer still sat blank after an hour of him staring at it. There was no reason he couldn't use it. Doing that would be like making the whole thing official, though. Instead he looked up Linda's phone number and saved it to a notes file on his phone. Then he googled her. She didn't have much of an online presence, just her listing on the school website – thirty-two years teaching history – and a Facebook page. He clicked and found it locked down and private. But that got him thinking. He went to the log-in page and entered Marian's personal email address. Then Duncan's name and birthday, and Maggie's name and birthday. Then he flipped the order of both. Still no luck. He went through middle names and her maiden name. Still nothing. Marian hadn't been particularly security minded – she wasn't the type to use a random string of numbers and letters as a password. He tapped on the computer mouse and thought. And then kicked himself. It took him three stabs at it before he got the right iteration.

Maribel_Benny.

Her grandchildren.

And he was in. She was a typical sixty-something with a job and outside interests. There were photos from her and Duncan's last trip, a tour of the fall colors in New England. Pictures of her garden and her Toastmasters club. Memes about teachers' gratefulness for holiday breaks and wisecracks about the broken vending machines at the school. And most recently, messages of condolence on her passing.

So sorry for your loss, Duncan.

I can't believe it. God Bless.

I just saw her last week. So sad. Thoughts and prayers to her family.

Terrible to hear. Maybe all those changes were too much for her.

What did that mean? What changes? It was posted by Tom Barstow, the football coach. Hank thought he also taught science. He clicked on the man's page and started pecking through posts from two years ago. That led to other pages, and some unhappy football families. It seemed that school policy was to have changed, and players were going to have to keep a higher GPA in order to compete. Or maybe they were just going to be held to an existing grade point average standard that wasn't then enforced. Hank couldn't tell from the comments. Either way, people were upset, foremost among them good ol' Coach Barstow.

Asking Linda about Barstow gave him a place to start. It would probably amount to nothing, but it could lead the conversation to other topics, other people. Other suspects.

SIXTEEN

'Oh, my goodness. Hank, it is you. Come over here.'

He took his coffee and walked over to the table where Linda Ghazarian sat. Her fellow church ladies had just gone and she was pulling something out of her purse. He knew it was the newspaper crossword and he knew she did it every Sunday here at the Roark Diner. And he knew Clem in the kitchen would make him breakfast to-go if he showed up and asked. So here he was.

'My dear boy. Sit down. How are you doing – with all the horribleness?'

Hank slid into the booth across from her. 'That's a tough one to answer. I'm OK. I've been really busy, so I haven't had much time to think.'

She took off her reading glasses and studied him. She had dark gray hair swept softly back from an oval face and blue eyes that matched the glasses she was now pointing at him. 'You have to take care of yourself, too. Or let Maggie do it. Because I know she must be concerned, too.'

'I'm following doctor's orders right now.' He pointed toward the kitchen. 'And getting some breakfast before I head out to the site.'

'Aren't those outside law folks supposed to be doing that?'

Even with all the things pinging around his brain, Hank registered the compliment – she hadn't included him as an outsider.

'Yeah. But I've told the families that I'll keep an eye on things. Know what's going on so I can keep them updated.'

He thought of the long list of victims. So many different circumstances, different ages. And then it came to him – that was his way in.

'Talking with some of them, you know, has made me think about Marian. And that some of them, the young ones, might have been her students.'

He could barely keep from cringing. Using disaster victims to further his own ends. He hadn't intended to bring the topic up this way. He hadn't known how he would broach it, actually. When he left home this morning, he'd decided to wing it. Well, he was flying now. In a dubiously ethical direction.

'Oh, I've thought the same thing. Because I certainly did. Pete Ustus. A nice kid. I had him in junior year history. Very quiet, but a good writer. And I know Marian had Lamont Rydell, must've been her last year teaching before she became principal. He was a bit of a star. Good grades, good athlete. I heard he quit just in time?'

'Yeah, he did. He's been really helpful. With his knowledge of the warehouse, that kind of thing.' He paused. 'I hadn't realized he was an athlete. What did he play?'

'Oh, goodness. Everything. Football, baseball. Maybe basketball, I can't remember.'

'So it sounds like he'll be a good fit for the Marines.'

'Oh yes, I expect so.'

He thought quickly. He had to keep this line of conversation going.

'All that physical conditioning. Especially football. Coach Barstow seems the type to have a program that prepares kids well for that kind of life after high school.'

She chuckled. 'I see you've met the man. He's definitely got a militaristic streak to him. Some kids it works well for, and some kids it doesn't.'

He rotated his coffee cup on the paper place mat.

'How did that jell with Marian? She always struck me as more of a case-by-case kind of person. You know, meeting people where they're at.' He launched into the story of her halting Spanish conversations with his grandmother, both of them cheerfully shouting over the wedding reception music and the crowd on the dance floor. By the end, Linda was dabbing her eyes with a napkin.

'Oh, lordy. I'd never heard that one. That's a tear of joy right there.' Another dab. 'Because that's pure Marian. I've got similar stories. Do you know she always remembered all three of my grandkids' birthdays? Especially after my husband died and with my daughter being a single mom . . . well, it just always meant a lot that she took the time. She even got the oldest one the cutest little wolverine stuffed animal when she decided to go to Michigan for college. It helped when she got homesick.' She paused. 'She always did know what people needed and how to get it to them. That's part of what made her such a good principal.'

'Did everybody think so?' He prayed the question wasn't too blunt.

She eyed him. Emotionally manipulative asshole that he was, he made sure he had an innocently interested look on his face.

'Well . . . it's a big staff. Lots of personalities. Some didn't appreciate her making changes when she took over.'

Some? More than one? He kept the interested expression but she fell silent. He nudged. 'I can just see her at a faculty meeting.'

'Oh, yes. Polite as anything, but wouldn't give an inch. Especially on the grades.'

Hank tightened his hand around the coffee cup and tried to look puzzled. *Please keep talking.*

'I'm sorry. I forget you all weren't down here then.' She gave an exasperated sigh. 'Such a tempest in a teapot. Marian was going to enforce the GPA requirements for sports. Some of the coaches had been letting things slide.'

'And her changes would've made kids ineligible?'

She nodded. 'I think it would've been only the most egregious ones. Which wasn't that many, honestly. But the rules are set by the state school activities association, and we're supposed to follow them.' She bit her lip and then took a sip of her own coffee. 'She never seemed stressed about it, but I often thought afterwards – after she passed – that the strain of it might have contributed. To her heart giving out like that.'

'People were putting that much pressure on her?'

'Barstow was. It was a good junior class that year. Lots of talent. They'd be seniors in the fall. Barstow and also Frank Hallinan, the baseball coach . . . they had a few players who might go on. College, or getting drafted, or whatever happens at that stage. But they didn't have the grades if Marian started enforcing the rules.'

As she spoke, Hank's hand had gradually squeezed his paper to-go cup to where it was threatening to collapse. He realized what he was doing and loosened his grip. 'Then what happened when she died?'

'It all . . .' She searched for a word. 'Evaporated. That's it. It all evaporated when she died. Herb Narwall came in to replace her and he was so green, he had trouble getting a handle on the job as a whole. He made so much work for the three of us who rotated as teachers-in-charge because he was always off "in training". So he sure wasn't going to take on the GPA fight. So, poof, it vanished into thin air.' She let out a puff of breath to punctuate her point.

'And the kids played their senior year?'

'Oh, yes. The whole town was thrilled. That must've been right about the time you and Maggie moved down here. I don't expect you took much notice, though, with everything you had going on.'

'That's definitely true. I had other things to focus on.'

She reached across the table and laid her hand on his. 'Oh, honey, and it hasn't stopped for you, has it? All those murders one after the other since you came, and now this explosion. You need to take some time off after this is all over.'

He nodded and smiled as Clem came out with a boxed breakfast of sausage biscuit, hash browns, and a side of salsa. He topped off the coffee to-go cup and gave Hank a pat on the shoulder before heading back to the kitchen. Linda started to reach for her crossword and, with no further excuse to stay, he slid out of the booth.

'Thanks for keeping me company,' he said.

She beamed at him. 'Oh, you're the one who brightened my day, talking about my dear friend. You just please think of me smiling as you go back to that explosion. Maybe that'll help brighten your own day a little bit.'

He said goodbye and headed out to his car. Once out of the parking lot, he turned left toward Highway 65 just in case she was watching him drive away. But then he took a quick series of turns that pointed him in opposite direction of the blast site. He had no plans to go there today.

There were other things that needed his attention.

His copy of the Marine Map was getting worn and grubby. The nicotine-stained fingers currently rubbing at it weren't going to help any.

'So you're saying that room had been there about a year?'
Sam said.

'About that long,' said the truck driver. His name was Andy
Wallace and he'd been with Skyrocket for seven years. He was the
last of the three surviving delivery drivers to be interviewed. The
other two hadn't paid much attention to anything. Two minutes in,
Mr Wallace already seemed more promising. 'It was definitely there
last Fourth of July. Cuz I remember thinking, "Why you taking out
space, Lyle?" Right at the time when he had the most stock.'

'Did you ask him about it?'

'In passing. He said something about future business moves.'

Sam thought about that. 'Did him saying that – did that fit in
with him? Like, was that out of character, or was he someone
who typically did sudden things like that?'

Mr Wallace handed back the map and fished a cigarette out
of the pack in his breast pocket. 'Little bit of both, I think. He
was usually a chatty guy, so to give that kind of short, corporate-
bullshit-speak answer was out of character, yeah. As for doing
sudden things, I guess he would. He sure wasn't like a plodding,
slow type. He was always moving, always thinking, working on
the business. So him coming up with a new idea wasn't surprising.
Shutting me down was, though.'

Now the money question.

'Did you ever see inside the room?'

'Nah. But I didn't ever really go into the warehouse anyway.
I'd come in to use the bathroom, get some coffee while they
loaded the truck, then I'd be on my way.'

'That seems like a pretty fast turnaround. They could load
everything up that quickly?'

'Well . . . I would take a walk. Down the drive to the road.'
He pulled out his lighter and grinned. 'Have myself a cigarette
or two.'

'Ah. Can't smoke in the truck?'

'Nope. Not near the warehouse, neither.'

Sam looked at the Marine Map and thought of the other one,
with all the little black body-part dots. 'Anybody else at the
company smoke?'

That got him an amused scoff. 'You think smokers all know
each other?'

Sam flushed a bright red he could feel burning his cheeks.

'Eh. I'm messing with you, kid. We kinda do, nowadays. Randy would walk down with me sometimes. Have a cigarette with me. I don't know his last name.' He swallowed hard. 'I feel kinda shitty about that now.'

'That's OK. I can figure it out. Anybody else?'

He wagged a finger at Sam. 'Paula. She did. Secret smoker. She was good at hiding it. Or was trying to quit. She worked up front and that's where the coffee machine was. So I'd see her pretty regular. I teased her once, said she should just walk down the drive with me. Nobody would have to know. She didn't take me up on it, just laughed. She was a sweetheart.'

He froze. 'I'm not getting anybody in trouble, am I? Nobody ever did anything wrong.'

Sam refrained from pointing out that the poor guy had no way of knowing that. Instead, he assured the driver that he was only trying to figure out what Lyle kept in the newly added room.

'I'm sorry I'm not more help. Me and the other drivers were always a little bit apart from the rest of the employees, not really friends with anybody cuz we were never there.' He finished off his cigarette. 'Now I'm standing here awful glad it was that way. And that makes me feel shitty, too, all the way down to the bottom of me. All the way through.'

SEVENTEEN

Hank hoped to beat Maggie out of the house, but she was already up and fixing the kids' lunches when his alarm went off. The wonderful woman had also brewed an extra full pot of coffee. He filled his travel mug, wishing he could stay. But he could barely look at her. He had to get out of here.

'How's Derek Orvan doing? Have you heard from him?'

He stopped with his hand on the door to the garage. 'Uh . . . fine. I think he's fine. Not back to work yet, obviously. But doing well.' He actually had no idea how his deputy's broken leg was healing. He should probably check on that.

'Good. He is following up with an orthopedic surgeon, right?'

Hank thought he could be honest about that. 'I'm not sure. I'll ask him.'

She nodded as she slapped globs of jelly on to a line of bread slices. 'If he has problems getting in, tell him to call me.'

Now he couldn't help but turn and look at her. 'Thanks, honey. I will.'

She grinned at him, licked the butter knife and lobbed it into the sink. 'Now that I'm not holding a deadly weapon, can I at least get a kiss?'

He took the three steps across the linoleum and leaned down. She put her arms around his neck and made him forget everything for thirty seconds. Then she pulled away and it all came back. And he thought of something.

'Derek did tell me to thank you, for all you did for him that day.'

She batted the air dismissively. 'Good heavens, of course.'

'Yeah, he said it was a lot better treatment than he's gotten in the ER before. It made me wonder what your predecessor was like. Was he any good?'

She considered that for a minute as she wrapped up the sandwiches. 'He was no great shakes, I guess. Fine, but not spectacular.'

'No great shakes? What'd he do, miss things?'

She waggled her hand in a 'kind of' gesture. 'He just wasn't the smartest guy, from what the nurses tell me. I always got the feeling they were glad to see him retire.'

Interesting. And very, very pertinent. He kissed his wife again and fled before she thought more closely about what he was asking.

The prosecutor was a man Sheila didn't know from some place up north. Because they snatched the whole thing away from Branson County so fast there hadn't even been time to file paperwork. Which was actually a little amusing, because local prosecuting attorney Andy Gibson *loved* paperwork. And she supplied most of it – arrest reports, returns on search warrants, jail records. They had a direct pipeline and a mostly good working relationship. Hence the northern guy.

Malcolm Oberholz was unaffiliated politically, unknown to local law enforcement, and apparently from a county prosecutor's office with too many lawyers because he had enough spare time to be specially assigned to Branson's jurisdiction for one particular case. *The State of Missouri vs. Edrick Fizzel, Jr*. Or, more accurately, *The State of Missouri vs. The Little Shit Who Ambushed a Deputy in the Woods and Beat Her Half to Death*.

He'd proven very lawyerly so far, requesting search warrants for Fizzel's house and filing charges of first degree assault and harassment, which would hopefully net the little bastard at least ten years in prison. But they hadn't yet spoken. She grudgingly granted that most of the delay was due to her hospitalization. And Tyrone's self-appointed role as nursemaid/gatekeeper. But now he was back to his normal schedule at work – thank God – and Sheila had a guaranteed block of time to herself. She'd wasted half of it staring at the phone and watching her tea grow cold. Finally she took the notepad from the side table next to her recliner, turned to a fresh page and slowly smoothed her hand across it. She didn't know why. He would be the one taking notes, not her. But it felt good in her hands. Normal. So she kept hold of it. Then she listened to the voicemail once more and dialed.

'Great. Thanks so much for getting back to me. How are you doing? They're letting you recuperate at home, right?'

'Yes, I've been home for a bit.' She didn't say it had been three weeks. That'd be admitting she was avoiding him.

'I know there were a few comments you made in the hospital before it was transferred to me, but that's it, as far as I can tell,' he said. 'You haven't given any statements?'

'No. Plus, there wasn't anybody unassociated who could take it. I know most everybody around here.'

'Yeah. I'll bet. How long have you worked for the sheriff's department?'

'Eighteen years.'

He let out a low whistle. 'Awright. And this is the first time you've been injured?'

She scoffed. Injured didn't quite cover it. She told herself to play nice. 'I sprained an ankle about seven years ago, chasing a suspect. Otherwise, no. Never been injured.'

'OK. So I want to take you through what happened. If you need to take a break, or want someone there with you, please let me know and we can stop.'

She didn't want touchy-feely. 'I will be fine, young man. You just conduct your interview.'

'Yes, ma'am.' She thought she heard a smile in his voice. 'Why were you in the Lakeside Forest Wilderness Area?'

'I was meeting a jail employee, Earl Evans Crumblit. We weren't able to speak at work, because he was providing intel on the insubordination campaign being done by some of my jail officers. So we met at the park, he gave me an update and I started walking back to my car.'

'And were you parked close by?'

'Not really. I always parked on the far side, away from the parking lot. So no one would see me and Earl's cars together.'

'And how far a walk was it?'

It usually took less than ten minutes. There was a path – it was a park in the middle of Branson, after all. Not out in the wilds somewhere, despite its name. But the path was through genuine woods, with limited visibility and sightlines. And it was nightfall. She tripped on a cable strung across the path at ankle level and went down hard. She immediately got to her feet and started searching the surrounding area.

'I felt certain the wire was there for me specifically. The path isn't heavily used, but there are people there every day. To put it out in hopes of tripping some random jogger? It seemed unlikely.'

She chose her words carefully. 'Unlikely' really meant impossible. She had known it was for her. So she left the path and walked along beside it, looking for any other tripwires. Then she saw a flash of white shirt and started chasing the person.

'What did he look like?'

'Stocky. Dark hair. Definitely a man. Didn't move like he was young. Otherwise I couldn't see much. It was almost dark, especially in the trees.'

'And was it this person who attacked you?'

'No. It was the other one. I'd almost caught up with the white shirt when I got hit.'

'Did you see this second person?'

She took a slow breath. Here was the rub. 'No.'

'Did you realize there was a second person at all?'

'Not until I got hit.'

'How many times did you get hit?'

'I don't know. Many.'

'What did he hit you with?'

'A tree branch.'

'Did you lose consciousness?'

'Yes.'

'Do you have any idea how long you were out?'

'No clue.'

These short answers were OK. She could do them fine. Just respond without having to think about it.

'Describe to me what happened when you came to.'

Shit.

'Well, um . . . that's pretty hazy. The men were gone. I know I couldn't really move. They told me later that I called 9-1-1. I don't remember that. I do remember thinking I had to get to the road. I guess somehow I did.'

Now the pause came from his end of the line. 'You crawled. Almost four hundred yards. The knees of your uniform were almost torn through and the ER doc reported your palms were scraped all to hell.'

She didn't know that. She hadn't thought about the logistics of it, she supposed. How she got to the side of the road so the ambulance could find her. An empty memory wasn't such a bad thing. She didn't necessarily want it filled. Time to focus on something else.

'Yeah, about that report. Just so as you know, that ER doctor is my sheriff's wife. We're friends. The other side will probably harp on that.'

He groaned. 'I was not aware. Huh. And her take on things is pretty key to helping prove the severity of your injuries. That's . . .' He let out a whoosh of breath. 'Well, that's par for the course with this case so far. And you're right. Fizzel's attorney will definitely use that to try to claim bias.'

Now there was a subject she was glad to change to. 'Who's representing the little weasel?'

'He's got a defense attorney out of Springfield named Dolores Jacobsen. She's been doing it a long time, knows every trick in the book.'

Sheila contemplated her tea and the youthful sound of the prosecutor's voice. 'And do you? Know every trick in the book?'

Oberholz chuckled. 'I'm not as young as I sound, ma'am.'

Sheila couldn't help the skeptical sound that came out of her mouth. He chuckled again. 'I know it's got to be tough for you to sit on the sidelines. I promise I'll keep you updated about everything along the way.' She heard paper shuffling on the other end of the line. 'At this point, the only other thing of note is who they're going to bring in to hear the case. Apparently all the judges in your area know the dad.'

An unwelcome image of a slight man with porcupine hair and a red nose forced its way into her brain. 'Yeah. Everybody knows Edrick Senior. He's been on the county commission for a long, long time.'

'Hmm. "A long time" like a bump on a log? Or "a long time" like fingers-in-a-lot-of-pies?'

Well, now. That was an astute question. She almost smiled. 'Fingers, definitely.'

She told him a bit about the kinds of pies, and he gave her some more information about Junior's next court dates before ending the call. She settled back into the recliner with a wince and stared at the ceiling. He hadn't come right out and said anything concrete, but there was some nice professional interest in his voice when he talked about Daddy Fizzel.

She slid her palm over the blank notepad paper and smiled.

EIGHTEEN

The woman on the phone was barely comprehensible. Dean at dispatch broadcast the address, with no guarantee it was the right location. The lady had been crying too hard to understand. Dean thought she was reporting a theft. Or maybe a burglary. Definitely something about the last straw. Sam rubbed his eyes and sighed. He was the closest, even though he wasn't on patrol, but rather assigned to help catalog blast site evidence at the feds' rented building off Sunrise Drive. He swung the squad car into a U-turn and headed back toward town.

Dean's best guesstimate was an apartment complex near America's Best Campground off Buena Vista Road. He cruised by slowly and saw no one out front.

'And you told her to go outside and stay put, right?'

'Of course I did. After making sure she wasn't in any danger. Cuz I do know what I'm doing.'

'Sorry. Just that I don't see anybody.' He rolled around back and came out the other side. From that angle, he could see a slightly open door. He braked. 'OK. Hang on. This might be it.'

He got out of the car and climbed the stairs. Aside from the door at the end of the balcony walkway, there were no signs of activity, which wasn't surprising for a Monday morning. He approached cautiously. Not that he didn't trust Dean's ability to translate hysterical babbling, but . . .

'Ma'am? Hello? Branson Sheriff's Department here. Ma'am?'

He stopped outside the door, his back against the wall. He was about to call out again when he heard the sobbing.

'Ma'am, I need you to come outside, OK? Can you do that for me? I'm going to help, but I need you to come out, please.'

There was a bunch of sniffling and the door opened a few more inches. Sam frowned. He sidled closer and used his foot to give it a kick. It swung open and he poked his head around the door jamb. The splintered door jamb.

'Jesus.'

He pulled his service weapon and moved quickly through the tiny apartment, making sure no one was hiding in the little bedroom or the bathroom. Then he holstered the gun, stepped through the ransacked belongings and knelt next to the woman huddled on the living room carpet. 'Ma'am?' he said softly. 'I need for you to come outside with me now. Here we go. Nice and easy.'

He wrapped an arm around her waist and helped her to her feet. She sagged against him and they tottered along the walkway and down the stairs. He put her in the passenger seat of his car and gave her a bottle of water. Then he stepped away and updated Dean. By the time he was done with that, she had calmed down enough that she was no longer hyperventilating. He knelt in front of the open car door and thought about what Hank would say.

'You're safe and we're going to stay here as long as you need to,' he said. 'Can you tell me your name?'

'Carrie Watson.'

'OK, Mrs Watson. It's nice to meet you. Is that your apartment?'

She shook her head.

'Whose apartment is it?'

'My daughter's.' Her breathing started to get worrisome again. He patted the air with his hands in a way he hoped came off as reassuring and not dismissive.

'OK. That's great. When you got here, it looked like that? All messed up?'

She nodded.

'And was the door open?'

She shook her head, the tears still running down her face. 'It was closed, but it was broken. So not closed, not all the way. But not open.'

It was a miracle Dean had been able to decode anything this lady said. Sam could barely do it and he was a foot away. 'That makes sense.' He smiled encouragingly. 'Now, do you know where your daughter is?'

She stared at him. And stared and stared. Like he was the lowest form of dirt. He felt the red crawl up his neck to his face and stay there. He cleared his throat.

'I'm real sorry, ma'am. I don't mean any disrespect. I'm trying to help.' Should he know something? He didn't think so. Why was she just sitting there like that?

'She's. Dead.'

Oh, no.

'Blown up.'

Oh, God, no.

There was no Watson among the dead. The daughter must have a different last name. He ran through the victim list in his head. Based on age, it could be any one of three young women. He was *not* going to guess which one.

'Oh, ma'am. I'm so sorry.'

They stayed like that for a bit, until her breathing slowed and his knees ached.

'I need to ask you some things, OK? It's going to help me investigate this.'

She snuffled at him and nodded.

'Is this the first time you've been here since . . . since it happened?'

Another nod.

'OK. And do you know if anyone else, any other family members or friends, have been by in that time period?'

'I don't think so.' She wiped her nose on her sleeve. 'I live about an hour away. So this was . . . her apartment wasn't the most urgent thing, you know?'

He'd need to talk to the neighbors, see if he could narrow down when the break-in occurred.

'When you went inside, did you happen to touch anything, go in the bedroom, anything like that?'

She shook her head. 'I couldn't move. I turned on the light and just stood there and couldn't move. Why . . . who . . .?'

The water bottle fell to the ground and she hid her face in her hands. It took ten more minutes for him to coax her into unlocking her cell phone and telling him which number to dial. It turned out to be a friend who rushed right over with a box of tissues and a repertoire of soothing murmurs. Sam had never been so happy to see a complete stranger. He helped her bundle Mrs Watson into the car and then pulled her aside.

'I need any information you can give me. What's her daughter's name?'

'Jordana Beckett.'

Twenty-four. Worked at Skyrocket for eighteen months. Long brown hair with a blue streak down one side, a nose ring, and a beautiful smile. Her picture was in the center of the bulletin board in the incident room, surrounded by her co-workers. Sam knew the whole board by heart.

'Do you know if she had a roommate or anything?'

'No. She lived by herself. Had for quite a while. She was a real smart, responsible kid.'

He asked her to help Mrs Watson get together a list of what Jordana had in the apartment then watched them slowly drive off, the friend with one hand on the wheel and the other on Mrs Watson's shoulder. They passed a familiar van, which pulled up next to Sam's cruiser. Alice Randall hopped out, slapped a baseball cap over her spiky gray hair and zipped up her coveralls all in one well-honed motion.

'Upstairs or down?'

Sam pointed and then held out the water bottle he was carefully grasping from the bottom. 'Here's this, for elimination prints. The mom's the one who found it ransacked.'

'Excellent.' She whipped out an evidence bag and he dropped it inside.

'Where's Kurt?' Usually the two evidence techs worked together.

'He's on his way to another scene. It's going to take precedence. I'm just here to seal this one. I'll come back later to process it.'

'Oh, no way,' Sam said. 'This one is the priority. The girl who lived here was one of the fireworks explosion victims. I think whoever broke in knew that.'

Alice froze, her equipment bag suspended halfway between the ground and her shoulder. 'What was that?'

Sam said it again. She dropped the bag and put her hands on her hips. 'Kurt's scene is a home burglary. Ron Dowder.'

Victim number six on the bulletin board.

They stared at each other then both turned to look at the still-gaping door on the second floor.

'I should call Hank.'

'Yeah,' Alice said. 'I think you probably should.'

NINETEEN

Hank left Maggie at the house and drove the minivan to a side street near the high school so he could watch the morning traffic flow in and out of the campus. He could choose to walk in and start asking questions. And within thirty minutes, the entire town would know that Marian McCleary's death was now a homicide investigation. And people would start scrambling. They always did. Even if they didn't do it. They'd scramble and hide things and prevaricate and dissemble and a bunch of other ten-dollar words. And he'd get nowhere.

The final bell rang and the students vanished inside and there was silence. His gaze swung from the front entrance to a poster at the edge of the parking lot advertising the next school baseball game. White butcher paper and red tempera paint. Even with all sorts of technology at their young fingertips, old-fashioned basics remained the best choice. He'd smile about it if he weren't in such a bad mood. The sign fluttered in the breeze and he noticed a paper attached to the bottom corner. He pulled into the parking lot and circled around so that he drove past the sign. The paper, stapled to the edge, was a printout of a news article from the *Daily Herald*. A profile of one of the starting pitchers. He drummed his fingers on the steering wheel. That wasn't a bad idea. The library would have an archive of the local newspaper that went back decades. What was it covering two years ago? Did it know about the athlete GPA fight? Everything about the town's only high school was a big deal. Had there been any other controversies worthy of news coverage?

He decided to leave the parking lot before someone pegged him for a loitering pervert and called the cops. He headed toward downtown and the library, stopping first at Donorae's for coffee. He'd only had one cup before sneaking out of the house, and that wasn't going to be enough after last night's tossing and turning. He got a large and sipped carefully as he navigated the short blocks to the library, where he pulled into the parking lot at the same time as librarian Jean Utley, who also happened to be married to the city's police chief. She tapped on his window and told him there wasn't any point in him waiting the half-hour until opening, so come on in and keep her company. She pointed him toward the microfilm reader and the filing cabinet that held the archives of the *Branson Daily Herald*.

It took him fifteen minutes and half of his coffee to figure out how to thread the damn machine. The reel whirred and squeaked its way back to the day she died.

POLICE BLOTTER: *Authorities Called to Branson Valley High School.*

Officials stated no students were involved in an emergency at the school Thursday morning that drew both city police and paramedics. Sources said a staff member collapsed and was taken to a local hospital.

And three days later:

BVHS Principal Was Devoted Educator

Marian Geary McCleary, a teacher for more than forty years who had recently moved into the Branson Valley principal job, died Thursday morning after collapsing at work. She was 64.

McCleary was chosen by the school board a year and a half ago to fill the principal vacancy after the previous administrator won a substantial sum in the state lottery and abruptly retired. She stepped easily into the role and was seen as a diplomatic leader liked by both staff and students.

'She knew how to work with everyone,' said algebra teacher Mary Kimball. 'And of course, she'd taught here so long that she knew the school inside and out. There've been some good things happening under her leadership.'

McCleary began teaching English at Branson Valley after graduating from what was then Southwest Missouri State University. Throughout her tenure at the high school, she served at various times as advisor for yearbook, student government, homecoming committee, prom planning and once, early in her career, for the audio/visual club, where she cheerfully admitted she didn't know a thing.

'That was just like Marian. If there was a hole that needed filling, she would step in and fill it,' said Bogart Cushman, a fellow English teacher. 'There were many times where kids couldn't find anyone to help with a club or a project, and she'd find out and make it happen for them. Even if she knew nothing about it. You should've seen the year we didn't have a cheerleading coach. My daughter was on the squad. Lord, did Marian not know what she was doing. But she was out there every day after school with them so they could practice. Those girls got their season and loved her to the end of the Earth. Still do.'

Hank had to stop and dig out a tissue. He'd never seen this article. Of course, the day it published, he was planning a funeral and dealing with a father-in-law made catatonic by grief.

He contemplated his coffee for a bit before his eyes would focus well enough to continue reading.

That same drive to help manifested itself when long-time principal Nick Denton won $2 million in the Missouri Lotto and quit the same day. Since it was halfway through the fall semester, the school board decided on an immediate replacement instead of an extensive outside search. McCleary was the nearly unanimous choice and, just like during the rest of her career, agreed to take on the job.

Marian Elisabeth Geary was born in Wellington, Kansas, to Gilbert and Mary Elisabeth (Hampstead) Geary. She moved to Springfield to attend SMS, where she majored in English and obtained her teaching credential. While there, she met and married Duncan McCleary, a Branson native. She began teaching at BVHS the next year.

'This school won't be the same without her,' said senior and yearbook editor Izzy Taylor. 'I mean, my mom had her as a teacher. Everybody had her. She was BVHS.'

McCleary is survived by her husband of forty-one years, daughter Margaret Elisabeth McCleary, and grandchildren Maribel Elisabeth Worth and Benjamin Fergus Worth.

He let out a slow breath. He hadn't known she was quite that involved beyond teaching classes. He did know it was a big deal when she was appointed principal. Duncan had been proud as anything, but made her promise she'd still take time off in the summers to travel. He'd wanted to see grand European capitals and little Scottish villages. Instead he was home with a first-grader who needed help with a Girl Scout badge and a four-year-old who refused to eat anything that didn't contain peanut butter.

Those thoughts got pushed to the side and the cold coffee dregs thrown in the trash. He resettled himself in the chair and started the microfilm reel spinning. He wanted a year and a half before Marian's death. He wanted that 'nearly unanimous' board meeting. The newspaper issues unspooled backward.

> *BVHS Baseball, Softball Have Worst Seasons in Years*
> *High School Christmas Play Draws Crowds*
> *Surprise Homecoming Loss; Football Team Will Regroup,*
>   *Coach Says*
> *Kids Set for Homecoming; Barstow Confident of Win*
> *Three Students Cited for Marijuana Possession at High*
>   *School Football Game*
> *New School Year, New Subjects Added to BVHS Curriculum*
> *Joy, Relief at Spring Graduation Ceremony*
> *Four BVHS Grads Will Head to the Ivy League*
> *BVHS Varsity Baseball Headed to State*
> *Drag Racing in Front of High School Results in Multiple*
>   *Arrests*
> *Drama Class to Present New Holiday Play; Tickets Available*
>   *After Thanksgiving*
> *It's College Application Time; Here's a Look at How*
>   *Students Decide*
> *BVHS Beats Republic in Homecoming Blowout*
> *Veteran Teacher Appointed to Fill BVHS Principal Vacancy*

There it was. There were seven board members and six voted to have Marian take over the job. Some guy named Jan Czernin disagreed. He said he wanted a wider search and refused to vote for Marian. 'We have a very fine school here and we need an experienced administrator. She might be a good teacher, but she has no experience running things.'

Hank inched the reel forward as the news article jumped to an inside page. Czernin gave a few more quotes, as did the talkative board president, but none of it was particularly informative. Until the very end.

Elected two years ago, Czernin was the board's newest member. He moved to the area from Des Moines and campaigned on the idea that the rapidly growing Branson school district should begin to institute policies used by bigger districts like the one he came from. He also highlighted the fact that his family – a wife and two grown daughters – were all educators.

Hank frowned. Educator teachers? Or educator administrators? He pulled out his phone and did some quick googling. A woman named Lesley Czernin was listed as principal in a four-year-old Des Moines high school graduation program. And she also popped up on the current web page of a tiny high school in the county neighboring Branson. As principal. He closed the Google search and got to his feet. He did love uncommon names. He didn't love thinking the worst of people, but at this point, he had no choice.

TWENTY

Ron Dowder had lived with a roommate near Ellison Street, south of the downtown business district. The guy got back from a weekend camping trip on Table Rock Lake to find the back door jimmied and multiple items missing. Two TVs, a PlayStation, a laptop, an iPad, a dartboard and, worst of all, a St Louis Blues Busch Beer neon sign. He was almost in tears over that last one.

'Not to profile or anything,' Kurt Gatz said as he stood in the middle of the living room, 'but the stolen items do suggest the thieves are a certain age demographic.'

The roommate, Ian Kiely, sat slumped on his couch. Sam looked from him to where the precious Blues sign used to hang and doubted that Ian's tears were caused solely by the empty spot on the wall. 'So, ah, you went over to Indian Point, huh? They got a nice campground by the lake there. You go with some friends?'

Ian nodded. 'And my girlfriend. She said I should get away from here. Get some space from Ron dying. That a weekend in nature would do me good.'

'That's pretty good advice.'

'And then I come back to this.' He flung an arm out despondently at the ransacked room. 'Half the stuff was Ron's. I was going to take it over to his little brother. Now . . . this world is fucked up, bro.'

'Yeah, man, it is.' Sam stepped out of Kurt's way as the evidence tech headed for the hallway and the house's two bedrooms. He opened his notebook. 'How many people knew what you two had in here?'

Ian put his head in his hands and started to identify people. Turned out him and Ron weren't exactly social recluses. The list grew to dozens of names, so many as to make the information almost useless.

'Did you know Jordana Beckett?'

'She worked with Ron, right?'

'Yeah. Did she ever come over here?'

'She might've come here for a party or something. She died, too, didn't she?'

Sam nodded. 'Can you think of anybody who's been here to your house and who also knew Jordana?'

Ian's head jerked up. 'Wait, did she get broke in to?'

'Yeah. I was just there.'

'Damn. That is so uncool. What do they call it – in salt to injury?'

'Um, something like that.'

'No. Salt in the wound. That's what they call it.'

'Yes. That's it.' Sam looked around at the mess. A lot of salt in the gaping wound of the explosion. 'So do you know if Ron and Jordana had any mutual friends?'

Ian rubbed at his sunburned nose. 'Maybe? I know that Ronnie would sometimes hang out with Pete and some other guy who worked with them. Walt? Will? I don't know. Maybe Jordana knew them, too.'

Pete Ustus. Victim number four. Sam pictured the bulletin board. There were no 'W' names. He'd need to look at the roster of former employees. Maybe someone on that list had a matching name. He poked at Ian's memory some more, until Kurt came out from the bedrooms. He moved to the side so the big guy could get to the front door, which he started dusting for prints. Ian looked questioningly at Sam and jerked a thumb toward the busted back door.

'They could've tried the front door first,' Sam said. 'So there might be fingerprints.'

'Damn. You guys must do a lot of thinking in your job.'

Out of the corner of his eye, Sam saw Kurt pause and hide a smile before resuming his work. 'I guess you could say that we do,' he told Ian, and then stepped into the kitchen as the other man's phone buzzed. He pulled out his own and sent another text – the tenth so far this morning, by his own increasingly irritated count – to Hank. None had been responded to, and this one wasn't either. He crammed his phone back into his uniform pocket and tried not to swear. Instead, he looked around. Kurt hadn't gotten to this room yet. He looked more closely. Ian might not have been in here, either, he thought as he considered a suspiciously rectangular void on the counter. 'Uh, hey, bro – did you have a microwave?'

'What?' Ian rounded the corner, red-faced and wide-eyed. 'Goddammit – they even took the *microwave*?'

The lady at the front desk stared in surprise. 'Aren't you the sheriff?'

Hank nodded. He had an appointment with the school district superintendent. The woman huffed at not knowing about it and showed him back to her boss's office.

'Sheriff. I'm Camille Getz. Nice to meet you.' She rose to her feet and they shook hands. She looked to be in her fifties, but with the thin, strong build and graceful movement of a ballet dancer that made her seem younger.

'Please, call me Hank.'

'You said on the phone you wanted to talk about emergency response?' She waved Hank into a chair across from her desk.

Hank nodded. 'Last week really brought home how wide-ranging an emergency can be. I want to start going through all the schools in county jurisdiction. Make sure that everything's up to date and we're prepared. Because . . .'

He trailed off and Getz took over as he'd hoped.

'Oh, Lord. So unexpected. I mean, we train for a school shooter more than we train for a massive explosion like that. Now, don't get me wrong, I don't want to stop that kind of training—'

'Oh, no,' Hank interrupted, 'sadly, I don't either. In this day and age, we can't. But I do want to make sure that everyone also has a swift evacuation in place for a disaster. Preferably a plan with a couple of options, depending on where the threat is coming from.'

'I know we've got one plan at all our schools, but I don't think we've got multiple. What do you suggest?'

They talked about various escape routes, parent pick-up centers, and where his deputies would have the most helpful impact.

'This is wonderful. I'm going to take this to Branson city PD and have the same discussion with them for our schools in the city limits,' she said. 'Although heaven forbid an explosion like that happen in a populated area.'

The thought made Hank's brain want to melt. Getz leaned forward and put her elbows on the desk blotter. 'How bad was it? At the fireworks place? There's so many rumors out there.'

How to put it into words? He let out a slow breath. 'It . . . it was massive. There's a crater. There's no part of the building left. Burnt trees. Burnt cars. And we . . . we're still working to identify the victims.'

Getz's eyes widened. 'You don't know who was killed?'

'Not that. It's that we don't know who's who.'

That took a second for her to compute. She blanched. 'Oh.'

Hank waited a beat before swinging the conversation back to schools.

'And how are your students doing? All those Creekside Primary kids, and Branson High – they heard the blast. I'm sure that was traumatic.'

Getz nodded wearily. 'Yeah. The little kids especially. Teachers have addressed it, and we've had counselors out there.'

'Do you happen to know how many students had relatives who died?'

Getz was aware of three. Her site administrators would have a better idea. Did Hank want a more definitive count? He demurred. He knew his time was almost up and he had other things to talk about.

'I do really appreciate your time. My mother-in-law always spoke very highly of you.' He had no idea if this was true. He hoped so. Getz had backed her for the principal job, so Marian at least hadn't been out there bad-mouthing her.

Getz snapped her fingers. 'I'd forgotten you were married to her daughter. Yes, Marian was a wonder. She should've been principal long before she was, in my opinion. But that old codger Nick Denton – I couldn't pry him out of there. It took two million damn dollars to get him to leave.' She leaned forward conspiratorially. 'Did you know that the day after he won on that Lotto ticket, he walked into work and started tossing fake dollar bills in the air. Then he shouted that he quit and danced a jig on the way out.' She shook a finger. 'And I seized the moment. Called Marian that very day.'

Hank made himself chuckle. 'I hadn't heard that about the money tossing. I am glad the school board agreed with you about

Marian being the right replacement. It was unanimous, wasn't it?'

Getz frowned. 'Almost unanimous.'

Hank tried to appear wide-eyed. 'Who voted against her?'

'Newer board member. Jan Czernin. He wanted to do a wider search. Said we needed a bigger candidate pool.'

'Oh. I had no idea.'

'Luckily, the board chair put him in his place. Said Marian's forty-year résumé was more than enough to assure they were making the best choice. Heh, heh. Don't show up here in town, pal, and start trying to throw your weight around.'

Sometimes – rarely, but sometimes – Hank did enjoy the insular world of Branson politics. He phrased his next question carefully. There'd been nothing in the *Daily Herald* about Narwall's appointment. 'Did this Czernin guy do the same thing after Marian died? When you all had to find someone to replace her?'

'Well, now.' Another finger shake. 'That's a different story. We had some interesting information by that point. Kept it hush-hush, because it would've made the board look silly. But we found out that Jan's wife is a principal. Was one up in Iowa and had no job down here when the Marian vote happened. By the time the board picked Herb Narwall, she was working out near Nixa. Getting the BVHS job would've been a big step up from that. So, ah, the other board members "suggested" that Jan recuse himself from any vote this time around.'

The way she said it made it sound as if the 'suggestion' had been offered by people armed with baseball bats in a dark and otherwise empty parking lot. Hank decided not to delve any further in that direction.

'How did you even find that out about his wife?' Because clearly, no one had done any preparatory googling of the opposition before the Marian vote. Had they wised up the second time around?

'We got a tip,' Getz said. 'Anonymous. I bet you come across that type of thing all the time in your profession. In mine, well, it was . . . out of the ordinary, that's for sure.'

'Mmm . . . even with anonymous tips, we usually have a pretty good idea of who it was.' That wasn't true at all. 'Was it the same for you?'

Getz steepled her fingers and eyed Hank for a moment before coming to a decision. 'I'll tell you, I did have a feeling. No proof. But just the way the message was phrased to be more about Marian than about Herb, and who was at Marian's funeral . . . I think it was Marvin Sedstone.'

Hank sat back in his chair, honestly astonished. The county's most prominent judge. Someone he dealt with all the time. 'What makes you . . . Marian's funeral . . . I don't understand.'

She nodded sadly. 'You were concentrating on your family – of course you wouldn't have noticed too many other people there. But nobody seemed more devastated than the judge. The man was absolutely rocked.' She shrugged. 'Like I say, I've no proof of any sort. But that's my feeling. Guess that's why I'm an educator, not law enforcement.'

She rose to her feet and Hank did the same. They shook hands again and exchanged business cards and a promise to meet with school principals regarding evacuation drills. He left the modern glass-and-concrete building with a ball of manipulative lies roiling his stomach again. He was getting used to the feeling, and it worried him.

TWENTY-ONE

Three more burglaries. One called in Monday afternoon by another sobbing parent and two that Sam found when he checked on apartments where young explosion victims lived by themselves. The older ones, he was figuring out, tended to have families or roommates. So their houses weren't vacant and easily looted like the kids' places were. He scoffed at himself. Kids. They were his age. He had no right to be calling them 'kids'. Except that right now he felt much older than his twenty-six years. He rested his head on the steering wheel of his squad car and took a long, tired breath.

He'd sealed the apartment in this little building off Green Mountain Drive. It would keep until Alice could get to it tomorrow. He certainly couldn't stay. He had four addresses left and they needed to be checked today. He couldn't take the chance that someone's home would sit overnight with a busted-down door and easy access for a second round of thieving. And it was still only him. There were no other deputies to spare. He wanted to call his colleague Ted Pimental in early, but he didn't have the authority. Only two people had that power. He refused to call Sheila. She would help, no doubt about it. But she'd also stress about the overtime costs. And she'd want to know where Hank was.

He had no answer to that.

There was no Hank. Anywhere. He wasn't answering his phone. He wasn't in a squad car to be reachable by radio. Sam even drove by his house, where the only sign of life was old Mr McCleary visible through the kitchen window washing dishes. Probably the dinner dishes. Normal people ate that meal. He, on the other hand, hadn't eaten since breakfast. He lifted his head off the wheel and started the car. Maybe he could grab something after he checked out this next location, a house out near Walnut Shade.

'House' was a generous term, Sam thought as he pulled up to

where twenty-six-year-old Bryan Reynolds (bulletin board number nine) lived. It was a ramshackle structure on a deserted stretch of road, set far back and tilting to one side on a definitely not code-compliant block foundation. He pulled into the dirt driveway, shut off the engine and waited. Nothing, and no one, came out. He got out of the car and stepped off the drive into the trees. A minute later, he emerged with a yard-long branch and a better feeling in his gut. He'd been rushed by enough guard dogs to know better than to approach a property like this empty-handed.

The front door looked intact. He didn't knock, making his way instead around the side to the back.

'Oh, shit.'

He'd been right, and too late. He tossed the tree branch aside and knelt next to the dog. It was a male, a pretty gray mixed breed who'd gotten strangled in the tangle of his chain. He'd probably been trying to free himself, or at least reach the shelter of the back porch. Sam unhooked the chain from the post and gently unwound it from the dog's neck. It was rubbed raw. He laid the big head back down on the ground and let the chain fall in a clinking heap. The water and food bowls were empty. Did Reynolds not have any friends? Anybody who knew he had a pet? One more death caused by the explosion. He didn't even have the energy to stand.

The sun was setting by the time he finally got to his feet. He pulled the flashlight off his duty belt and approached the house. The back door swung open at his touch. That didn't necessarily mean anything. Lots of people left their doors unlocked in this county, especially in isolated spots like this. He called out and then stepped inside. The moldy plate of food on the table was likely Bryan's mess, but the dumped-out dresser drawers in the only bedroom probably weren't. And the empty cigar box tossed on the floor definitely wasn't. Sam knew Bryan would've taken much better care of the contents, which – based on the smell – included a particularly aromatic strain of pot. He shook his head. The stuff was legal in Missouri now. That didn't mean people weren't going to keep right on stealing it, though. He pulled on a pair of nitrile gloves and carefully put the box in an evidence bag. The beat-up container might be their best shot out of all six locations for thief fingerprints. He didn't want to risk leaving it here until Alice came tomorrow.

He called her as he walked back to his cruiser. 'Hey. I found another one. TV's missing. Probably a stereo sound system, too. And a lot of weed. Can you make this one first tomorrow? It's really isolated. I put up crime scene tape in the back, but that's not going to stop anybody.'

Alice laughed in agreement and said she'd head there first thing in the morning. 'You did good today, kiddo. Really nice work.'

His face turned red as he mumbled a 'thank you' and hung up. He checked the time and blew a sigh of relief as he dialed Ted Pimental. He gave the older deputy – who was a little bit of a mentor and always a lot of help – two of the remaining three addresses and asked him to check. 'I'll go by the last place in Forsyth, but there's something I gotta do first.'

He hung up and walked around to the trunk. He rooted through his emergency gear, found the blanket, and trudged back toward the house. Five minutes later he was back, sliding a wrapped object on to the back seat. He pulled out of the driveway and pointed the car toward Forsyth. He no longer wanted to stop for dinner first. He wasn't hungry anymore.

Hank had avoided being home since Saturday morning, when Aguta had turned his world upside down. He was sneaking in late and leaving early and hopelessly praying the whole thing would just go away. It was exhausting. And ridiculous. He powered down his work computer and stared at himself in the black of the monitor screen. Then he turned out the lights and drove home. If he hurried, he'd be in time to tuck the kids into bed.

They were thrilled to see him, which made him feel even worse.

'You haven't read us bedtime stories in forever.' Maribel dropped a Percy Jackson novel in his lap.

'Wait, I thought we were going to do one of the "Little House on the Prairie" books.'

They both stared at him. 'We never agreed to that.' She had the same don't-argue-with-me look as her mother. She hopped on to her brother's bed and sat there, cross-legged and expectant. Benny, already tangled in his Spider-Man sheets, grinned at him and started bouncing.

'Calm down, Benny.' He looked at the book. 'Guys, I don't think this is right for your age so – wait, and it's book two.'

'Grandpop already read us the first one.'

'Oh, he did, did he?'

'Yeah, and it was awesome.' Benny drew out the word. It was the highest praise the four-year-old could think of. 'There's monsters.'

Hank sighed. As with everything about Duncan, you took the bad with the good. On the one hand, patient help with homework and fun outings to the park. On the other hand, double chocolate brownies for breakfast and letting them jump on the beds when it was too cold to play outside. And monsters.

'Are you sure this isn't going to be too scary?'

They both shook their heads. He sighed again and opened the book. Thirty minutes later, he had to admit it was more entertaining than reading about Pa building a sod house. He refused to start a new chapter, straightened out Benny's bedclothes and leaned in to kiss what looked like his freshly bathed head. It wasn't. 'You didn't wash your hair did you?'

'How can you tell?'

'It stinks, Benny.'

'I put my head underwater.'

'That's not good enough. We're going to need to wash it with shampoo in the morning.'

Benny huffed and rolled over to face the wall. Then he whipped back around and wrapped his arms around Hank's neck. Stink or no, he held his son tight and then crossed the hall to Maribel's room. He settled her under the covers and they talked about what she'd done at school – Monday was the day for their weekly trip to the library – and how in math group she had to sit next to Jesse Thompson, who always had a gross runny nose. He started to lean in for a kiss but quickly pulled back and cocked an eyebrow at her.

'I washed my hair all the way,' she laughed, then turned serious. 'Grandpop does try to make Benny do it. He's just sneaky.'

'Yeah, well, that's a little brother's job, you know.'

She rolled her eyes and gave him a hug. 'Night, Daddy.'

'Good night, Bug.'

He quietly closed her door and fled to his bedroom so he wouldn't have to talk to Duncan, who was out in the living room listening to Johnny Cash albums with the dog. He couldn't sit on the couch and chat like everything was normal while 'Bury Me Not On the Lone Prairie' played in the background. He could barely even look his father-in-law in the eye. He was terrified the old man would look at him and somehow see what happened to Marian. That his face would give it away and destroy Dunc's whole world.

So instead he locked himself in the bathroom and took a scalding shower. When he came out with several fewer layers of skin, his wife was sitting on the bed.

'Hi, stranger.'

He startled and dropped his dirty laundry. 'Oh, hey. I didn't think you'd be home this early.' He'd planned on being asleep when she got off shift. He bent down and scooped up his clothes, using the moment it took to put them in the hamper to collect himself. He turned and pulled her to her feet. She wrapped her arms around his neck and kissed him. He buried his face in her long brown hair. 'You're lucky. A half-hour ago I smelled like Benny.' She laughed, that from-deep-in-her-chest sound he loved and was so afraid of taking away. She drew away just a little so she could look at him.

'How was your day? How's the investigation?'

She was talking about the explosion. So he wasn't lying when he told her everything was slow going and they were a long way from figuring anything out. Even though he was really talking about Marian. He had no idea how the blast investigation was going. He considered Sam, whose calls he'd ignored all day. Then Maggie kissed him again, long enough to chase that and every other thought from his head. He gratefully wrapped his arms around her and took her to bed.

TWENTY-TWO

Hank was up early, the impossibility of his task taunting him as the coffee-maker spluttered and steamed. Maybe he should come clean. Not with everybody. Ideally just one person. Someone who could keep his secret, and someone who could ask questions without raising suspicion.

It would have to be Judy Manikas. Marian's closest friend was the only one who met both criteria. He rose and poured himself a cup before the pot was done. The machine spit at him in response. He leaned against the counter and watched the sun rise out the back window. He wanted to call her now, but she taught second grade at Bee Creek Elementary and was likely already on the way to school. He looked at the time. He should be on his way to work. Get out of the house before Dunc came up from his bedroom in the basement. He filled a travel mug with the rest of the pot. Then he couldn't find his car keys.

'Leavin' early again?'

Hank looked up from his search of the catch-all desk in the corner. 'Uh, yeah. Still helping out with the blast investigation.'

Dunc's slippers shuffled on the tile floor as he crossed to the refrigerator. 'I don't know how you survive on just coffee all day.'

He heard a jingle and dug under a pile of papers, finally pulling out his keys. 'I was going to take some of those leftover whatever-they-are.'

'Whatever they are? That's some good chicken Parmesan right there.'

Hank busied himself with straightening the desk so he could avoid looking Dunc in the eye. 'Great. I'll get some.'

'Eh. Here.' Dunc scooped some into a plastic container and handed it to him. 'Bring this dish back, though. It's the only one we've got. The kids used the other one this size to start a worm farm in the backyard.'

Hank met Dunc's gaze in spite of himself. 'Thanks. I appreciate it.'

Dunc waved him off. 'You go save the world now. I'll be here with the harder job, trying to keep the damn worms alive.'

Hank fled into the garage before his face could give anything away to Dunc. He'd been lucky to get out of there so easily. The old man hadn't even quizzed him on the fireworks investigation or asked what else he was up to. So the worst lie he'd been forced to tell was saying he wanted the chicken. Maybe today would be better than yesterday was.

He set the dubious-looking entrée on the passenger seat and backed out of the garage. He was halfway down the driveway when his phone chimed with Sam's specific ringtone. He groaned with guilt. He knew he'd been ignoring the Pup, hoping they could just talk when he got to the office. But that clearly wasn't going to work for Sam. He sighed and answered it with the button on the minivan steering wheel.

'I'm here, Sam. What do you need?'

'Where the hell have you been? I tried you all day yesterday.'

Hank was taken aback. Sam seldom swore, and never, ever swore at him. 'I had things to do. I'm really sorry. What's up?'

The information came in a torrent – burglaries, victims, crying, moms, a dog, TVs, broken doors, microwaves. Hank didn't absorb even half of it. 'Wait, whose homes were broken into?'

He heard Sam take a huge, exasperated breath. Then the kid slowly laid it all out. Hank grew more and more angry until he smacked at the steering wheel and accidentally made the horn blare. 'Have you been able to check all the victims' houses?'

'Yes. And no. Some lived alone and there were obvious signs of break-ins. But there are two people who lived alone and their houses are locked with no break-in signs. I can't believe though, that the burglars didn't hit them. I'm trying to find relatives who can give us permission to go inside and check to make sure. I didn't want to call Sheila for help.'

'That was absolutely the right decision,' Hank said, even though she'd likely be able to find them in a heartbeat. 'I'll meet you at the office to help. I think that's . . . wait.' A smile started to spread across his face. 'There's another option. We'll get search warrants. Just for permission to go in and make sure no one got in, burglarized the places, and then locked the doors on their way out. That way we're not spending all day trying to track down relatives they probably don't even have.'

Now Sammy swore at himself. 'I should've thought of that. I'll go right now and—'

'That's OK. I'll do it.' He whipped the minivan out of the driveway and pointed it toward the county courthouse in Forsyth and Judge Marvin Sedstone. And, unlike with Linda Ghazarian or the poor school superintendent, this meeting wasn't even going to be a manufactured coincidence. Sedstone was always the judge Hank used for search warrants because, while a stickler for procedure, he was always available, even in the middle of the night. And he rarely denied a request.

Come trial time, though, he was known for being crushingly hard on both the prosecution and the defense. But that even-handedness hadn't stopped the public from permanently associating him with one particular prosecution victory. Ten years ago, a jury convicted Kirbyville resident Ramson Blaine of capital murder and agreed he should get the death penalty. It fell to Marv to pronounce the official sentence. He'd been known as Judge Headstone ever since.

The judge was in between court hearings and welcomed Hank into his chambers with a surprised look.

'My boy, I didn't think I'd see you anytime soon.' He waved Hank into a chair and settled himself behind his huge oak desk. A solid and fit sixty-nine-year-old, the judge had gray-white hair whose diminishing volume was counteracted by the enormity of his eyebrows. He raised them questioningly at Hank. 'I thought you were out at the explosion site.'

'I have been. But the specialist forensic teams are really the ones working it right now.'

'Not a job I'd care to have.' They talked about the damage for a bit and then he pointed at the folder in Hank's hands. 'It looks like you've found other things to keep you busy. What do you need?'

Hank explained the rash of burglaries and pulled out the paperwork he'd completed in his office before walking to the courtroom. 'We want to just go inside and ascertain whether these two houses have also been burglarized. That's it. Some of the others that were hit had been locked up again, but the doors were damaged and the ransacking visible through the windows, so my deputies had cause to enter.'

The judge nodded as he perused the documents. 'Based on the pattern, and the unsuccessful search for people to give permission, I'll grant it. Any luck finding who's responsible?'

'Not so far. The entire state knew who the victims were. It's easy enough to figure out addresses.'

'Ain't that the truth nowadays.'

The way he said it pinged Hank's radar. 'Are you having problems, sir?'

'Nah. It's just kids being stupid. Probably some kind of a dare.'

'What are they doing?'

'They TP'd my hickory tree about a month ago. My wife was spitting mad, but it didn't do any real harm.'

'My wife would've been spitting mad, too.'

'Maggie? No. She seems the calmest young lady. I'd imagine you can't afford to rile up easily when you run a hospital emergency department.'

'Well, that's very true. At work. But when it comes to her plants, she gets angry as anything if they're messed with. Of course, it's usually deer or skunks – not teenagers.' They both laughed. 'Her main defense is a concoction of pepper and garlic and something else that she sprays all over the yard. It's Marian's recipe, and I've got to say, it works.'

He sat back and waited. The judge's beetle brows drooped. 'I'm not surprised. Everything Marian did worked.'

'She was very good at her job,' Hank agreed. He studied Sedstone's face as the older man hid a sniffle and then busied himself with the search warrant paperwork. He couldn't lose the momentum. 'How did you and she know each other?'

'Oh. Um . . . we served on a panel together. Juvenile justice. We made – the panel made – some good recommendations.'

'I know Marian had been worried about the direction some of her students were headed.' He actually had no idea, but it seemed a reasonable assumption. 'I hadn't realized she had help in trying to find solutions. That's great.' He gently pressed and got Sedstone to list off some of the panel's findings. Once the judge warmed to the subject, the conversation led where he needed it to – the title of the panel and the years it operated. Marian had served on it as both a teacher and as principal. He would look up other panel members as soon as he got back to his office.

'Were there any specific things at the high school she was concerned about? I've often wondered if maybe stress had something to do with her heart giving out like that.'

Sedstone straightened the stack of papers as he thought. 'I've wondered that, too. I know she had a couple students who were in juvenile detention, but that wasn't out-of-the-ordinary, honestly. So it wouldn't have been too stressful.' He paused. 'She did make some comments, after she became principal, about a staff revolt. The way she said it, though, she sounded like she thought it was funny. I suppose it could've been her just putting a brave face on a stressful situation. I wish . . .' He trailed off and then sniffled again, mumbling something about allergies. He cleared his throat and signed the paperwork with a flourish. 'I wish she were still here. And I wish you luck on these burglaries.'

Hank had no choice but to accept the documents. He stood and made his way to the door, sneaking a last glance back at the judge. He saw him staring out the window, a sad and wistful smile on his face. An icy shiver ran along Hank's spine. It was the exact smile Duncan wore when he talked about his wife.

TWENTY-THREE

'I was hoping it could be settled nicely. But they kept not paying.'

'Did they explain why?' Sheila asked.

'I kept getting a song and dance about their retailers being late with payments, so they didn't have the money to turn around and pay us.' The man gave an exasperated snort. 'That's great, but I got factories in China I gotta pay. They aren't going to wait for some middle-man distributor to get its shit together.'

Sheila jotted that down on her notepad next to *Eric McGlinchy, importer, chief financial officer.* She'd given up any pretense of convalescence and now had an entire workstation cobbled together next to her damn recliner. After her call with the prosecutor yesterday, she made Deputy Boggs bring her a phone headset and laser printer from the office, along with a stack of fresh notepads and her squishy purple stress ball. Then she talked the young woman into setting up Tyrone's folding card table and threading power cables to the outlet behind the couch. Boggs grudgingly did it, but not before giving Sheila that nonplussed stare she did so well. 'It's your funeral. Ma'am.'

And it almost had been, when Tyrone got home from work. 'Are you fucking kidding me?'

'It's either this, or I go into the office,' she said.

'No, it's this and you don't get better.' His deep baritone rose in volume with each word. He wagged one of those long, beautiful fingers at her. 'And then you're here longer. And then you're more miserable. Which makes me more miserable. Which I'm really getting sick of.'

He stomped down the hallway and slammed the bedroom door. She hadn't seen him again all night. He was asleep by the time she scooted her walker the length of the house and climbed into bed beside him. And he was already gone when she woke up in the morning. But he'd left her breakfast. Love in the form of toasted Eggo waffles. She smiled and thanked her lucky stars again that she'd met him at that street fair twenty-five years ago.

Now the empty waffle plate sat on the carpet and its spot on the card table held Sheila's phone and the notepad.

'Mr McGlinchy, you said "middle-man distributor" a little derisively. What do you mean?'

He sighed. 'I didn't mean it as a dig. They were a good, solid business. But they don't import. They buy from the companies who actually work with the Chinese manufacturers, then sell to retailers. We've been in business with them for years. It used to be more common, the position they occupied in the process. But it's not anymore.' He paused. 'We have our own locations now. We import and we then do our own wholesale distribution.'

'So what did that mean for Skyrocket?'

'I'll be honest with you. When you combine that with them being delinquent, we were about to cut ties.'

'Faye Halliday says she isn't getting paid by her retailers, and that's why she's not able to pay you.'

She could practically hear him shrug. 'That's unfortunate, sure. But, here's the thing. We haven't had any problems lately. With the retailers that we sell to through our wholesale division. So I don't know what's going on.'

Neither did Sheila. 'Did you ever hear anything? About their performance, their timeliness, that kind of thing?'

McGlinchy was silent for a moment. 'There're grumblings. That they're slipping. In getting deliveries to folks on time. Getting orders right. Basically – pardon my language – not having their shit together like they used to.'

'How about their safety?'

'Oooh, no ma'am. I got nothing to say about that. That's way out of my purview. Our safety and inspection division is talking to the feds. Cooperating. We're cooperating with the feds. And the state marshals. That's the division who knows all about that. I just do the numbers.'

She didn't blame him for not wanting to touch the blast investigation. It was a multi-jurisdictional mess. That was why she was keeping her head down and sticking with her own little aspect of it. Even if she had to do it from her living room.

*   *   *

Yesterday, Sam hated his job. Today, he was back to loving it as he taught Molly March how to break into a house. More specifically, how to pick a lock. As soon as Hank got Headstone's sign-off on the warrant, they drove to the little cottage in Forsyth that Sam hadn't been able to enter last night. Randy Foulk, one of the oldest blast victims at fifty-four, lived alone and had no next of kin. Which was why Molly was currently kneeling at his back door and gingerly working the lockpicks back and forth in the keyhole.

'This is fricking hard. How do people do this fast?'

He laughed and showed her how to better angle the tension wrench. The tumblers fell into line and the lock rotated open to her delighted whoop. She stood and pushed the door open. Sam followed, fumbling for a light switch in the dark caused by Foulk's blackout curtains. His gloved hand found it and lamps at either end of a sofa flickered on. It would be a comfortable spot to watch TV – if there'd been a TV.

'Well, shit. What does that make us? Seven for fourteen?' Molly said.

'Yeah.' Sam glared at the empty spot on the wall. 'Half the victims burglarized.' He stomped around the small room, stopping in front of a table against the wall that held nothing but computer cords. 'I am going to catch these assholes.'

Molly gave him a wide berth as she went to check the bedroom. She came back with a framed photo of a man on a motorcycle. 'Well, this sure wasn't parked in the driveway. There's a nice helmet in the closet, though.'

One part of his brain applauded her blooming investigative skills. Another part boiled with anger at the sheer affrontery of the thieves.

'It would explain that random covered spot on the side of the house,' he said.

They both looked down at the photo. There was a grin on Randy's craggy face, probably made that way by years of riding into the wind. He looked to be in the Rockies somewhere. He was dusty. The royal blue Harley Heritage Softail was spotless.

'This . . .' Sam tapped the frame. 'This is their mistake.'

Molly moved the photo away from his pressing finger and stared at him.

'This one, you can't just put into the stream of televisions for sale on Craigslist. This is obvious. This, they're either going to keep or sell. Either way, it'll get used. On a road.'

'And hopefully seen by patrol. I see,' she said.

'Come on. I'll start sealing this place until Alice can get here. You go look up his registration and put out a BOLO.'

She handed him the photo and hustled out the lockpicked door. He looked down at the happy biker and carefully laid him on the table. Then he pulled out his phone and took a picture of the picture. This would go better on the bulletin board than the company ID photo currently there. This was the real victim number three.

TWENTY-FOUR

The days bled into one another and Sheila wept bored tears. Metaphorically. This was what she'd been reduced to. Thinking in poetic nonsense as she scrolled through resale websites for stolen goods. Sammy finally told her about the burglaries yesterday and she, like a damn fool, leapt at the chance to assist. Now if she saw one more listing for used houseplant pots or exercise bikes, she'd officially go insane.

She adjusted the recliner to ease the ache in her middle and pondered the blue sky out her living room window. She'd rather be out there looking for the Harley. That was a stolen good she could get behind. Electronics? Those could be hawked out of the trunk of a car by some zit-faced teenager. The bike would take more doing. The bike was adult. As were the burglaries, frankly. One or two opportunistic smash-and-grabs could be perps of any age, but this systematic raiding of every isolated victim house – that was thievery of a different level.

A bird flapped through her sliver of sky and interrupted her thoughts. Before she could scowl at its freedom, her phone rang.

'Tom. How are you?' She tried to keep the happiness out of her voice.

'I'm doing well,' the forensic pathologist said. 'And how are you?'

She chuckled. If it were anyone else asking, she'd demand they mind their own business. But with him, she felt like it was a conversation with a friend and not a worrywart nursemaid. 'I'm OK. Better every day. Definitely going stir-crazy. So please tell me you've got something interesting.'

She heard a half-sigh, half-groan. 'Well, interesting is one way to describe it.' The phone beeped for her to switch to FaceTime. She did and Watanabe's face filled her screen. He was clearly in the morgue – a row of metal tables stretched out behind him, laden with charred body parts.

'We're still working on which parts go with which ID,' he said. 'But the numbers no longer match up.'

Sheila peered at him through her phone. 'I don't understand. What numbers?'

He moved his phone so she could see the room better. 'There are fifteen.'

She blinked. And blinked again. Like it would help her with the equation he was asking her to compute.

'We have an extra body.'

'Are you sure?' She couldn't take her eyes off the carnage behind him. 'Wait, sorry. Of course you're sure. But how . . .'

He could both answer that and not. He said they'd been exceptionally methodical, for two reasons. First, it was a good teaching opportunity. He pointed to the end of the row, where two residents were working at an autopsy table. And second, there was no hurry – there were only a few possible causes of death and the identities were known. The blast investigators weren't necessarily waiting on Watanabe's findings to move ahead with their inquiry. If that had been the case, he would've sorted through and cataloged everything immediately, instead of slowly going through each body bag before moving on to the next one.

'I started to worry when the femur bone fragments weren't penciling out, so to speak. Then we opened this bag.' He walked over to a table. The only thing on it was a skull. 'After we did that, I stopped all work and we opened everything. And we have fifteen skulls. Or at least fragments of fifteen skulls.'

Sheila slumped back into her recliner. Who the hell was the extra person? No one else had been reported missing. She tried to think through what Tom just told her. 'Wait . . . so what's . . . this is . . . so one of these skulls is an unknown person killed in the explosion?' She could only speak in a stammer.

'Ah, no.' Tom waved over one of the residents. She slipped on a fresh pair of gloves and gently rotated the solitary skull so the back of the head was visible to the pathologist's phone. 'This specific person died beforehand.'

No amount of blinking was going to clear away the bullet hole Sheila saw in the bone. She just stared as Tom went on about a CT scan confirmation that the projectile was still lodged in the brain.

'We're doing DNA on the skull now. Rush request, obviously,' he said. 'It could be one of the known victims. It could be the unknown one.'

It could be, yes. It could be either one. It could even be some scenario they hadn't thought of yet. But there was one thing it definitely already *was*. A nightmare.

'I need to know more about Marian. And her work as principal. I can't tell you why, not yet.'

Hank hoped he was making the right decision. Letting someone even this far into his confidence was incredibly risky. He prayed Judy Manikas could keep her mouth shut.

She smiled at him and offered the sugar bowl for his coffee. He declined and placed it back on her dining room table. 'Of course I'll help any way I can.'

'And I need you not to tell anyone. I'm trying to . . . to figure something out. And until I do, I can't let people know about it.' He wrapped his hands around the *I'm a Teacher, What's Your Superpower?* mug. 'Does that make any sense?'

'I suppose. But it doesn't matter. I'm happy to help with anything having to do with Marian.'

Hank hid a sigh of relief and asked about the disagreement regarding athletic GPA requirements. Judy rolled her eyes and tucked a strand of curly brown hair behind her ear. She was a small woman vertically, but made up for it horizontally. She planted her large, dimpled elbows on the table with an emphatic thump.

'Tom Barstow's such an ass. He wanted to put a winning season ahead of kids actually passing classes.' And instead of sitting down with Marian and discussing the issue, he went whining to the parent booster club, saying she had no right to interfere with his domain. 'So then everybody got riled up, some on his side, and some on Marian's. And we talked about it. She wasn't going to back down. That next fall, she was going to enforce the state grade requirements.'

At the beginning, Marian found the whole thing funny. She figured Barstow would throw his tantrum and then fall in line. But he didn't. He got angrier and angrier. The fall semester that she started it, he came into the office with a chart of his players and yelled at her for ten minutes.

'And it wasn't voice-mildly-raised-in-a-professional-environment yelling. It was full-on fuck-you shouting.'

For a second-grade teacher, Judy used some pretty salty language. 'After that, Marian was pissed off. We talked about it. She was not going to be bullied around by a man with less authority than her. Well, any man, but especially a subordinate. She pushed it through and got her way.'

That sounded exactly like the Marian he knew. He could picture her sharp blue eyes and the wry look she had when standing firm against an opponent.

'And then she died, and the reform went by the wayside, didn't it?'

'Oh, yes. That little man who replaced her didn't want any troubled waters. So Tom sailed right over him, did exactly what he pleased and got the championship football team he always wanted.'

'Was he the only problem she was dealing with?'

Judy chuckled. 'There were normal things – the budget, student behavior problems, class schedules, stuff like that.' She paused. 'Wait. The class schedules. There was something going on there. Kids not getting the classes they should. Other ones being put in too high a level. Marian mentioned the guidance counselor a couple of times. Florence Dettinger.'

Her tone had been different when talking about that, Judy said. About Barstow, she was irritated or amused. About the class schedules, she had sounded outraged. 'She only mentioned it once or twice in passing. Said she was trying to figure it out. I thought she meant fixing some of the kids' schedules. Do you think she was talking about something else?'

Hank wrote down the counselor's name. 'Do you know anyone – a parent, maybe – who you could ask about it?'

She thought for a moment. There was a family at her elementary school with older children, smart ones, who'd gone through the high school.

'Just please don't let on that it has anything to do with Marian.'

She grinned. 'I feel like an undercover agent.' The grin dissolved and she leaned forward. 'Now I want to give you something.'

She walked into the living room and lifted a cardboard bankers box off the coffee table. She placed it on the polished walnut dining table and slid it over to him. 'This is Marian's. It's all the things from her office at school.'

Hank was astounded. He thought everything had been thrown out.

'Arlene Ostermann packed it all, taped it up like that, and gave me the box to take to Duncan. I didn't want to bother him with it before the funeral, and then there was the flurry of things going on and your family moving down here and . . .' She trailed off into silence. 'And then a year passed and even more time and I felt silly. And I didn't want to bring up memories that would be painful. So I just kept it.

'But then you said you were coming over, so I got it out of the garage. I think you should have it.'

Hank did, too. He very much thought he should have it. He wanted to rip into it right then. Instead he finished his coffee and said thank you. She walked him and the box to the door and stopped, pinning him to the wall with a look.

'I know you wouldn't be asking me all this if there weren't something bad out there. I'm praying it's not bad about Marian, but I can't imagine that it's not.' She took a shaky breath. 'Since I promised you, I need you to promise me. That you won't drag her through any mud. She's been at rest for more than two years and she's earned a peaceful eternity. That, and I loved her. She was my dearest friend. I want to protect her. From what you've just asked about, I don't know the best way to do that. So I'm depending on you to do it for me. I need you to promise.'

Hank nodded. 'I will.'

He fled to his car and pulled out of sight of Judy's house. Then he stopped and ripped open the box. A few framed photos and a couple of little ceramic figures sat on top. Underneath was a black-and-red coffee mug wrapped in tissue paper. He moved all that aside and found nothing but a stack of files. Everything appeared to be school-related as he rummaged through it. Just before his fingertips hit the bottom of the box, they grazed something that felt like leather. He tugged and a five-by-seven leather-bound book emerged from the stack. It was dark green and solid and had an attached ribbon bookmark. A journal. He slowly opened it to the bookmarked page covered in Marian's handwriting.

Duncan is starting to scare me.

TWENTY-FIVE

The driveway was short – and very, very long. Sheila's walker rolled down it slowly, her feet trying to keep up. She focused on the cross bar and the blue racing stripe she was shaming with her slow hobble. Up and down she shuffled in her lavender sweat suit, ignoring the spring flowers and the neighbors' side-eye. She'd finally reached the point where she couldn't think if she couldn't move. And the inside hallway and its damn carpet made wheeling more difficult than she could manage more than once. She stopped at the end and eyed the mailbox. Tyrone would be furious that she was out here. What he didn't know . . . as long as damn Mr Callahan next door didn't rat her out. She eyed his immaculate hedges and wondered if he was peering at her through his ugly plaid kitchen curtains. He wouldn't be the only one. They all kept a close watch on the only Black couple on the street. Then she laughed at herself. She had much bigger things to worry about. Which was why she was out here in the first place. Walking off her astonishment at a murder and her anger at Hank.

Where the hell was he? He wasn't answering texts, or calls. Hell, she'd even sent him an email. There'd be another murder when she finally tracked his derelict ass down. She inched her way into a turn and was halfway around when she heard the sound of a rickety car muffler. She was so relieved she sagged against the walker and waited for Sammy to come around the curve in the road. His Bronco pulled up and jolted to a stop as he saw her standing there. He climbed out with a look that was puzzled, frazzled and horrified all at once.

'Don't think I'm out here like some welcoming committee,' she said. 'I just needed some air.'

'Oookay. Can I help you back inside?'

'Do you want to join Hank on my shit list?'

That wiped all three emotions off his pinkish-white face and replaced it with irritated bafflement. 'I can't find him either. He's not anywhere. I don't know what's going on. I talked to him yesterday and told him about all the burglaries. He said he was sorry he hadn't responded, but he wouldn't say why.' He flapped his gangly arms in the air. 'He went and got the search warrants I needed, but now he's disappeared again.'

'That's better than what I've gotten, which is a big, fat nothing,' she said.

'Well, maybe he hopes that if he doesn't engage with you, you'll stay home recuperating like you're supposed to and not do any work.'

Sheila gripped her walker handles and glared at him. 'He and I have already had that argument, and he lost. So he knows better than that. And now I need to talk to him about the extra body.'

Sam tugged on his ear. 'Do the feds know?'

'Not yet,' she said.

'That'd kinda be Hank's job to tell them, wouldn't it?' It wasn't really a question. More an annoyed observation. Good boy. She resumed her turn and he followed her up the driveway, stopping repeatedly to bounce on the balls of his huge feet and keep himself from outpacing her. 'So what now?'

'Come inside. I'll tell you what Watanabe said.'

Sam held the door open for her and made sure her wheels didn't catch on the threshold. Thank God. She was exhausted. She caught a glimpse of herself in the decorative mirror in the foyer. She still looked like a scarecrow, with stick limbs and scraggy hair. But her skin had less of a sickly gray overlay to it. She'd tell Tyrone the sunshine did her good.

Sammy somehow whisked away the walker and had her settled in the La-Z-Boy before she could even react. She gratefully caught her breath and tried to ignore the painful hitches in her torso where broken ribs met damaged organs. She gave him a pat on the arm and looked at her notes. Tom Watanabe had given her the number for the bulleted skull. Sam wrote it on the whiteboard and put a sticker on that spot on the forensic diagram. Then they translated that into where it would be if the building were still standing.

'That puts it right near that mystery room,' Sam said, stickering the spot on Lamont's map.

'And if we want to take a pretty safe leap, the body parts right around there are probably the rest of the guy,' Sheila said. Sam nodded and penciled a circle around the cluster of numbers.

'So if he – or she – was a visitor, what were they doing so far into the warehouse?' he asked.

'Good question. And if the skull belongs to an employee, then which of the other bodies is the extra person?'

They both stared at the wall. 'Who's already got a confirmed DNA ID?' Sam asked.

Sheila listed five names, including Paula Timmons blown clear of the building and Ned Wickham by the loading dock. 'Tom obviously moved the skull to the front of the line. He's hoping to have results later today.'

'So now we just wait.' He turned to her with a look of apprehension. They both knew how much she hated that.

'Yeah, but don't worry.' She shrugged and gestured at her home confinement. 'I've become an expert at it.'

> *I don't do this kind of thing. I don't have time. I don't have the need. But . . .*
>
> *A to-do list is not an outlet. That's what Judy tells me. I need a way to bitch about Coach Barstow and football parent boosters and that mess with the advanced honors classes and the leaky faucet in the bathroom that Duncan won't fix and my balky knee.*
>
> *Look. Right there. A list. There's no changing me.*
>
> *So how should I do this? Spout out like a broken sprinkler? Take it one by one? Both feel incredibly foolish. Either way, I'm talking to a piece of paper.*
>
> *But – how often has paper talked to me? How often has a book talked to me? A student essay? So I guess this is me making it a two-way street. I'm going to talk. Try to, at least. Probably mostly about what's irritating the hell out of me. In a form that isn't a list, right, Judy?*

Hank laid his hand on the first page and looked around his office. Carefully labeled evidence bags covered every surface. He'd somehow managed to resist reading the entire journal right there on the side of the road in Judy Manikas's neighborhood. The whole box needed to be processed first. He had now finished and could get on with invading Marian's privacy. That was always an abstract thought for him in a murder investigation. Now, with this victim, it was a concrete violation. He knew and loved this woman. He felt awful reading her personal thoughts. And thrilled that a journal existed. Which made him feel guilty on top of awful as he turned the page.

The next several entries were dated two months before Marian died and were about Barstow and the athletic GPA fight. She sounded plenty annoyed, but also seemed to be enjoying her ability to take on the football coach. She definitely seemed to think she would win the battle. That matched with what he'd heard from others.

He came to the end of a page but instead of turning to the next, he moved forward to the entry he saw in the car. He'd planned to go in order, but he couldn't help himself. He had to read this.

> *Duncan is starting to scare me.*
>
> *He's moody and cranky and he looks at me like I've spit in his food. I don't know what's wrong. He's been at loose ends since he retired. Maybe he's bored? Of course he's bored. He needs a hobby. He needs to get out of the house. He needs to get out of my hair.*
>
> *He was never observant before. Now . . . he notices everything. Where've you been? Why are you working late again? I need to distract him. From everything.*

And a week later:

> *Had lunch with Marv. Duncan found out. I told him it was about the committee. He threw in my face that I'd promised. How am I supposed to avoid working on a committee I've been part of for years? What does he want from me? I've said I'm sorry.*

What the hell did that mean? Sorry for what? Why on earth would Dunc be upset she had lunch with Judge Sedstone? Clearly they were friends. Hank leaned back in his chair and pondered Marian's neat penmanship. His head started to hurt. Because his brain was dragging him to a place he didn't want to go. A place that was an easy logical jump away. If it were a normal case, one with a victim he didn't know. But it was incomprehensible with Marian. He tried to pull his thoughts away, but they wouldn't cooperate. She'd apologized for something and made a promise. And it involved the man who had been visibly distraught at her funeral. The man who was not her husband.

TWENTY-SIX

They both stared at him. Sheila with an expression hard as mahogany wood, and Sam angry as a treed raccoon.

'Where have you been?' He tried not to spit out the words. It didn't work.

'I had some stuff I had to take care of. I'm so sorry.'

'I do not like that you're in my house,' Sheila said. 'But since this is where we have to be, so be it.'

Hank stood in the foyer. He seemed afraid to come any farther. Hell yeah. Sam tried again. 'Where have you been? Do you have any idea what's going on? What you haven't been helping on?'

Hank shifted from foot to foot. 'I got the search warrants for those other two burglaries. Did you have a problem executing them or something?'

'The burglaries are not the problem.' Sheila ground the words out through a clenched jaw.

'That wasn't what you wanted to talk to me about, too?'

She tried to fold her arms emphatically across her chest, her standard pre-assault response to someone else's idiocy. Now she had to stop halfway because of the pain. Both men quickly looked away. Sam caught Hank's eye and knew his own heartbroken expression mirrored his boss's. Sheila responded with a scornfully curled lip and quickly directed their attention away from her with a point at the Marine Map.

'Noooo.' She drew out the word and swung her point over to Hank, where it seemed to pin him to the wall. 'I wanted to talk to you about the murder.'

Hank snapped back like he'd been punched. It was quite satisfying.

'See that nice little red dot amongst all the black ones?' Sheila said. 'That's your murder victim. The skull at least. Body number fifteen.'

He looked from Sheila to Sam and back again. 'There's an extra body?'

'I'm surprised you even remember how many there're supposed to be.' Sheila arched an eyebrow that practically dared him to protest. Thankfully, he wasn't that stupid.

'I deserve that,' he said instead. 'May I ask you to get me up to speed?'

Sam held his breath. He honestly didn't know whether she would or whether she'd toss him out on his ear. They both waited through the long minute it took her to make a decision.

'Dr Watanabe called me yesterday,' she began. Hank's shoulders slowly started to relax but he remained in the foyer as she laid out what they knew so far. While she was talking, Sam went over to the diagrams and updated several of the dots with names the pathologist's office had confirmed earlier in the day. There were still way too many with only numbers, though. Hank said the same thing as he came over and stood next to Sam, who pointed at a cluster of parts right in the center of the warehouse. 'That's Jordana. Jordana Beckett. She liked koalas.'

Hank shot him a sideways glance of confusion.

'There were a bunch of little figurines all over her apartment. I saw when I responded to the burglary. At least the assholes didn't take those.' His voice hitched as he said the words. Hank turned and gave Sam his full attention.

'And how are you?'

'What? Me? Uh, fine?' Not exactly an honest answer, but Hank didn't seem like he could handle a heart-to-heart at the moment. 'Just, you know, it'd be nice if we had some more deputies to help with it.' He thought of Ted and how the two of them had spent the week scrambling from one burglary crime scene to another. Hank went in a different direction.

'I'll find someone to monitor the pawn shops and online,' he said.

'Um . . .' Sam deliberately kept his gaze away from the occupied recliner. Which led Hank straight to her. He frowned and turned. 'You're doing that aspect?'

She didn't deign to respond, just patted at her hair and then folded her hands in her lap. Hank sighed. 'OK. That's . . . well, that's . . . fine. Please just let me know if anything pops up. And when you hear from Watanabe about the skull ID.'

She nodded once, a queen acknowledging that a subject had

spoken. Sam cringed, but Hank took it. He looked like he couldn't put up a fight even if he wanted to. There were dark circles under his eyes and his posture seemed to have folded inward like a poorly done origami swan. Sam wanted to say something, but Sheila picked her notes back up and resumed listing newly identified dots, the activity Hank had interrupted when he arrived. His boss gave him a sad smile and left without another word.

Judy hustled her second-graders out of the classroom as quickly as she could when the bell rang. That it was Friday helped. Once free of the building, they tumbled forth like a spilled bag of marbles. She navigated her way through them with expert ease as she scanned the parking lot for the Bostwick minivan. There, at the end of the pickup line. She walked over and Mrs Bostwick rolled down her window. She took a nervous breath and started with an easy topic, asking about Winston, the now-third-grader.

'Oh, he's doing so great. He still misses you, though. He loved your class.'

Judy looked in the back. A toddler napped in the middle seat. 'And how long until I get this little guy?'

'Four years. It'll go by in a flash. For me anyway.' Both women laughed. The line moved and Mrs Bostwick rolled forward, Judy keeping pace beside the van.

'I . . . ah . . . I was hoping you could help me.' She'd come up with a story last night as she lay wide awake in bed. 'I've got a nephew who'll be moving down here in time for the next school year. He'll be a sophomore. His folks don't know whether to send him to Branson Valley or take him up to Springfield Catholic High School. He's really smart. Lots of accelerated classes. And I remembered that your older boys are the same. Can you tell me how it was for them at Branson Valley?'

Mrs Bostwick's divided attention snapped together and focused completely on Judy. She started to speak but then looked over her left shoulder. Judy's breath caught in her throat. Had she somehow said something wrong?

'Hang on,' Mrs Bostwick said. She swung out of line and pulled the minivan into a parking spot. Judy trotted after, still praying she hadn't screwed up anything. Mrs Bostwick turned off the engine and twisted in the driver's seat so she could look at Judy full on. 'You need to tell them to go to Springfield. Absolutely. Don't send them here.'

Judy took a step back at the force in her voice. She'd had no idea that would be the response to her made-up dilemma. 'What makes you say that? What happened with your boys?'

'It depends which one you're talking about.'

The oldest went through all four years just fine, getting most of the advanced classes he wanted. Every once in a while, there wouldn't be space in a class, but the chances of that happening seemed to get spread around amongst all the students, so none of them were left completely high and dry, so to speak. Then her next son went through, three years behind the first. From his sophomore year on, the poor kid couldn't get any of the accelerated classes he wanted.

'That counselor was the biggest idiot I've ever seen. I know it was her, because the problems started after she came to the school. Which was poor Henry's freshman year. So he had horrible schedules the next two years. We had hope for his senior year. Mrs McCleary was made principal when he was a junior, and that spring she was doing the class registration for the next school year herself. I think because she knew full well how much of a moron Mrs Dettinger is. But then she died. And the scheduling went back to the counselors. The other one helped him get into calculus, thank God. But that was all he got. No other good classes.'

Judy was so drawn in by Mrs Bostwick's story, she'd physically had the same response and realized her face was practically inside the woman's window. She pulled back and tried to smile.

'And there was never any explanation?'

'Nope. We even went in and complained. Several times. I had to find a babysitter and everything.' They both glanced at the snoring three-year-old. 'And that darn woman said everything was the luck of the draw. That if he wasn't lucky, we should consider an outside readiness program and that would get him into the advanced classes. I stopped her right there.' She blew a raspberry and ran a hand through her short, no-maintenance mom hair. 'We got no money for that stuff. All six of ours are gonna go to Missouri State. We're not angling to get into some private college somewhere.'

Which would also explain why they hadn't pulled Henry out and paid to send him to Springfield Catholic, like Judy's fictitious nephew was considering. 'Do you have any in high school now, or are your middle two still in junior high?'

She rolled her eyes. 'The twins? They're freshmen this year. I don't know that they're quite honors-track material like their brothers. So at least we won't have the horrible counselor issue. We'll just keep seeing more of the principal since all they do is get in trouble.' She pushed a button and the door slid open as her third-grader ran up, dragging the school's beleaguered crossing guard by the hand. Judy hurriedly got out of the way, thanked Mrs Bostwick for her advice, and vacated the area before the eight-year-old ball of pent-up energy woke up his little brother.

She walked back to her classroom in a daze. Marian had been doing the class scheduling herself? That was such a big job it usually took multiple counselors working full time. No wonder she'd been furious the few times she talked about it with Judy. But those had been vague mentions at best. Mrs Bostwick's specific information definitely shed more light on why Marian was so upset – and stressed. And it was stress that everyone figured caused the heart attack, or cardiac arrest, or whatever they called it.

But the sheriff wasn't investigating cardiac arrest. Judy'd done some extrapolating during last night's sleeplessness. The sheriff was interested in what was going on with Marian right before she died. The only reason for him to be interested was if a law had been broken. Ergo, Marian's death involved a crime. Cardiac arrest was not a crime. Unless it wasn't cardiac arrest. In which case her best friend had been murdered. Judy made it the last little way back to her classroom and closed the door. She leaned back against its cool metal surface and started to cry.

TWENTY-SEVEN

I f he'd missed news of a murder, what else did Hank's unheard messages contain? He drove away from Sheila's house and pulled his squad car into the Country Mart parking lot. He turned off the engine and deleted the nine messages from Sam and the six from Sheila without listening to them. He was still reeling from their in-person condemnation, mostly because he completely deserved it. And tangentially because now he had another murder on his hands. He pushed that thought aside. Nothing could be done until Watanabe came back with either the ID of a warehouse worker or confirmation that the skull was the unknown fifteenth body.

His phone buzzed in his hand. He still had three texts and two voicemails.

Duncan: *You need to get cookies for M class. She says we can't make them ourselves. Stupid.*

Maggie: *We're out of milk. And Maribel needs twenty-seven individually wrapped treats for school tomorrow. Some spring celebration thing. Make sure they don't contain nuts.*

Duncan just now: *And milk. And a leash. Guapo just chewed through the one you got last month.*

Of course Guapo did. The damn mutt loved to gnaw on anything long and thin. Several belts and his set of very nice tie-down straps met their end that way. And this made the fourth leash, because the kids kept leaving them on the floor. A week ago, that was his biggest family problem. Now, not so much. He put off responding and went to the voicemails.

Yesterday: 'Sheriff Worth, this is Angela Alvarado. I heard about the extra body. Call me.'

Today: 'Alvarado here. I know you must be busy revving up your homicide investigation, but I need you to give me a call.'

Her choice of words made it seem like a request, but her tone of voice made clear it was an order. Feds weren't used to being ignored. He sighed and hit the call-back button before he could talk himself out of it.

'Your response time leaves a little bit to be desired, Worth.'

'Sorry. It's been a busy couple of days.'

'Yeah, no kidding.' She had to be out at the blast site. He could hear engines rumbling and people talking in the background. 'I wanted to let you know that we've confirmed that the side stretch of the warehouse – where that room is drawn on the Marine Map – was full of fireworks. There's significant damage in that area.'

'More significant than other areas?'

'Uh huh. A lot of explosive power in a small-ass space. Which doesn't make much sense. There was room throughout the warehouse for more inventory.'

'So why cram it into one smaller room?'

'Exactly.'

He heard movement and then the background noise muted as a car door slammed. There was a pause as her phone linked into her car's audio system.

'I want to take another run at Faye Halliday. I want to know why they were storing things so strangely.'

'You're welcome to use my interrogation room again,' he said.

'Thanks. I think I might. What I really want, though, is to use your deputy again.'

Hank had to force his mind back to last week and think about it. 'You mean Sam?'

'Is that his name? The tall, gawky kid who went out to the Halliday house with me? That's who I need. He was a good counterpoint to me. And she seemed to trust him.'

If he hadn't had so much on his mind, he would've swelled with pride at Sammy's good work. Instead he said, 'You gonna do some good-cop, bad-cop?'

'I'm going to do some good-cop, very-pissed-off-federal-agent. It's a variation of yours, but it ends with the word "penitentiary".'

A chuckle broke through his bad mood. He gave her Sam's phone number.

'You're welcome to come, too, you just got to promise not to ruin our good-bad routine.'

'No. That's OK. I've got a lot to do with this extra body.'
While that was entirely true, it wasn't what he would be doing.

'I get it.' There was a squeal of tires that sounded like she
took a corner too fast. 'Oh, speaking of. Do you want me to
bring that up with Faye? The extra body?'

What the hell. 'Sure. You might as well. It's going to get out
soon anyway. It'd be better to spring it on her and assess her
reaction.'

Now Alvarado was the one chuckling. 'That'll be fun. OK,
I'll brief you afterward.'

Hank hung up to the sound of more tire-squealing and a muffled
honk he had to assume was directed at her. He stared at the
bloom-laden trees lining the parking lot and then rubbed at his
eyes with the heels of his hands. He would never pass up the
chance to be part of an interview like that. Before. Now he had
more pressing things to do.

He started his car and pulled out into traffic, Marian's green
leather journal on the seat beside him.

Judy stood at her kitchen sink and rehearsed what she would
say. Hank hadn't asked her to do more than talk to Mrs Bostwick,
but she didn't think he would mind her doing this, too. She'd
always marveled at how lucky Marian got with her son-in-law,
even if he was half-Latino. Hers was a do-nothing 'entrepreneur'
with get-rich schemes and a bad haircut. Marian, on the other
hand, got a tall, dark and reliable lawman with kind eyes and a
fabulous smile. If only Judy and Mitchell's daughter had made
such a good choice.

She wrapped the curlicue cord of her landline around her
fingers and dialed Linda's number. Her friend picked up with
a cheerful hello. They chatted about the husbands for a few
minutes, and then Judy took the plunge. Mitch was cleaning
out the garage recently and came across a box Judy forgot she
even had. It was Marian's, can you believe it? Can't even
remember how it came to be in her possession, let alone how
it ended up on the shelf with all the camping equipment. Maybe
Marian left it in her car after one of their Bunco nights?
Anyhow, the nice sheriff son-in-law stopped by to pick it up
and they had a good chuckle about the whole thing. It sure

had got her reminiscing, though. Did Linda ever think about Marian?

'Oh, goodness, yes,' Linda said. 'It's hard to believe it's been more than two years since she passed. I still miss her all the time.'

'And you know, I just have to say, I'm so disappointed that the school didn't stick with her changes,' Judy said. 'I saw in the paper the other day that the softball team is going to State. I bet there are kids on that team who aren't passing their classes.'

Linda let out a very un-Linda-ish snort. 'I can tell you flat out that's exactly what's going on. I have the shortstop in one of my senior classes. She hasn't turned in a paper all semester. I hear that about other players, too. And they're not even half as bad as the football team. Tom Barstow had eleven players with GPAs below the cut-off that Marian was enforcing.'

Judy hadn't expected such specific information. 'Wow. You know those numbers well.'

'Well . . . I went into the computer and looked it up. The whole thing made me so angry, I wanted to know. Now I'm tracking all the players' grades. Not that I can do anything about it.'

'Yeah. I bet nobody's able to go up against Barstow.' Judy nervously stretched the phone cord straight and prayed she wasn't being too obvious. 'He was so mean to Marian, remember?'

There was a long pause. 'Oh, Jude, you don't know the half of it.'

She let go in surprise and the cord sprang back toward the wall. 'What do you mean?'

'It was horrible. Just a few days before she died, he stormed into her office and accused her of ruining kids' lives. I was at the front desk sorting out some attendance issues with Arlene and heard the whole thing.' Linda sounded like she was about to start crying. Judy kept quiet. 'He said she was unqualified for the job. That she had no idea what was important to a school. That it was her fault all the sports teams were having losing seasons.'

Linda told Judy that she and Arlene's conversation had stopped mid-sentence. They had stared at each other in shock. But then Marian had given it right back to him. 'What's important to a school is producing literate graduates who'll become functioning members of society. Not young men who'll have no prospects once they blow their knee out in some community college football game.' She sounded calm as anything despite the irate man in her office. She reminded him that all the athletes had gotten plenty of warning in the fall. It wasn't like she'd tightened the rules in the middle of the season. 'She said she'd offered Jacob Delaney help in English. "He didn't take it. Not last semester, not this spring semester either. He'll have a fresh slate in the fall, Tom. And you're the one who can convince him to go to tutoring. All he needs to get is a C. You can get that just by actually doing the homework."'

That was when Barstow exploded, shouting that his star player wasn't going to be controlled by the administration. Linda said she and Arlene had looked at each other, all worried-like, and walked over to the door of Marian's office. They could see her standing at her desk with Tom in front of her, right up in her face. Arlene had tried to interrupt but he'd kept at it, threatening to stick the parent booster club on her. She'd laughed at him. 'I taught half of those parents when they were in high school. They love me.'

Barstow got so red Linda had thought he might burst a vein. Marian just crossed her arms and leaned back against her desk. 'I had lunch with the club president on Saturday. He knows what I'm trying to do. He's fully behind me. We're going to work together to institute a tutoring program for any athlete who needs it.'

Linda let out a shaky breath. 'He almost hit her. I swear, his hand came back and he almost laid her out. Lord have mercy, if Arlene and I hadn't been standing there, I'm positive he would have. His arm stopped just in time. Marian didn't even flinch. She stood up straight and said – I'll never forget this – she said, "You want to win a state championship so badly, try encouraging their minds as well as their bodies. Now get out of my office." It was the most bad-ass thing I've ever seen. I was so proud of her.'

Linda was full-on crying now. Judy felt terrible. She wanted to console her but couldn't think of anything to say. And now she had to switch subjects and possibly make it worse.

'So, um . . . how are your classes going this semester? Is that new advanced psychology class still fun to teach?'

Another snort. At least that was better than the crying. 'No. It's very much not fun anymore. Half of the class doesn't care. I don't know why they took it in the first place.'

'Is there any tutoring for those kids? You know, like college prep stuff?' She strummed the kitchen counter nervously. Was her steering of the conversation too obvious?

'Those kids? My lackadaisical ones? They could use it, but it's never really been a thing at this high school. Although our college credit tests have had higher pass rates the last few years. It'll be interesting to see if that'll happen with my class. It's the first time we've taught this subject here.'

There was indeed a separate college prep program, but Judy didn't mention that Pamela Bostwick had been offered it by the school's own guidance counselor. Linda didn't seem to know anything about that aspect of Dettinger's activities. Judy wondered if Marian had kept the high school teacher in the dark while she looked into the matter. It made sense. Why stir up something before having all the facts? Judy figured the only reason she knew about it was because Marian needed to vent, and a best friend who worked in an entirely different school was a good person to use.

She took a deep breath and tried for a jolly tone of voice. 'Well, you make sure to avoid Barstow until the end of the school year. No sense ruining your last few weeks before summer break by having to interact with him.'

That got a chuckle out of Linda, thank God. They made a promise to meet for lunch and Judy unwound the phone cord from her hand and hung up. Then she got out a notepad, sat down at the dining table, and started to write.

TWENTY-EIGHT

The bulletin board needed updating. No one had been coming into the main office, way over in Forsyth. All the investigation was happening in Branson. Sam was only here to finish his burglary reports and catch his breath after talking to Sheila. But instead of sitting down at a computer, he was staring at fourteen faces. And one big question mark, written in black Sharpie on printer paper and tacked into the corner.

'Yeah, I just heard. Another body. That's a pisser, isn't it?' Alice walked into the conference room and dumped a stack of folders on the long table.

'But a very professional placeholder on the board. You must have spent so much time on it.'

'Oh, shut up. I've been busy. And you're going to want to know why.'

That got him to turn around and look at her.

'I was going to text you, but since you're here.' She flipped through her paperwork and plucked out a mug shot.

'Don't tell me this is our question mark?'

'Ha. Funny. This is a man who visited burglary victim Bryan Reynolds. Aidan Welby. I know that because his fingerprints were all over Bryan's house.'

'Including the cigar box that smelled like pot?'

'Oh, yeah.'

He assessed the smug look on her face. 'What?'

'That box was only the tip of what me and Kurt think is a drug iceberg.'

'A drug *what*?'

'You're taking all the fun out of this. A stash. In the backyard shed, evidence of a lot more pot.'

'You think he was moving product?'

She waved a hand dismissively. 'Probably. And without the proper licenses. That's not the good part, though.'

'There's something better than him violating the new recreational use laws by not having the right permits?'

'Yeah. The cocaine residue.'

He sank into a chair and stared at her. 'Keep talking.'

'In the shed. And in a hidey-hole we found under the floorboards in the bedroom.'

So fireworks employee Bryan Reynolds had a side hustle. Sam looked at his photo on the board and then asked Alice for the mug shot. Aidan Welby was white, mid-twenties, scruffy, with brown hair and eyes and a weak chin.

'What's on his record?'

'All kinds of good stuff. Class B trafficking, Class C delivery of a controlled substance, Class D possession, and – just for variety – a few counts of forgery and passing bad checks.' She handed Sam the printout.

'He's quite the model citizen.' He went down the list. 'Eh, looks like the trafficking charge got tossed. That explains why he's not in prison.'

'Unfortunately,' Alice snorted.

'And now he's probably walking around with who-knows-how-much cocaine.'

'Don't forget the pot.' She grinned at his scowl and pushed the stack of folders in his direction. 'Here's everything on the other six burglaries, too. No Welby fingerprints, but I don't think that means anything other than he started wearing gloves.'

'You think he wanted some TVs to go with his drugs?'

'I think he wanted the powder. And then maybe hit all the other victims' apartments to cover up that that was his goal.'

'But we never would've known that Reynolds's house was burglarized if all Welby took was the drugs. He could just walk off with them.' He shuffled the folders and thought. 'Somebody would know, though. Somebody is probably expecting the drugs, or expecting payment. A whole string of burglaries could give Welby plausible deniability. He could say he doesn't have the drugs and doesn't know where they are.'

'Then turn around and resell them,' Alice said. 'It's not a bad plan, to be honest.'

Sam wasn't so sure. Leaving the dog to die? That was especially cold if the burglar had been a frequent enough visitor to know the poor thing. And know that Reynolds had no family who would arrive to care for it. Ignoring a pet seemed more like something a complete stranger would do – one who was stealing from every explosion victim possible. He absentmindedly sorted the folders as Alice handed over a few more documents and left the room. He drummed his fingers on the table for a moment, then swiveled his chair around and stared at the question mark, wondering at her theory and developing his own.

The lady agent came across as a hard-ass, but Sam figured that if he could survive Sheila, he could survive anybody. Especially somebody who'd specifically requested him. Hank had said only that Alvarado thought he was a good interviewer. But Sam wasn't an idiot. He knew he was here because of the contrast. Gangly, nonthreatening young local beanpole versus sharp-edged, black helicopter, government Gen Xer. It was a smart play and he had no problem with it. To be honest, he was excited, even though he knew how unpleasant it would be for Faye Halliday.

They walked up the path to her door and Alvarado gave it a sharp rap. She even knocked like a fed. He stood next to her and tried to look like the human version of a Labrador retriever. The old cousin answered the door and didn't buy it for a second.

'Whatcha want?'

'We need to speak with Faye.'

'She's busy.'

'Not anymore, she's not. So you can send her outside or you can let us in. Your choice.'

Sam patted the air with his hand. 'Ma'am, we just have some things to clear up. I'd hate to have Mrs Halliday have to stand out here in this heat, because it might take a while.' It was the equivalent of dropping a slobbery tennis ball on the front step. *Please engage with me.* He turned his hand palm-up. 'Could you see your way to letting us in?'

Alvarado crossed her arms but stayed quiet. The cousin contemplated them both with a blank expression. Finally she moved to the side and allowed them into the foyer. 'Take your shoes off. Don't want you dirtying up the carpets.'

Alvarado frowned and bit back a comment. Sam just started in on his boot laces. It was going to take a while. Once the cousin was satisfied they would follow through on her orders, she pointed toward the living room and then disappeared into the back of the house. Alvarado finished with her own boots and straightened. 'I got to admit, that's a nice move. It thoroughly pissed me off and now I'm standing here in my stocking feet like a defenseless moron.' She rubbed her hands together. 'So let's get some of my authority back. You try to start things, and I'm going to cut you off.'

When Faye finally appeared, they were comfortably ensconced in chairs on one side of the coffee table. She sank on to the sofa and stared at them. Sam cleared his throat. 'We're real sorry to bother you, ma'am, but there are a few things that have come up and we—'

Alvarado gave his leash a yank. He was glad she'd warned him. 'You, *ma'am*, have not been very forthcoming with us. We've been analyzing what's left of your warehouse – because, you know, the explosion and all – and we've been able to determine that the left side had a very high concentration of fireworks. Can you explain why that is, when you had a very large building with lots of space to spread things around?'

'I told you, I wasn't in charge of that stuff. Lyle told everyone where to put things.'

'Well that would make sense, *ma'am*, except that this inventory was packed into that add-on room, the one put up in the corner of the warehouse. A room no one has been able to explain to me. Including you.'

Sam had been slowly leaning forward with his elbows resting on his knees. It was a posture Hank used when he needed to appear sympathetic. Now Sam clasped his hands together and interrupted. 'What we're confused about is how many fireworks were in there. Cuz they did some calculations, you see.' He shot a hassled look at Alvarado, like he and Faye were the ones on the same team. 'And they tell me the huge damage in that part of the warehouse couldn't have been caused by your inventory.' He needed to tread carefully here. 'Unless your inventory was more powerful fireworks than you were supposed to be selling.'

Mrs Halliday blinked at them. That was it. She was supposed to respond. His clasped hands tightened. Alvarado stayed silent.

Sam swore to himself. What now? Make it a question. 'So . . . why did your company have such big fireworks in there?'

Mrs Halliday shook herself out of her stupor. 'How many times do I have to tell you, Lyle—'

'Enough.' Alvarado's hand sliced through the air. 'I'm done with this. You paid the invoices. You handled all the bookkeeping.'

'Yeah? And what did you find? Huh?' Mrs Halliday was almost yelling. 'Nothing. That's what you found. I know you've been going through everything.'

'Damn straight we've gone through everything. And you know the only thing we learned from it? That you weren't stupid enough to keep records of illegal transactions.'

Mrs Halliday snapped back like she'd been slapped. 'We didn't do anything illegal.'

'Yes, you did. It's the only explanation for why that corner of the warehouse – that room – exploded like it did. So, you're looking at an indictment for—'

'Whoa, hold on.' Sam sat back in his seat with what he hoped was a surprised expression. 'There's no need to start threatening folks. Let's all just slow down here.' He shifted away from Alvarado and focused on the shaking Mrs Halliday. 'You told me on the day of the explosion that you and Mr Halliday had an argument that morning. What was it about?'

The shaking stopped. 'I don't remember saying that.'

Out of the corner of his eye, he saw Alvarado stiffen. He fought the urge to do the same. 'You certainly did, Mrs Halliday. What did you argue about?'

She shook her head. 'We didn't argue. He just went to work like normal.'

Sam practically bristled with indignation. She'd said exactly that, when they were at the library. Under the coffee table, he felt Alvarado's sock-clad foot nudge his. He cleared his throat to buy himself a few seconds to calm down. 'And why didn't he wait?'

Both women looked confused.

'Why didn't Mr Halliday wait? Right after the explosion, when we were still at the site, you kept saying, "why didn't he wait?" over and over.'

She looked at her hands. 'I don't remember that.'

'Bullshit.' Alvarado spit out the word and stared at Mrs Halliday like she was pinning an insect to a science exhibit. 'It's bullshit that you don't remember saying those things, and it's definitely bullshit you don't remember the argument and the reason Lyle was in a hurry.' She leaned back and brushed invisible lint off her slacks. 'I think he was in a hurry to go admire fireworks that violated your federal licenses. Or maybe . . .' She drew out the word and then paused. 'Maybe he "didn't wait" to do something? Or to meet with someone? There at the warehouse that morning.'

Mrs Halliday shrugged weakly. 'I don't know what you're talking about.'

Alvarado sighed. 'Well, that's too bad. I guess we're just going to have to keep working to figure out who the extra body is.'

This time Mrs Halliday's jaw fell open all the way and stayed there. Sam watched silently. Now was not the time for a sympathetic interjection.

'The what? An extra body?' She stammered around for a full minute. 'There was somebody else in the explosion?'

'Yeah. Who was it? Who came to see Lyle that morning?'

She stared at them. Shook her head. 'I don't know. It could've been anybody.'

'No.' Alvarado still had her hands pressed together. 'I don't think so. I think it was either someone who you owed money, or someone who owed you money.' She turned to Sam. 'What's your bet? Which of those two do you think?'

He tried not to look startled at the question. Did she want an honest answer, or a manipulative one? He decided to straddle the line. 'I think,' he said slowly, 'it would be somebody who was real concerned about your finances. To come all the way down here to Branson. To show up in person.'

'How do you know that? It could just be an employee's friend or something. Pete or Randy or somebody.'

'Oh, really?' The sarcasm dripped from Alvarado's words. 'Was that a thing? That you allowed random people into your warehouse and let them wander around? Near a room that ordinary employees were forbidden from entering?'

Sam wished they knew whether the murder victim was the

extra body or an employee. That would certainly help direct their questioning. Either way, one piece of information could be useful.

'Did Lyle own a gun?' he asked.

Off to the side, the cousin snickered. Mrs Halliday sneered at him. 'Of course he did. Everybody does.'

'Would he take it to work?'

'I don't know. Sometimes, probably. He could. You don't need a permit in this state anymore. Why do you want to know?'

'Oh, we're asking everyone,' Alvarado said. 'We have to look at every possibility for why the warehouse exploded.'

'The explosion wasn't his fault.' She started to tremble.

Alvarado gave her a smile that made no effort to be friendly. 'That, Mrs Halliday, remains to be seen.'

TWENTY-NINE

I don't have enough time. The class schedules are eating me alive. I don't know how I'm going to get them done by the deadline. Lovely Candice Williams keeps asking me what's going on. How can I tell her that her counseling partner is committing crimes? Because I'm starting to think that's what's going on. I had to take the scheduling work away from both of them, so that Florence wouldn't suspect anything. She does, of course. How could she not? I'd hoped when I replaced that work with taking care of the students coming out of the juvenile justice program, she would believe me that the whole thing was just a shifting of job duties. Ha. Silly me. She knows that I suspect. But I don't know exactly what I suspect.

She's been putting the same set of kids in the advanced classes. Not mixing it up like we've always done in the past, so that all the accelerated students get a chance for at least some of what they need. (Lord, I wish we could offer enough classes for all of them. Damn school board.) And she's even throwing in some kids who shouldn't be in there at all. But why? *Her way is slightly less work, but not enough to make it worth it. So something else is driving it. I'm tempted to ask one of the parents whose kid hasn't been getting in. See if they know anything. Even if it makes me look like an idiot. I know it's favoritism, plain and simple. But this many 'favorite' kids? There has to be a reason.*

ank closed the journal. This fit with what the high school parent told Judy earlier today. College Readiness Programs? Did Florence Dettinger run them, or just funnel kids into them in exchange for a kickback? He started to flip through the journal's pages to see whether Marian had talked to a parent. Then his phone buzzed.

Dinner is at 6:30.

If the text had come from Duncan, he could easily disregard it. But the other adult in his household? He hadn't found a circumstance yet in which he dared ignore her. He wouldn't right now, either. Especially since he'd soon have to break her heart. He laid a leaden hand on Marian's journal and then locked it in his office desk drawer. He couldn't risk taking it home, even though he desperately wanted to finish reading it.

He sleptwalked through Wal-Mart, forgetting the milk but remembering the leash. Maribel snatched the cookies from his hands the minute he walked into the house. She skipped away and started separating them into decorated paper lunch bags lined up on the kitchen counter, a hopeful Guapo trotting along after her. Maggie worked around them both, moving from sink to stove. She sighed when she saw only a leash left in his hands. 'No milk?'

'Shit. Sorry.'

'That's OK. Dad can make them fried eggs or something in the morning.' She leaned up and gave him a kiss. 'How're you doing?'

'OK. Busy. They figured out that too much explosive was in part of the warehouse. Too much to be just consumer fireworks.'

Her eyes widened. 'So what's that mean? Illegal stuff?'

'Yeah. That's what they're thinking. Sammy went with the lead ATF agent to interview Faye Halliday again. I haven't heard how it went.'

She arched a surprised eyebrow. 'You didn't go?'

Dammit. He needed to get his head in the right place. Which was telling Maggie only what she needed to hear. Not cavalierly tossing out the truth. 'Yeah, we figured Sam made a good counterpoint to the hard-ass fed. I would've just muddled that dynamic.'

She pulled away with an odd look. 'That's never stopped you before.'

He had to maintain eye contact. The woman had small children. She knew how to spot a lie. 'I thought you'd be proud of me – delegating,' he managed to say.

She rolled her eyes and moved back to the stove just as Benny

barreled into the room and threw himself against Hank's legs
with more force than Hank expected. The two of them staggered
backward and Hank grabbed the laundry room door to keep from
toppling over. He dropped the leash as Benny latched on to his
belt and tried to climb up. Guapo darted away from Maribel and
snatched it. His stubby legs shifted into the highest gear they
could and he bolted toward the safety of the living room. Maggie
dropped the pasta strainer in the sink and yelled at him. Maribel
startled at the noise and the package slipped from her grasp,
scattering cookies all over the floor.

Guapo made it as far as the doorway into the living room.
Where he got a face full of slippered foot. His momentum flipped
him over Duncan's plaid Isotoner and into the air. The leash
flew separately and hit the carpet a few feet away from where
Guapo landed on his side. The dog was on his feet instantly,
even more delighted at this new game. Maggie rushed in and
grabbed his collar before he could choose between the leash and
the cookies.

'Well.' Duncan sucked at his teeth and turned to look at Hank.
'Figured you were home. Nobody else can create a mess this
fast.'

Hank sighed, detached the four-year-old clinging to his shirt
and started picking up cookies. 'You could help, you know.'

'Oh, no,' Dunc said, calmly folding the newspaper he was
holding. 'I no longer bend down. That's why I have
grandchildren.'

'Yeah,' said Maribel as she crawled out from under the table
with a handful of mildly smashed cookies. At least they were
individually wrapped. She put them on the counter. 'He says his
knees are old and his back is older.'

Hank rose to his feet. 'Does that mean your head is oldest?'

Maggie laughed as her father glared. Last week, Hank would've
basked in both reactions. Now he wondered how much of Dunc's
expression was playful cantankerousness and how much was a
glimpse at something else. Some other emotion the old man held.
Jealousy? Anger? Why else would he have been so upset that
Marian was friends with Marv Sedstone? What was hidden in
their marriage to make him feel that way?

'Hey.' Maggie, hands full of plates and silverware, nudged

him with her hip. 'Pay attention. I said, "Would you grab the bread?"'

He had no idea how long he'd stood there staring at Dunc. He apologized to his wife and moved to the oven as the old man shot him an odd sideways look and shuffled to the table. Hank rested his hand on the oven handle. He had to focus. Compartmentalize. Get a grip. He was never going to solve Marian's murder if he didn't. So keep the secrets and act like normal.

'Before it burns, honey. Please!'

He yanked open the oven, pulled out the bread and joined everyone at the table. He had to move aside Dunc's copy of the *Daily Herald*, which made him think. 'Is there anything in there about the burglaries?'

'Yeah,' Dunc said as he spooned spaghetti on to Benny's plate. 'Talk about capitalizing on tragedy. Those poor victim families.'

Hank glanced at the article. 'And there are actually two more than what this says. We were later getting into the houses because I had to get search warrants first.'

'But you didn't need warrants for the others?' Maggie said.

Hank explained how the other break-ins had been visible from outside. 'But for the last two, I had to go to Marv Sedstone. He signed off so we could get inside. And yeah, both places had been hit.'

He spoke to Maggie, but his attention went to the man in his peripheral vision. Dunc's grip on his fork tightened and the corners of his mouth grew white and pinched.

'Old Judge Headstone, huh?' Maggie chuckled.

'Yeah.' Hank pressed further. 'He's always a kick to talk to. Very interesting guy. This time we somehow got talking about yards and plants and whatnot. I tried to give him your mom's recipe for deer repellent, but I couldn't remember all the ingredients.'

The fork clattered on to Dunc's plate. 'And what did he have to say to that?'

Hank tried to look puzzled. 'To me forgetting?'

'No.' His now empty hand curled into a fist. 'What did he have to say about you bringing up Marian?' His voice hitched on the last word.

Maggie stared at him. This was – or would have been a week ago – completely out of character. Now it was the reaction Hank expected. He spoke slowly. 'Just that she was good at everything she did. I hadn't known they served on a committee together.'

Dunc fought the pinch and managed to stretch his mouth into a smile. 'It was some juvenile justice thing.'

'Oh. Just while she was principal?'

'No. Longer than that.'

Maggie moved the bread plate away from Benny's greedy hands. 'I think she started that – what – about ten years before she died? Right, Dad?'

Dunc picked up his fork and focused on swirling his spaghetti. 'Something like that.'

Hank pushed down the sympathy bubbling up in his chest. 'They must have done some good work. Did it take a lot of her time?'

'At the beginning,' Maggie said. 'Or maybe she just talked about it more when it started. But I was at college, so I wasn't around.'

They both looked at Duncan and the rictus still marring his face. 'I think it was always about the same.' He stuffed a mass of pasta into his mouth.

'Who else was in the group with them?' Hank kept his voice light.

Dunc shrugged. And chewed very slowly. Hank didn't let him off the hook. He kept his eyes on his father-in-law's face until he finished his mouthful. 'Somebody from the junior high school. Somebody from some law enforcement someplace. Maybe probation? Maybe City PD?'

Clearly bringing all this up was as welcome as a sharp poke to the eye for Duncan. Hank took a deep breath. He had to go after the other eye, too. 'It must've been pretty smoothly run if she and Sedstone were in charge. I'm sure they had a great time.'

Dunc made a strangled squawking sound that had Maggie turning to him in alarm. He waved her off and took a drink of water. 'Enough about the old days.' He cleared his throat. 'Maribel, sweetheart, why don't you tell them what you're going to do at your spring party tomorrow?'

Well played. By the time Maribel finished her lengthy predictions, most of the table had forgotten about Marv Sedstone.

Except the two men sitting across from each other. One tried to keep his expression neutral and feign interest in family banter. The other forced a lid on to clearly boiling emotions and concentrated on his food.

Both suspected the conversation wasn't over.

THIRTY

The birds hushed as Sam stepped outside and sat on his back porch step. They waited until he settled himself and wrapped his hands around his coffee mug before starting up again. This early morning time was usually his favorite part of the day. But today the birdsong was an unpleasant cacophony that echoed the one in his head.

'There you are.'

He turned. Brenna came around the corner of the house and sat down next to him. She pulled two pastries out of the bag she'd brought and got a grateful kiss in response. Sam devoured his as she soaked up the backyard sunlight. He saw when the white wood near the fence caught her eye.

'Why is there a cross under that bush over there?'

He shrugged.

'Did you bury something?'

He stuffed the last chunk of bear claw pastry into his mouth and swatted the air with a sticky hand. He didn't want to talk about it. His girlfriend pondered him as he worked his way through the almond filling.

'How'd that interview go yesterday?'

He answered quickly, grateful she'd dropped the other subject. 'Pretty well. We're now pretty sure the owner was meeting with somebody that morning. But the wife is refusing to say who. The feds are going to go back to everybody though, on both ends. The importers they buy from and the retailers they sell to. When they interviewed them first, it was just about the explosion. We didn't know about the murder then.'

'So then what's got you out here all pensive and everything?'

He scoffed. 'Pensive' made his thoughts sound a lot better than the jumbled mess they really were. He tried to put them in order and instead just wound up vaguely gesturing at his backyard.

'Sam . . .' Her tone made his name a warning.

'No, no . . . I'm not trying to keep my job away from you.' He'd done that before on horrible cases and it had ended with glares and slammed doors and *I'm not a damn snowflake* at high volume. 'I'm just having a hard time articulating it.'

'It's Hank, isn't it?'

'He's disappeared. Just *phffft*, disappeared. Not answering messages, not asking for updates, not being part of interviews. Nothing. He doesn't even seem to care there's a murder.'

'OK. So let's think.' She leaned back on her elbows and stretched her long, lovely legs out on to the lawn. 'Has he been this way since the explosion happened, or did it start before?'

'Definitely after.'

'What about the explosion would have him upset? Or wanting to avoid it? Did he know somebody who died?'

'No. Nothing like that.' He took a big swig of coffee. 'And something like that, we would know. Like when those teenagers died in the car crash, he was doing really badly and he kinda went to ground. But even though we couldn't get a hold of him, we knew why and we knew he was investigating the case. This time . . . I got no idea.'

'So maybe it isn't the explosion at all. What else does he have going on?'

He stared at her. 'Nothing. Absolutely nothing important is going on in this county except that.'

'Then it has to be something personal.'

'Like with his family?' he said.

'Yeah. What else would be so important that he ignores the biggest damn thing to happen here in years?'

It was a good point. Oh God, was one of his kids sick? Did someone have cancer? Was old Mr McCleary dying?

'Calm down,' she said at the look on his face.

'But if something's that wrong, where he's given up working a fricking murder . . .' He trailed off.

'Then he needs your help,' she said. 'So you find him, and you find out what's going on.'

'I think Florence Dettinger is running a scam.'

Hank was once again using his squad car as an office, taking rapid notes on a clipboard as Judy rattled off the results of her conversation with Linda.

'How?' he asked. 'Do you think Dettinger's selling spots in these advanced classes?'

He heard her take a deep breath. 'Kind of. In a roundabout way. I think they sign up for a "college readiness" program. Only I looked, and there's nothing advertised out there like that. You know, where anybody could enroll.'

There were, of course, college application advisors and folks who tutored for the college entrance exams. But that didn't seem to be what Dettinger offered the Bostwick mom, Judy said. Mrs Bostwick made it seem like it was specifically tied to BVHS advanced classes. A quid pro quo. 'I bet Marian was on to it. I bet she'd even figured out how many families were paying. I'm sure it's added up over the last five years. I think that makes Dettinger just as much of a suspect as Tom Barstow.'

Hank dropped his pen. 'What?'

She sniffled. 'That's what we're doing, isn't it? Trying to figure out who killed her?'

He sat there speechless. He hadn't intended for her to put it all together. He groped around the footwell for his pen, trying to buy some time. Finally he decided that was stupid. He was stupid.

'Yes. That's what we're doing. I'm sorry I didn't just level with you in the first place.'

'What happened to her?'

'We think she was poisoned.'

'Dear God.'

Hank had no response to that. His attempts at communication on that front had not been successful lately.

'Do you have a next step? I have an idea, if you're interested.'

He sure as hell didn't, and he told her so.

Her voice firmed up and he imagined her expression doing the same. The annual high school science fair was tomorrow. The public was welcome. She'd already told her students they should go and see all the exciting things they'd learn when they got older. 'Most of the high school teachers will be there.'

'Like Tom Barstow?'

'Exactly. I could . . . well, I could try to talk to him?'

Absolutely not. A man with anger issues like that was not someone he wanted Judy chatting up. 'You say the public is invited? Then I'll be there. You don't have to handle Coach Barstow.'

There was a relieved sigh on the other end of the line. 'I'm sorry. I don't mean to be a wimp, but—'

He cut her off. 'You're not anything of the sort. You've been incredible. You'd make a good detective. You want a job?'

That got a chuckle. He said goodbye and hung up, glad one of them was still able to laugh.

'The murder victim was not a warehouse employee.'

Sheila absorbed that information as Tom Watanabe kept talking. Something about the skull's DNA not matching any of the samples provided by the victim's families.

'Of course, that doesn't give us an identity for this Doe. But I can tell you it's a man.'

Well, that was better than nothing. 'The ball's in my court, now, Tom. I'll keep you updated on our investigation.'

'Please do. I'd like to stay in touch. And you're always welcome to come up for a visit. Get out of Branson for a while.' The way he said it confirmed what Sheila already suspected. He knew exactly how she'd been injured. It wasn't hard to track down. Plenty of news coverage regarding *Deputy Sheriff Ambushed, Beaten by Commissioner's Son*. Amazingly, it didn't bother her. She didn't feel he was defining her by the assault, treating her as if it eliminated everything else she was. A wife. A friend. An investigator. With everyone else, all those parts of her had been replaced with two simple identities. Invalid. And victim.

She was neither. And Tom, God bless him, acted like it. 'I'll give you a tour of a real morgue. Show off some of my fancy university equipment.'

That got a chuckle out of her. 'That'll just make me jealous,' she said.

He heaved a theatrical sigh. 'That's the curse of the forensic pathologist. Inciting professional envy wherever I go.'

That got a gut-busting laugh out of her. She hung up and clutched her abdomen. It hurt, but it felt great. She hadn't laughed like that, spontaneously and uninhibitedly, since before the attack. She caught her breath and, energized, started making phone calls. She was in such a good mood, she wasn't even furious when Hank didn't answer. Fed up, yes, but not furious. She struggled to her feet and limped over to her whiteboard, talking to herself the whole way.

It was time to make some assumptions.

First, that the killing likely happened very close in time to the explosion. Otherwise someone would have reported it. If it happened overnight, say, somebody would've discovered the body that morning and called the cops. And there was no report of a dead body or a shooting during the two hours the warehouse was open before the blast occurred. So that was assumption one.

Assumption two – John Doe knew someone in the warehouse. It wasn't a random gun-wielding maniac out to shoot as many people as possible. If that was the case, somebody in that building likely would've had the opportunity to call the cops once the shooting started, even if only for a split second. And that didn't happen.

And all this led to assumption three. The murderer would not have had the chance to flee before the whole place blew up.

So the murderer was also a victim.

She finished writing and capped the dry-erase marker. She was no longer laughing.

THIRTY-ONE

D r Aguta couldn't hold them off any longer. The state regulators were coming on Monday and would tear Whittaker's whole operation apart. Hank stood in the middle of the morgue and watched the young doctor wring her hands. It was fine, he told her. She'd given him more days to investigate than he'd expected.

'Have you figured anything out?' she asked.

No, not really. Only that secrets had been buried with Marian and were stubbornly refusing to return to the surface. 'I have some suspects. But it's slow going.'

'Well, I do have some definitive news for you. I finally got her medical records. I asked for six different Branson residents, so hopefully that kept people from suspecting anything about her specifically.'

'Thank you.'

She looked around the cold, sterile room. 'Let's take a walk.'

That wasn't a good sign. He followed her out the front and on to the path ringing the parking lot. They moved in silence until they hit the far end. Then slowly, methodically, she told him that Marian took no heart medications. In fact, her only prescription was for acid reflux. A routine checkup six weeks before her death showed normal kidney function. Normal everything, actually. Until the emergency room ECG.

'The hospital doctor looked at her and saw a demographic. Mid-sixties, post-menopausal, high-stress job. So he listed it as natural causes, cardiac arrest.'

'Even with the weird heartbeat?'

She nodded. 'I do want to say that we don't know what was going on in that emergency department that day. It could've been crazy busy. Maybe he had ten other patients and no time to consider the ECG of somebody who died very quickly once she reached the ED. But that's why we have backup systems.' She stabbed a finger in the direction of the morgue building. 'Like autopsies.'

'So what is your final opinion?'

She stopped walking and turned to face him. 'It wasn't natural causes. It was definitely digoxin toxicity. What I can't determine is whether it was an accident, suicide or homicide. So if it gets reopened, I'm going to have to say undetermined.' She assessed the look on his face. 'I'm sorry. I know that doesn't make for a strong court case. But I'm confident – and Dr Watanabe is too – that she ingested a large amount of poison four to six hours before she died. If you can figure out who had access to her in that time period . . .'

That would be his next step. No more tiptoeing around. Instead, he'd have some direct conversations. And let the rumor mill chips fall where they may.

Sam sat in the dark office for an hour before he heard the key turn in the lock. The door swung open and Hank flipped on the light switch. Then he dropped his bag, reflexively put his hand on his service weapon, skidded on the raggedy carpet, lost his balance, and stumbled back into the wall. From the look on his face, Sam was glad he hadn't managed to draw his gun.

'What the hell, Sam? Why are you here?' He shoved himself off the wall and scooped up his computer bag, his face redder than Sam had ever seen it. He walked behind his desk but didn't sit down. Sam decided to stay right where he was in the little chair in the corner. He cleared his throat to force down the laughter that threatened to burst loose.

'I wanted to talk to you.'

'By lying in wait?'

'Well, that wasn't my intent. But you're not exactly returning phone calls.'

Hank responded by tossing the bag on to the desk. Sam hoped there wasn't actually a laptop in there. 'How did you even get in here?'

'Sheila told me where she hides her key.'

'And how the hell does she have a key to my . . . never mind. I don't want to know.' Hank took a deep breath. 'What is so important that you felt the need to ambush me?'

'I don't know. That's why I'm here. To find out what's so important that you won't help us investigate a murder.'

Hank stared at him. Didn't move, just stared. Sam started to worry he'd gone too far.

'I'm sorry. I know . . . I know that I've been MIA. That I've left you guys alone to handle this,' Hank said. 'I haven't been able to . . . I'm really sorry.'

He trailed off and stared at his desk. Sam forced himself to continue. 'Here's what I think. I think something's going on. Because you normally would be all over an investigation like this. So what's happening that makes you need to disappear like you've been doing?'

More silence. Sam leaned back in the little corner chair and tried to look relaxed. 'I know there's nothing else going with work. So it has to be personal. And I'm here to ask if you want help.'

Something shifted. He was still standing, but not pine-tree straight anymore. He hadn't swayed like a willow – more like he cracked, a brittle silver maple in a wind storm. He stayed up for a minute and then sank into his desk chair. A dozen horrible possibilities went through Sam's head as he sat there, willing himself to be quiet. Finally, Hank got out his keys and unlocked his desk drawer. He slowly pulled out a slim green book and carefully laid it exactly in the center of his blotter. Then he started to speak. The pathologist filling in for the dead Dr Whittaker. The discovery of incompetence, laziness. The reexamination of certain cases. One fatality in particular. Not natural causes. Investigation needed. Quietly, so as not to alert potential suspects. Quietly, so as not to alert family just now getting over the death. His family.

Sam followed along just fine until that last part. He squinted in confusion as Hank fell silent. His boss looked at him with unreadable eyes.

'Maggie's mom? Was murdered?'

Hank nodded.

'Poisoned? With heart medication?'

'Or with a plant. Foxglove has the same compounds as digitalis-type medications. Something like lily-of-the-valley could've done it, too.'

Who had motive? Who had access? What would the timing have been – over a long period or a single dose? He didn't realize he was speaking out loud until Hank shrugged.

'Dr Aguta thinks it was more likely to have been one, or maybe two, large doses in order to get that severe and acute of a response. So it's who had access to her the day of her death. And maybe the night before.'

Sam paused. 'Do you know that?'

Hank shook his head. 'No. Those questions will give away the fact that I'm investigating. So I haven't started asking yet.'

'But you do have suspects?'

'Yes.' The angry football coach. The corrupt school counselor. The board member with the underemployed wife. Sam swore softly. He never would've imagined a high school principal could have so many problem acquaintances. He rubbed his ear as the list settled uneasily in his mind. That's what they all were. Acquaintances. Which was a problem. Suspect lists never started with acquaintances. They started closer. He looked at his boss. Hank met his gaze.

'Mr McCleary?'

Hank laid his hand flat on the green book. 'Yes.'

'Oh, shit.'

'Yes.' He offered nothing further.

Sam's thoughts raced. 'Is that her diary?'

'Basically.' His hand didn't move.

'And what – they were arguing?'

'Not exactly. He didn't like her friendship with someone and was getting angrier and angrier about it.'

Sam had intruded this far. Might as well keep pressing. 'What kind of friendship? And with who?'

'Marv Sedstone.'

Sam felt like an anvil just dropped on his head. You always suspected the husband, but the county's senior judge, too? He wasn't sure how long he sat there before he was able to speak again. 'So at least five suspects. How can I help?'

Hank told him what he needed. Sam cringed inwardly, outwardly nodded, and left in a daze. He'd sat here in the dark determined to get the truth, vowing to help. Now he wished he'd never asked.

THIRTY-TWO

The woman on the other end of the call sounded as exasperated as Sheila had been for days.

'I can't get a hold of your boss.'

'I'm sorry to hear that. It's a familiar situation lately.' Blowing off his own staff irritated the hell out of Sheila. But him ignoring a federal agent? That brought a smile to her face. 'How long have you been trying?'

'Just now. He didn't pick up.'

Sheila rolled her eyes. *Honey, you got no idea.* 'Well, Agent Alvarado, is there something I can help you with instead?'

She'd secretly had all calls to her office phone forwarded to her cell. It was working wonders for her information-gathering capabilities.

'No. I'm the one who was going to help you.' Alvarado paused, like she expected a thank you. Sheila stayed silent. Alvarado resumed, oozing irritation. 'There's a retailer missing. Hasn't been seen in twelve days.'

Sheila straightened in her recliner. 'That is very pertinent. What's his name?'

'William Buck. Buck Fireworks Corp.'

'Those "More Bang for Your Buck" billboards.'

'Yeah. Whatever. He's been officially reported as missing.'

'What the hell took twelve days?' Sheila said.

Alvarado scoffed. 'I know. Apparently he was supposed to be backcountry camping along the Buffalo River. Nobody expected to hear from him until two days ago. He never came home.'

Sheila's fingers were flying over her computer keyboard. 'He's one of the ones who owed Halliday money.'

'Yep. And one of the ways to get down to the Buffalo is right past a now-nonexistent warehouse.'

'Exactly. It would've been easy enough for him to stop in and have a chat with Lyle.'

'And Lyle shot him over an unpaid bill? I don't know.'

'Maybe he was angry? Maybe tempers flared?' Sheila would much rather be talking this out with Hank.

'That's plausible. Especially if it involved the illegal inventory in that special room.'

They both pondered that for a minute. 'Have you determined that's what was in that room?' Sheila asked. 'Illegal fireworks?'

Alvarado sighed. When she spoke again, she actually sounded like a human being instead of a force of nature. 'We think so. I *know* so, but not yet to where we can definitively say so in a court of law. My CFIs are still working on their analysis.' The ATF's certified fire investigators were the gold standard. 'But there is no way the force of the blast in that area could've been caused by retail fireworks, even if that room was packed with them.'

'So was Lyle giving him "more bang for the buck" in order to pay off his debt?'

Alvarado cackled. 'Nice. And yes, that's my operating theory at the moment. That's why I'm going to have a chat with Lamont Rydell. He has to know more than he's saying. Seen something inside that room or heard Lyle talking about it.'

Sheila stared out at her slice of sky. She was liking Alvarado more and more, but there was no way she wanted the woman anywhere near a poor kid who'd just lost fourteen friends and coworkers. 'You know, maybe we could divide and conquer. You take the retailer. I know the homicide is my investigation, but you'll be a lot more qualified to zero in on the pyrotechnic details than we would.'

There was a pause. 'Go on.'

'And I'll take Lamont,' Sheila said. 'He's a local. We share that, and another demographic that I think will make for a more productive interview if I do it.'

Alvarado gave a soft laugh. '*Entiendo. Gracias.*'

'What?'

'I understand completely. We will play to our strengths, you and I. It's been a pleasure talking to you.'

Sheila hung up after honestly saying the same. She even felt a little guilty about not sharing the other possibility – Sammy's theory that employee Bryan Reynolds had a falling out with a drug associate, a man who might've come to the warehouse to settle things on a clear Tuesday morning.

Access to criminal records from the office was easy, but civil cases required a trek across the parking lot to the courthouse. Sam said hello to the lady at the front counter and sat down at the public computer terminal. He pulled out the list of names – *the list of Mrs McCleary's potential killers, sweet Lord* – and started entering them into the search fields.

Coach Barstow. Named in the estate trust filing of someone who must have been his mother. Then a property sale that appeared to be associated with it. He must've sold the family house.

Jan Czernin, the new school board member. Nothing. He hadn't been in town long, so that wasn't surprising.

Sam expected the same with Florence Dettinger. She was a newcomer as well, only local for five years. But her name popped. Two rent and possession cases and an unlawful detainer. She fell behind on rent at an apartment complex on Shepherd of the Hills Expressway within a year of moving to Branson. Her financial problems continued – another landlord sued for rent a year later and then filed the unlawful detainer, which accused her of refusing to move after the lease expired. Sam requested the case files. Dettinger finally moved after getting served with the unlawful detainer, but the landlord had no luck collecting the back rent until a full year after that, when the legal action was suddenly withdrawn. Was it Dettinger's then-new 'college readiness' program that gave her the ability to settle the debt? It made sense. She'd gone from not being able to afford a place to live, despite her school salary, to being able to write a check for more than ten grand in back rent. That was an income stream anybody would want to keep flowing.

Sam pushed the files aside and stared at the computer screen. The blinking cursor dared him to type it. He wasn't sure how long he sat there before he finally did. McCleary. The family had been in town a long time and it showed. The filing of a will sixty years ago. Some property actions in the 1970s. Then again, thirty years ago, a will for one Fergus McCleary. That must have been Duncan's father. Four years later, Flora Duncan McCleary.

Definitely the mother. And then a little more than two years ago, Marian Geary McCleary. The screen started to blur and Sam bit down on his lip until his eyes stopped watering. He requested the files. The clerk asked if he was joking. The sixty-year-old one was on microfiche somewhere, the machine was broken and upon further thought, he didn't really need to see it, now did he?

Sam bit his lip again and made do with the more recent wills. All of them were completely standard. Everything got left to the family. He put aside the older two and read Mrs McCleary's in its entirety. All property went to the surviving spouse. Her retirement accounts were liquidated and split equally between Duncan and Maggie. Her jewelry went to Maggie, with some to be held for Maribel. And there were little bequests. Judy Manikas got 'the potted rosebushes in the side yard'. Linda Ghazarian got a framed fake dollar bill and Mrs McCleary's signed copy of Diana Gabaldon's *Outlander*. Bogart Cushman got all of her English teaching materials.

The clerk rolled her eyes when he returned the files. He was tempted to ask for his own great-grandpa's 1945 will, just to see the look on her face. Instead, he sat back down and entered the last name on the list. Only one entry appeared. Alma R. Sedstone v. Marvin H. Sedstone. Petition for Dissolution of Marriage. Filed five years ago. And withdrawn four months later. Sam leaned back in the rickety lobby chair and let out a low whistle. Mrs Sedstone wanted a divorce, during the exact time the judge was working on that committee with Mrs McCleary. Was that also the time when Mrs McCleary apologized to her husband? Was she sorry for the same reason that Mrs Sedstone wanted out of her marriage? And what made the judge's wife change her mind? Sam went back to the counter and the clerk who clearly wanted to hit him. She huffed out and returned with a wafer-thin folder. He didn't even return to his seat, just opened it.

'Sealed by order of the court?'

'If you're going to start reading them out loud, I'm going to have to ask you to leave.'

'No. Wait. This says the case has been sealed. That's all that's in here.'

'Yeah.'

'They can do that?'

'Obviously.'

'But this isn't signed.'

She raised an eyebrow and pulled the file across so she could see it. 'Eh. Guess not.'

'So it's not legit.'

'It's filled out, stamped and dated.'

'But there's no judge's signature.'

She shrugged.

'So let me see all of it.'

'I don't know where it would be.'

'It's not back there in some envelope marked "sealed"?'

'If it is, you're not opening it.'

'But there's no signature.' He knew his voice was getting louder, but he couldn't help himself. 'So this order isn't valid.'

'I'm not deciding that. And you're sure as hell not deciding that.'

'Then who do I go to?'

'You'll have to go to court.'

'Which court? Which judge? Cuz it doesn't say.'

She crossed her arms and stared at him. He resisted the urge to throw the file at her and instead took a picture of the lone paper inside the folder. She snatched it back and stomped away in one direction as he stomped away in the other. He was halfway across the parking lot before he calmed down enough to realize it didn't really matter that no one had signed the order. What mattered was who had the pull to remove the documents and who would care enough to do so. And that was an easy question to answer.

THIRTY-THREE

They'd already argued about the wheelchair. And the walker. It wasn't until Sheila threatened to whack her with the cane that Boggs gave in and let her totter out to the driveway. Sheila looked at the squad car. That wouldn't do. She handed Boggs the keys to her Forerunner.

'They're still going to know we're the sheriff's department.' Boggs gestured at her uniform.

'Yes, but I'd rather whisper it than shout it.'

Boggs chewed on that while Sheila made her very slow way to the car. It took her longer to do that than it did to drive to the Rydell house, in a neighborhood just north of the Strip. It was small, with a grassy yard surrounded by shrubs.

'You wait in the car.'

'Why?'

'Because you unnerve people, child. That's handy in some circumstances, but not this one. We want to have this boy cooperate, not scare him.'

She knew Boggs wouldn't take offense. She wasn't wired that way. The young deputy looked at her and shrugged. 'OK. It's your call. But I'm guessing you still need my help getting out of the car?'

Damn it. Thank God smugness wasn't a part of her limited emotional repertoire. Sheila answered the matter-of-fact question with a testy yes, and five painful minutes later finally stood on the doorstep. Lamont's mother opened the door immediately and ushered her in as if she were made of finely spun glass. Lamont was already seated on the couch, with a ramrod spine and his hands on his knees. Mrs Rydell clucked and fluffed her into a pillowed wingback on the other side of the coffee table. Sheila tried to smile and refrain from swatting her hands away.

'When do you leave for boot camp, Lamont?'

'Two days, ma'am.'

'And how you been doing since the explosion?'

Behind her, Mrs Rydell sucked her teeth and started to fidget.

'Ma, stop,' he said, then looked back at Sheila. 'I'm OK, I guess. I don't think it's sunk in yet, that they're all gone.'

'I'm sorry for that. Were a lot of them your friends?'

'Some of 'em. I mean, like, not the old guys. There's some my age, though, who were friends.'

'Can you tell me about Bryan Reynolds? Was he a friend?'

His posture seemed to soften a little. 'Bryan? Uh, we didn't hang out or nothing. He was, you know, a coworker.'

Sheila thought about Sam's description of Reynolds's house. 'That backwoods lifestyle not your thing?'

A grin split his face. 'That's one way to put it. And the pot. I wasn't going near something like that.' He gestured at the suitcase in the hallway.

'So Reynolds used marijuana – did he deal it?'

'Oh, yeah.'

'Was that all he was into?'

'He was way into his truck. Is that what you mean?'

'No. I mean like other kinds of drugs.'

His back was relaxed enough to actually touch the couch now. 'Damn, really? I didn't know about that. He kind of didn't bother with us. Me and Ron and Pete would eat lunch together. Jordana, too. They were all real nice to me when I started. It was some older ones weren't too happy with Lyle hiring a Black kid. Bryan was kinda in the middle. Didn't seem to care, but couldn't be bothered to hang out.'

'Did he ever mention somebody named Aidan Welby?'

Lamont met her gaze and shook his head. There was no reason to doubt he didn't know anything about the cocaine. Now it was time to get him to come clean about the rest. She pulled a copy of the Marine Map out of her cardigan pocket. 'You were real helpful with this. Because of you, we been able to get people identified a lot quicker. That's a big consolation for their families.'

She unfolded the large sheet as she spoke and smoothed it out on her lap, her hand coming to rest on a square in the western corner of the building. Lamont's spine starched right back up.

'You talked with Deputy Karnes.'

'Yes, ma'am. He was nice.'

'You told him that you never saw inside that room. That right?'

He nodded.

'You worked all over that warehouse, right? Why wouldn't you have gone in there?'

He shrugged. 'It was always locked.'

'By who?'

'Lyle.'

'He ever say what was in there?'

Lamont shook his head.

'You never walked by when the door was open? Never saw in there? Never saw people carrying things into there?'

'No, ma'am. Could've been empty for all I knew.'

'OK. Then you might like to know – for curiosity's sake, I guess – that we've figured it out. Well, those fire explosion experts did.'

Lamont didn't move. Behind Sheila, Mrs Rydell started to fidget again. Sheila ignored her and pointed at the room.

'The crater right here is too massive to have been caused by just legal fireworks. Even if the room was packed to the ceiling with the most powerful canister shell party packs on the market, it wouldn't have caused that much damage. Only illegal product could have.'

'He said he never saw it,' Mrs Rydell said.

'Yes, he did say that. And I'm going to choose to believe him, because I think he's a good young man with a bright future. Who wouldn't lie to the police during an investigation.'

Lamont's hands curled so tightly he looked as if he would pop off his kneecaps. Sheila leaned forward as far as she could without splitting her middle open. 'So I'm going to ask you another question now. And I want you to think on the whole big picture before you answer. Think on the folks who lost loved ones that day, who need to know what happened. Think on the safety officials, trying to sort out whether illegal fireworks are out there, maybe even in retail stores, just waiting to kill somebody else.'

She paused. The boy swayed slightly, still unbent. He looked above Sheila's head, at his mother. Then he stared at the map before finally meeting her eyes. 'You never saw, but did you know?' she asked softly. 'Did you know what was in the room?'

He nodded. 'Most of us did. Kind of. It was big stuff. Definitely illegal without the right permits. Ned Wickham would drive it in after hours. I guess it was him and Lyle unloading it.'

'How do you know that?'

'I forgot my phone one day. Went back for it and saw them two unloading unmarked stuff. Big-ass stuff. I left before they saw me and just got my phone in the morning. Then I asked around. Pete said he got a peek at what was in there. Salutes – those huge in-the-air things. He said he saw M-80s, M-1000s, too. I don't know I believe that.'

The packaging was homemade. And the shells weren't big, properly manufactured ones used in large display shows like the one put on every Fourth of July over the city of Hollister and Lake Taneycomo. That would've been against the law just because Lyle didn't have the proper permits to sell them. The shells Pete saw, Lamont said, were things no one could get a permit to sell. Straight up illegal.

'Why do you think Lyle was messing with that stuff?'

Lamont nervously rubbed his hands on his pants. 'Ma'am, I . . .'

Before Sheila could start cajoling, Mrs Rydell stepped in.

'I know you think you're disrespecting Lyle if you talk. But baby, you're disrespecting all your dead friends if you don't.'

Her son dropped his head into his hands. 'He owed so much money to them two companies. Ones that import fireworks, then Lyle buys from them. He was behind on his payments so bad.'

'How did you find that out?' Sheila asked.

'Him and Faye had a huge fight one day just before I quit. The whole warehouse heard it. Then Pete told me they had another one a couple days before the explosion. Right there in the front office. About them being in so much debt.' He eyed Sheila, guessing the question on the tip of her tongue. 'They never said it out loud though. No names or yelling out "illegal fireworks" or anything. Just "we've got to earn more money" and "you're the one who got us into this mess". So I don't know who he was wanting to buy them from or sell them to.'

Off to the side, Sheila saw his mother nod approvingly. She gave them both a minute before she began to fold the map. 'Thank you, Lamont. This is going to help. A lot. I just have one more question. Were there any regular visitors to the warehouse? Anybody stop by a lot? Or maybe even just once in a while?'

The warehouse was in the middle of nowhere. He never saw anybody other than the folks who worked there, he said as he helped her to her feet. She thanked him and patted his strong young hand with her skeletal one. 'Don't forget we're proud of you. You get out of here and see the world. See what else it's got to offer.'

'Yes, ma'am. I plan to.'

She made her slow way out and down the porch steps, glad that at least someone was escaping this place.

I took away all of Florence's scheduling today. Not just the advanced classes. Everything. She was furious. She came storming in, saying that I didn't know what I was doing. I told her I would do it this year, because we were returning to a randomized assigning of accelerated courses. She said that was what she'd been doing. I looked straight at her and told her I didn't believe her. She turned white and left all in a froth, as my mother used to say. I didn't get a chance to ask her the other question I have. I wanted to have it out right then, but as I sit here now, I'm actually glad. Now I can go in Monday and pull some records, see if I'm right before I confront her about it. I'm positive there's more going on than just her getting a kickback.

Hank leaned back in his chair. It was the last note in the journal where Marian talked about her school worries. The final two entries were about Duncan. Then she must've packed it in the banker's box and given the whole thing to Judy. And a few days after that, she was dead.

I suggested therapy again, but he absolutely will not do it. He says there's nothing wrong with him. It's a stab right at me – what's wrong with us is because of what's wrong with me. But there would be no problem with 'us' as a couple if there wasn't a problem with us as individuals. He doesn't see it that way. I don't know if he ever will.

What was going on in your marriage, old man? He thought about the Sedstone divorce filing Sammy had unearthed earlier that afternoon. Thank God for the Pup. He was being a huge help, even though his discovery certainly hadn't lessened Hank's fears. Neither did this:

He won't talk to me.

God I wish he were still working. At least then he would have something to occupy him. Now he just sits all day and broods. I don't know what to do. Do I get Marv over here? Have him swear on his courtroom Bible that nothing happened? Ha. I think Duncan would probably hit him. And that wouldn't be fair to either one of them.

I'm just so tired. Flat out worn out, as Daddy used to say. I'm getting hit from all sides. I'm angry at some and sad at one. Which is worse? I don't know.

THIRTY-FOUR

The house belonging to Aidan Welby's girlfriend was even worse than where Bryan Reynolds lived. Falling-down rickety with a yard full of junk. There wasn't a guard dog like Bryan owned, although the woman who answered the door had a pretty fierce growl.

'Ma'am, all I'm asking is when was the last time you saw him?'

'I don't got to talk to you. Get off.'

Sam glanced over at Ted Pimental, who was trying to avoid the sharp edges of a sheet metal box on the tiny front porch. He finally gave up and stepped down into the dirt. Then he handed Sam the warrant. In the past several days, they'd tried three different locations where Welby was known to hang out and had come up empty every time. Then they learned about the girlfriend. She glared at them and tried to shut the door. Sam stuck out his boot to stop it swinging shut. Then everything went to hell.

She howled and spun around just as shouting started from inside the house. Deep, angry male shouting. Ted was on the radio in an instant. Sam tried calling for calm but the noise rolled closer and a man twice the size of the doorway appeared.

'We have a warrant to search this property.' Sam held up the paper. He could sense Ted shifting position behind him. 'I need everyone in the house to come outside.'

'You got no grounds. We ain't gonna do shit.'

'This document says you will.' Sam's boot was still holding open the door, which put him very close to the refrigerator-sized gentleman in the dirty *Down With Big Brother* T-shirt. 'This is Aidan's residence. We're looking for Aidan. So you step outside here, and we'll leave you alone.' Maybe.

The man worked a few words past angry spittle before a clattering crash sounded from the depths of the house. The woman started yelling again and another man joined in. Sam pointed toward Ted and ordered the man outside. The guy stayed put, his only movement a wince at the high pitch of the woman's yelping. Then a screen door slammed open in the back. The refrigerator's unibrow shot up and he swore. He quickly stepped back and put his full weight into the door, easily dislodging Sam's boot. It was almost closed when two new sounds filled the air. The throaty gargle of a motorcycle engine started behind the house and the welcome crunch of wide squad car tires on gravel came from the driveway.

The man stopped pushing on the door and fled into the house, shouting obscene threats at his absconding housemates. Sam threw the door open but didn't follow. There was no telling how many people – and how many weapons – were still in there. The back screen door slammed open again just as the motorcycle rounded the front corner of the house. Ted, gun drawn, moved to intercept. Sam turned and jumped down off the porch, seeing not the driveway but last year's bullet-riddled forest and Ted bleeding out in front of him. He screamed that it wasn't worth it.

Ted ignored him. Austin Lorentzen, behind the wheel of his squad car, didn't even hear. He saw the fleeing bike and spun the vehicle hard to the right, blocking the exit route. The bike, with the woman clinging to a wiry bald man, swerved to its left and dodged through the scattered shortleaf pines along the side of the driveway. Leaves sprayed everywhere as they slowed in the deeper soil. Austin whipped his car back toward the road, pulling even with them as the man tried to find more solid ground. The bike wobbled along, scraping against trees as the woman shrieked. Ted ran after and Sam had to turn away, for reasons both past and present.

He ran to the corner of the house and checked to make sure the side was clear. The refrigerator was still out there. He scurried along the side, ducking below the two windows, and peered around the next corner. The man was trying to get an old Nissan Sentra to start as another person came out the back door, flapping arms and hollering.

Sam stepped into view and leveled his Glock at the refrigerator, who slowly raised hands that didn't have far to go to touch the car roof. The other one skidded to a stop but kept flapping. Sam ordered them both to lie on the ground. It took three repeats for the wannabe bird to comprehend. He cuffed the big guy then fought through skunky BO to pat down the other one. He would need more handcuffs from his squad car. He got them up and marched them quickly around to the front because God knew what was going on out there. The shrieks were turning to wails and the motorcycle sounded like it was dying. Wedged ingloriously under Austin's cruiser, it went quiet just as they got there. The two riders were sitting on the driveway gravel, the bald guy cuffed and the woman holding her bleeding leg. Austin was digging around in his trunk.

'That was not me, man,' he said when he saw Sam. He pointed at the bald guy. 'That was all Harley-Davidson's fault. Scraped her up against a tree.'

Ted tossed him a pair of cuffs. Sam put them on the flapping bird and put him in Austin's back seat, even though they'd been standing closer to Ted's car. Ted nodded in solidarity. Rookies always got the smelly ones. Then they both turned to the big guy.

'Anybody else in the house?'

Silence.

'OK, George Orwell, you're going to ride with me,' Ted said. The refrigerator looked at him in confusion. 'That's what I thought. Let's go.'

He had the guy fold himself into the back seat and then he and Sam cleared the house. Three shoebox bedrooms, one bath, no other inhabitants. Unless you counted the five TVs, brand-new video game console, half a dozen marijuana plants, and small collection of baggies filled with white powder.

'At least we can give Ron Dowder's roommate his PlayStation back,' Ted said.

Sam kicked half-heartedly at a lump of clothes on the floor. 'Yeah. I wish it was the St Louis Blues neon sign. I bet they sold that soon as they took it off his wall.'

'Probably.' He looked over at Sam. 'What was up out there? I wasn't going to get run over or anything.'

Sam dug a boot toe into the laundry pile. 'I know . . . it was nothing. Just a knee-jerk . . .'

'Look, kiddo, I'm fine. My leg works fine, it's healed up fine. I didn't die last year – because of your quick thinking. And that's a gift I'm not going to be careless with. OK?'

Sam nodded without looking at him and pulled out his phone to call Alice and Kurt. Then they walked outside to ask a few questions of *Down With Big Brother*, who had a worrisome glint in his eye.

'Aidan dropped all that stuff here,' he volunteered.

'Well that's great, Mr Nate Riggs,' Ted said as he went through the guy's wallet. 'Then you're able to tell us the last time you saw him.'

Riggs shifted uncomfortably in the back seat and considered what answer would best shift trouble away from himself. 'Two weeks ago, maybe.'

Which was before the explosion. And before all the burglaries.

'So two weeks ago, Aidan dropped off stuff that was stolen one week ago? That's what you're telling me?'

Now the guy was confused. He didn't have enough information to know what lie would sound like the truth. Sam bent down so he could look him in the eye. 'We've already got you on the stolen goods. And drugs. And you're on what, probation? Parole?'

'Parole,' said Ted as he typed away on his car's computer. 'Drugs, car theft. Been doing pretty well since you got out. Your parole officer's going to be disappointed, Nate.'

'Things could go easier on you if you give us everything you know about Aidan,' Sam said. 'Where is he? What's he into?'

Sam waited while the big guy appeared to think through various self-serving scenarios. His patience wasn't rewarded when Riggs decided to stick with his original line.

'I didn't know that shit was stolen. Aidan dropped it here and took off. That's all I got to say.' He glared at Sam and then spat through the open window, just missing Sam's poor abused boot. 'Oh, and I want a lawyer.'

The other two also demanded attorneys – one with an added 'fuck off' and the other with an 'I'm gonna sue you for ruining my leg.' That left only the highflier. All he asked for was a bag of potato chips. Sam promised they'd stop on the way back to town, if the guy answered a few questions. 'Thanks, bro. Super hungry. Haven't seen Aidan.' He tried to focus on Sam.

'Where'd the cocaine come from?'

The bird thought about it. 'I never did see any. They wouldn't have showed me though. Aidan was smart like that. I might consume the merchandise, you know?'

Sam sighed and shut the car door. Aidan was either 'smart like that' and off somewhere selling powder he hadn't paid for, or he wasn't smart at all as he lay in pieces in the Columbia morgue.

THIRTY-FIVE

I t took Hank ten minutes to find who he needed in the crowded high school gym. Arlene Ostermann was in the corner by the Student Debate Club's fundraising booth – coffee and donuts. He wanted one of each, but the school secretary came first. She was as stout and formidable as she'd been two years ago. Only the reading glasses lodged firmly in her short gray hair had changed, from blue to a bright pink. He re-introduced himself.

'Of course I remember you, Sheriff. You came to see us after poor Mandy Bryson was killed. I still can't believe she was murdered so soon after graduating, and so soon after you came to town. I'm glad to see you under better circumstances.' She swept a hand out toward the festivities. Tables laden with science experiments lined the walls. Some had water tanks, others jungles of plants. One appeared to have an actual functioning robot. Computer monitors showed student-generated animations explaining physics and biology and some kind of worrisome chemical reaction that made Hank glad it was on screen and not an actual hands-on demo. The tennis team was selling helium balloons by the entrance and the Student Council's face-painting station had a line of both adults and children. Benny and Maribel would be having a ball. He should've brought them. Except.

'I'm wondering if I could ask for your help again,' he said. 'It's about Marian.'

Her eyes widened in surprise.

'I know. It seems out of the blue. But we've recently found out that the medical examiner, well, he didn't investigate heart attacks properly. A lot of cases, all over this part of the state. So I need to take a new look at the Branson County ones where the cause of death was cardiac problems.'

The poor woman almost dropped her donut. She stuttered a bit as she secured it with her napkin. 'I don't understand. A new look? Wouldn't another doctor do that?'

He was getting very good at lying straight to people's faces. 'Absolutely. I'm just gathering the information for them. Trying to reconstruct these folks' last days. And then the doctors will use that, in connection with the medical records, to reevaluate the cases. But the review hasn't been announced yet, so if you could keep it to yourself for now.'

She nodded slowly. 'So . . . you want to know about her last day at work?'

'Yes, ma'am. What time she got into work, who she saw, what she ate. If you know any of those things.'

Her expression said she thought he was both nosy and crazy. He stuck his hands in his pockets and attempted to look as benignly innocent as possible. 'You need to know these things to confirm she died of cardiac arrest? Because she collapsed right there. Alone in her office. I was right outside. It wasn't like anything else happened.'

'Oh, I know. Nobody disputes that. It's just that a proper autopsy wasn't done. So what caused her to collapse is what we're trying to figure out.'

'Oh, I see. I guess.' She took a bite of sprinkled glaze and chewed furiously. 'I say stress. You want cause of death, just put down "High School Politics". That's what killed her.'

She moved slightly to the left and pointed subtly toward the other end of the gym and Tom Barstow, standing with one of his biology classes. He'd been relentless in his pressure to reinstate the lax GPA enforcement for athletes. And then there was the scheduling. You'd think the counselors would be pleased to give up the workload, but no. Florence Dettinger kept sticking her fingers in, despite Marian's instruction to stay away. 'That meant even more hassle for Marian. She was working on it that morning, in fact. Came in mad as a wet cat.'

Hank tried to appear nonchalant. 'Why's that?'

Arlene poked at her few remaining sprinkles. 'She said she had a few more families to pull, then she'd tell me.'

'I don't understand what that means.'

'I didn't either. But after, when I was cleaning out her office, I found a list. Of students. Ones who were in the advanced classes. Some were highlighted.' She never figured out why, and she always wondered what happened to the list. She couldn't find it the next day when she boxed up Marian's personal items and gave them to Judy Manikas.

Hank moved to the side as a teenager with a large posterboard display shuffled by. 'When she came in all mad, was she carrying anything? A coffee mug, a lunch bag?'

'Oh, definitely a lunch bag. Because I packed it up, afterward. She always brought a sandwich from home.'

'Was the sandwich still in it?'

'Yes. I threw it out. But her soup was gone. She had a little Thermos, and that was empty.'

Hank fought back the bile suddenly in his throat. 'What about coffee?' he said hoarsely. 'I know she drank a lot of that.'

'We have a pot for the office staff. She'd always pour herself some when she got in.'

And obviously the whole pot hadn't been poisoned. He pressed further. Marian kept her mug by the machine or in her office. And yes, it was obvious which one was hers. Black-and-red plaid – the school colors and a nod to Scotland. That brought a pained smile to Hank's face, because the mug now sat in an evidence bag at the sheriff's department. She, however, thought he was merely sad. She patted his arm. 'I know, hon. It's still tough, isn't it?'

He tried to regroup. 'Do you remember if anyone was in her office that morning?'

Plenty of people, unfortunately for Hank. Mrs Ostermann ticked them off. A few students for various reasons, the head custodian and Linda Ghazarian about some problem with her classroom windows, Mary Kimball with some problem about her algebra class, someone from the English department – maybe Bo Cushman? She couldn't remember – and then that malevolent Tom Barstow trying to bully her again.

They both looked across at the coach, holding court under the basketball hoop. 'The sad thing is, it's all gone back to how it was. He got the low GPA threshold he wanted, and Florence Dettinger is back to screwing up class placements.'

And somehow making money off it, if the records Sam unearthed at the courthouse were any indication. Hank paused. 'You said the coffee pot was for the office staff. Are the counselors considered office staff?'

She nodded. Hank bit back a sigh and stepped to the side as a pony-tailed teenager came barreling through the crowd. Her group needed Mrs Ostermann to unlock a classroom. The secretary pulled out a ring of keys, gave Hank's arm a final pat and led the anxious student away.

'Hi, Mrs Manikas. Are you here to see how great all your old students are doing?'

That was exactly why Judy, armed with her notebook and a growing faith in her Columbo abilities, stood in front of Marty Albertson's display. She'd taught second grade to a third of the teenagers here and she planned to hit them all. She oohed and aahed over his biogeochemical cycle experiment and then got down to business. Yes, he was in advanced classes – calculus, physics, literature, psychology. Yes, all that would indeed help him get into a good college. And that's so funny she would mention it, cuz yeah, he was doing a college readiness program. It wasn't tutoring or anything, more like having a consultant for which classes were the right fit. It was all done by Ms Dettinger. He wasn't sure how much it cost. His parents took care of that, but she made everything easy.

Judy walked away with her blood boiling. Marty had always been whip-smart, so she had no doubt he belonged in those classes. But for his parents to have to pay for that access? She took a breath to calm herself and moved along to Shelby Carver, long dark hair striped with pink and a table full of bamboo plants. She was in advanced biology. That was it. There wasn't room in any of the other classes. The only reason she was in advanced bio was because Ms Garcia made room. 'She said I'm her student who loves it the most and the counseling office could stuff it,' Shelby said with a grin. Judy sidled closer.

'So how do some of your friends manage to get in all the classes?'

Her face fell. Judy wanted to wrap her in a hug. She knew the girl's parents worked in the town's service industry and didn't make much money.

'Some of them enroll in this college prep thing. Mrs Dettinger told me about it last year, but I didn't even ask my parents.'

'Did she say how much it would cost?'

Shelby lovingly adjusted one of her plants and avoided Judy's gaze. 'It was two thousand for a year.'

'That's obscene.' The words came out before Judy could stop them. Shelby's head came up and the twinkle in her eye was back.

'I know, right? I'm glad you think that, too.'

The recent graduates who made it to Ivy League schools, did they do the college prep? Shelby nodded. Judy itched to write it all down but held off.

'I heard one of them say that the tests were easy when you have all that extra time. That was the key, just as much as the advanced classes.'

Shelby said that with a shrug, but Judy's jaw dropped. She tried to cover her shock and ended up asking several idiotic questions about sustainability and pandas. Finally she gave the precious girl a hug goodbye and moved on. An hour later, she'd talked to eleven kids and three parents. Some had paid, some hadn't. Some hated Dettinger, some loved her. There was one person left. Judy walked outside and found a bench near the gym entrance. She settled herself and enjoyed the fresh air while she waited. It didn't take too long. The woman sat down on the other end and smiled.

'I hear your nephew is moving to town.'

THIRTY-SIX

Nine years distance had helped. Coach Barstow wasn't nearly as intimidating as he had been when Sam was in high school. He'd always been one of those larger-than-life campus figures. That hadn't changed, from the look of it. People flowed past him in a steady stream, quick with a handshake, a backslap, a selfie. Sam gritted his teeth and joined the line.

'Karnes. How you doing? Still playing some basketball?'

'A little. Mostly doing some hiking and hunting.'

'Excellent. Good to hear.'

'You're still teaching biology, I see.' He'd been Sam's teacher junior year. It hadn't been a very rigorous class. It was clear Barstow's priorities lay on the football field. But to be fair, so did half the town's. 'I'm looking forward to another good season this fall. It's too bad that Tim Lewesky has to graduate, though.'

Barstow's laugh boomed into the gym rafters. 'That's the God's honest truth right there. I've never had a better running back. And he's going to play for Nebraska. So if he's gotta leave here, I'm proud he's going to a good program.'

'Yeah, we're all real proud of him. I can't imagine if he'd been ineligible.' Sam hoped the topic swing wasn't too abrupt. 'Like that scare with those kids a couple years ago.'

Barstow snorted with laughter. 'We came through that just fine, though, didn't we? A little divine intervention, and we were back to the roster we wanted.'

The callous comment rocked Sam back on his heels. Thank goodness Hank, across the gym and deep in conversation with the fiercely competent Mrs Ostermann, hadn't heard. He attempted to right himself, stuttering through an observation about the biology experiments along this wall of the cavernous space. He looked at a forest of bamboo, where the student was chatting with a short, round lady in capri pants and a patterned shirt, and a table with a robotic hand opening and closing a fist. 'Hey, remember when Billy Stevenson got sick eating all those raw potatoes from that battery experiment?'

It was just something to say as he tried to figure out how to end the conversation. But as he looked along the wall, at a display of roses with stages for extracting perfume and another table with something about the effects of ultraviolet radiation on yeast cells, Billy's stupid eleventh-grade stunt took on new meaning. He shook Barstow's hand and moved away. The man wasn't the best teacher, but that didn't mean he didn't know things. Things about plants. And about what kinds would make a person sick.

Florence Dettinger had the transactional smile of a car salesman. She knew you were shopping, and she was determined to convince you she had exactly what you needed. Even if you didn't know that yourself. So Judy pretended she didn't.

'My goodness, word sure gets around,' she said, shaking Florence's hand as the counselor introduced herself. She was a thin woman with bland brown hair that went to her shoulders and long limbs she arranged expertly as she sat down.

'I'd just hate to have him make that commute up to Springfield Catholic, when we could take good care of him right here.'

'I just worry.' She put on the wide-eyed look she used when reading a book to her class during storytime. 'He's such a smart kid. And my sister-in-law is . . . particular about making sure he has the best of everything. You know how that is.' Florence nodded in solidarity. Judy pressed on. 'Maybe you can tell me – how many advanced classes will the high school offer next year?'

'Well, it's less about quantity than it is about quality,' she said. 'We have a special college readiness program that will help with the classes he gets into and even get him ready for the tests.'

'The ones where – if he passes – he gets college credit?'

Florence nodded.

'So it's like study sessions or something?'

'Not exactly. It's more like optimizing what your nephew brings to the table. Sometimes flaws are assets.'

'Oh, he doesn't have any flaws.' Judy gave the counselor a broad wink. 'According to my sister-in-law, that is.'

They both chuckled. 'What I mean is that if there's something like anxiety or certain reading difficulties, he could be eligible for extra time on tests. And figuring that out would be part of the college readiness package.'

Now Judy nodded. *Why yes, maybe it does make sense to splurge and get the four-wheel drive. You never know when you might need it.* 'So it would cost money?'

'Unfortunately, yes. We do have costs that need to be covered. But the benefits to the kids are immeasurable.'

Judy barely kept from snorting in derision. The immeasurable benefits were easily measurable. Better transcripts, higher test scores. Things that shouldn't have price tags, just the sweat of hard work. Instead, Florence the sleazy car salesman was offering a lower loan interest rate, not because you had solid credit, but because you had enough spare cash to slip her a bribe under the table. Judy clutched her little notebook and hoped her expression was still friendly.

'This makes a lot of sense. And I think my sister-in-law is going to like hearing it. She will want to do some number-crunching, though.' She took a breath and said a silent prayer. 'Is there any way you could give me an idea of the college readiness cost? So I could tell her before she makes a decision between here and Springfield Catholic?'

Florence's posture stiffened. Judy worried she'd gone too far. She felt the notebook start to crumple in her grip. She forced her hand to relax and blinked calmly at the counselor. Florence bit her lip and then seemed to make a decision. It was five hundred per class, not a number she usually gave out until the student's family committed to the program. But Judy's nephew was a unique situation. So – five hundred, and then the 'test help' was an additional two grand.

Damn. Judy nodded like that was no big thing. 'So my nephew would wait until he had his class schedule and then pay by how many advanced classes he got?'

'No, no. He tells me which classes he'd like to take, just like every student does. He would just, as part of the college readiness program, pay at that time.'

Ah, she understood now, Judy said cheerfully. This was all so helpful. Florence, the sale almost finalized, pulled a business card out of her pocket.

'After they move here and enroll, have your sister-in-law call me.' She rose to her feet and disappeared into the crowd. Judy looked down at the stark white rectangle. Just Florence's name and a phone number. She carefully clipped it inside her notebook and went to find Linda Ghazarian. She had a hunch about that testing assistance and maybe her friend and fellow teacher could confirm it.

She found Linda selling cotton candy at the band boosters table by the locker rooms. She sat down behind the machine, choking on the unholy combined smell of sugar and sweaty gym socks. Linda nodded in sympathy and kept spinning pastel blue fluff. Finally she had a pause in customers.

'What'd you do, pick a flavor that matched your eyeglasses?' Judy said.

Linda guffawed and waved a cotton candy stick at her. 'Total coincidence. They already had it going when I showed up to volunteer.'

'OK, before you get more hungry kids, I got something to ask you.'

Linda put down the stick. From her tone, Judy was no longer joking around.

'Your new advanced psychology class – how many of your students have a 504?'

Linda stared at her and cocked her head. 'Huh?'

It was an out-of-the-blue question, Judy acknowledged, but she really needed an answer. How many kids had a plan under the federal 504 program because of a disability that required some kind of accommodation? Linda pressed her palms together and thought about it.

'I know I have a few.' She started silently ticking off on her fingers. 'Five, maybe? No, six.'

'In one class?'

Linda shrugged. 'I've got ones in my other classes, too.'

'How many?'

'Oh, good heavens – you want me to count them all?'

Judy was leaning forward in the chair, crowding Linda against the machine and turning herself into a pest. She moved back and apologized. 'I just got talking to people and it got mentioned, so I was curious. If there were more kids than usual.'

Linda turned away as a pair of teenage girls approached. She twisted them generous portions as Judy tried to breathe through her mouth. Why did they put a food stand this close to the locker rooms? The girls sauntered away and Linda wiped her hands.

'Of course there are more kids. I'm sure you have more kids than you did years ago. Everybody does.'

That was true. A 504 plan could be a force for enormous good. She had arranged it for some of her own second-graders, working with parents to come up with solutions to behavior problems or learning barriers. She remembered one poor boy with debilitating allergies. He couldn't go on the outdoor field trips and so needed a revised curriculum to compensate for the assignments the rest of the class did during those outings. She'd taught numerous children with ADHD who did better at desks in the front of the room, and worked to allow the little girl overwhelmed in noisy situations the right to wear noise-cancelling headphones during boisterous free time. All of these adaptations made for better learners and were some of Judy's proudest successes.

But.

The rules for a 504 were more loose than the federal standards on special education plans. All it took was a parent asking and the school signing off on it. An official like a counselor would have no problem coordinating 504s for high schoolers. 'Your 504 students – what kinds of accommodations do they need?'

Linda looked startled. Then she wagged a finger at Judy. 'You know I can't talk about that.'

'I'm not asking for names.' It came out snappishly. Judy tried to dial it back. 'I just mean that I'm curious if it's all for the same thing, or different things, or whatever.' She tried an airy wave to indicate she was only mildly interested in the answer, but it came off like she was swatting at a fly. And Linda was starting to look at her strangely. She sighed. 'I just have a parent who wants one and it's almost the end of the school year and it would be great if they'd wait until next year but I know they won't. And I know it will put a huge wrench in my class schedule and I just wanted to see if you had the same kinds of problems.'

None of that was true. And Judy didn't even feel bad about lying. She needed the information. She needed to be able to go to Hank Worth and tell him exactly what Dettinger was doing. She cast a forlorn look up at her friend.

'Oh, Jude, I'm sorry. I didn't realize.' She pulled up her own chair and sat down, ignoring an approaching customer. 'It's so tough, isn't it? All the competing forces we have to deal with. Mine isn't so bad. Testing accommodations, mostly.'

'Oh, like more time? I've had that with a few kids. But those were second-grade tests. You've got real tests.'

Linda chuckled softly. 'I do. And because of that, everybody's real picky about getting exactly what they're supposed to. So I get how you feel.'

She suddenly looked tired. Judy reached out and took her hands. 'Well, I'm glad I'm in this leaky educational rowboat with someone like you.' She would've continued, but a polite cough from the other side of the table had them both rising to their feet. Linda apologized as she whipped up a serving and Judy took his money. Two whole dollars. Multiply that by a thousand and you could buy extra time for a test, which would lead to a better score, which would get you into a more prestigious college. Which was horrible and wrong and very, very lucrative if you were a school counselor with the ability to make it happen.

THIRTY-SEVEN

P ercy Jackson was a miracle worker. The kids raced for bed now that it meant another chapter of *The Sea of Monsters*. Hank gave in tonight and read them even more. Just because it's Saturday, he said. They both nodded solemnly and swore it wouldn't start them whining for the same thing on school nights. He looked them in their guileless chocolate brown eyes and knew that promise would never hold.

He tucked them in and made his way to the living room, grateful Dunc was out at a Kiwanis event and Maggie was still at the hospital. He didn't want to deal with the first, and he couldn't bear to look at the second. He sank into the couch, too tired to even turn on the TV. He contemplated the fireplace instead. All those big river rocks from floor to ceiling, the center-piece of the house. Nestled together so securely he never even thought about it. But devastating if it came crashing down. All it would take was one crack. Just like with his fragile family.

The next thing he knew drawers were slamming in the kitchen and then Maggie was at the end of the couch.

'I'm glad you're up.'

He rubbed the sleep out of his eyes. 'Not really.'

She perched on the arm and looked down at him. 'I talked to Derek Orvan today. He hasn't been able to get into an ortho here in town. So I made some calls and found him an appointment for Monday up in Springfield.'

'That's really nice of you, honey. Thanks.'

'I'm not bringing it up because I want a pat on the back. I'm bringing it up because he and I got to talking. And now I have a question for you.'

He froze.

'Except for last week, Derek's never been treated in my emer-gency department. Not even before I started working there. Why did you tell me that he had been?'

'I . . . I must've gotten him mixed up with someone else.'

'No.'

He looked up at her in surprise.

'I'm not buying it. You asked me for a reason. You wanted information on my predecessor for a reason. What is it?'

He hauled himself into a sitting position and ran a hand through his hair. It gave him only a few seconds, not long enough to think of an excuse she would believe. 'Somebody asked about a case from a while back. Where they were treated in the emergency department by Al Preston. I just wanted your professional take on him.'

'If that were true, you would've just asked me that. Which means it's not true. Which has me asking, what the hell is going on with you? And don't you dare tell me it's the explosion, because it's not. You're avoiding me, you're avoiding Dad. You're so preoccupied you can barely take part in a conversation.'

That last one wasn't fair. He could hold a conversation, he just didn't want to. He tried to deflect.

'You can't hold it against me that I'm avoiding your father.'

'Ha, ha. Start talking, or I'm really going to get mad.'

He put his elbows on his knees and stared down at the carpet. It would come out this next week anyway. When Aguta reported Whittaker's malfeasance, all number of cases would be reopened. And a certain local doctor would tear into her mom's medical records and see exactly what the pathologist saw.

So even if the world didn't immediately know about Marian specifically, her daughter sure would.

He reached out and tugged her hand so that she slid off the couch arm and on to the cushion next to him. And he didn't let go. He started to speak and her grip grew cold and weak, until her fingers lay flat and motionless in his. He pressed his other hand on top, trying to warm them and knowing he wouldn't succeed.

'Heartbeat.'

He nodded.

'Somebody gave her a fatal dose of digoxin.'

'Unless . . .'

She was staring at the wall behind him. 'No. There is no medical reason she would have that in her system. No reason for those kind of heart readings. Someone poisoned her.'

He nodded again.

'How long have you known this?'

'A week.'

Now she looked at him. He almost wanted her to get mad at him. Anything to take her mind away from the pain.

'Why?'

He looked at her. Why did he wait a week? Or why did someone kill her mother? He went with the question he could answer. 'Because I was trying to investigate – before people found out. Before . . .'

'Before the killer knew that we know it's a murder,' she finished as he trailed off, still talking to the wall. Her hand grew colder. He didn't let go.

'You still could've told me.'

'I'm sorry.' It was all he could say. He would do it the same way again, but he certainly wasn't going to sit here and tell her that. Instead he fell silent and let her think. Finally she pulled her hand away and looked him in the eye.

'You have suspects?'

'Yes.'

'How many?'

Five. 'Three.'

'Three people wanted my mom dead?' There was no emotion in her voice.

'Well, three people have motive.'

'The same motive?'

'No.' He waited. She was feeling her way, asking precise questions. He knew how she processed things and he knew that meant she wanted precise answers and no more.

'What motives?'

'Two of them – to stop her from instituting new policies at school. The third – to open up the principal job for someone else.' That was Jan Czernin, the school board member with the wife who wanted the BVHS principal job, although Hank wasn't considering him anymore. The man hadn't been anywhere near Marian the day of her death. But telling Maggie that motive was better than divulging the one for suspects four and five. There was no way he could look at her devastated face and say the word *adultery*. Besides, maybe if he prayed hard enough, he would find out it wasn't true.

'She was murdered because of her job?'

'That's what I'm looking into.'

Her eyes narrowed. 'That's cop speak.'

Shit. 'I don't mean it to be. All I mean is I'm trying to figure out who had access to her, or her food and drink, that morning. I'm trying to nose around without letting anybody know what I'm after. So I haven't definitively found out very much.'

She let out a long breath. 'So what happens when they publicly slam Whittaker on Monday?'

'Then I start asking direct questions of these people.'

'Good.' She balled her hands into worried fists. 'But how long are you going to be able to do that? It happened within the city limits. It'll be Branson PD's case.'

He was worried about that, too. He'd need to pull some strings he'd never used before. He hoped they worked.

'I will make sure that everything . . . that everything gets done. I will do—'

She cut him off. 'I know how these things work. So don't make me a promise you might not be able to keep.'

He pulled her closer and made the promise anyway. *I will do whatever it takes.*

She crumpled then, sobbing in his arms. He held her and stared at the fireplace, feeling the cracks start to form.

Duncan picked up the ECG reading and then let it fall back to the dining table.

'This makes you sure? How does this make you sure?'

'It's a different kind of heartbeat, Dad. The pathologist is right.'

Maggie was worryingly pale, her face bleached overnight by grief and nonstop tears. Hank sat an arm's length away and tried to be invisible. The better to watch Duncan. His father-in-law stared in bafflement at the medical records, and his daughter.

'Why didn't they figure it out then? When it happened?'

'I explained why, Dad. The former ED doctor rushed it, and Whittaker didn't do his job.'

'Didn't do an autopsy?'

'Right.'

'This would've been found if he had?'

She nodded, but he still looked bewildered. That was understandable to a point. But Maggie had been explaining over and over for the past half-hour. And Duncan McCleary was not otherwise a confused old man. The codger was still sharp as a tack and had no problem poking people in order to prove it. That he wasn't poking now made Hank increasingly uneasy.

'So there's going to be an investigation,' Maggie continued patiently.

'For how this toxin stuff got to her?'

They both looked at Hank. He nodded.

'What . . . what if she . . . would she have done this to herself?'

The back of Hank's neck started to tingle. That scenario would be the perfect misdirection if Duncan had something to hide. He started to respond with his own question but Maggie got there first.

'Are you kidding me?' Her volume increased with each word. 'Why would you say that? Mom wasn't suicidal. What makes you even think that?'

Dunc snapped back in his chair. Even Hank leaned away a bit. Maggie smacked the table and demanded an answer.

'She wasn't the same.' He stared down at his hands. 'Work had been really stressful. And I maybe wasn't as understanding as I could've been.'

'What?' It came out of her as a snarl. Hank fought the urge to take her hand. Dunc fought the urge to flee.

'I had just retired and I was bored, and she was busy and productive. I wasn't those things any more, and I missed it. So I didn't want to pay attention to her being that way.'

Was that all he'd done? Maggie's softening spine and sympathetic sniffle showed she believed him. Hank sure as hell didn't. There was another reason Dunc might not have been understanding of his wife. And he planned on discussing it with the old man once they were alone. But for now, he thought, let's see who you toss at me to keep the focus off you.

'Was there anyone who was mad at Marian?'

Dunc rubbed the bridge of his nose. 'I'm sorry. Let me think. Um. The football coach. Barstow. He was so ticked off about Marian raising the GPA requirements for athletes. He kept cornering her every chance he could. Yelling at her to keep the status quo.'

Maggie bristled again, this time at Barstow's treatment of her mother. Hank let her rant for a minute then turned back to Dunc. 'Was that it? Anybody else?'

'That school counselor. I don't know if she was mad at Marian, but Marian was sure mad at her.'

Dunc didn't remember the woman's name, but she'd played favorites with the class scheduling for several years. So Marian took the task away from her. She was in the process of doing it all herself that spring. Then some parent of a sophomore came in and demanded certain classes. 'He said he'd already paid for them and so his son had better get exactly what the counselor had promised.'

'Wait – someone was selling classes? In a public school?' Maggie thumped a still clenched fist on the table. 'I don't even understand that. But oh, Lord, Mom must've been mad.'

Dunc half-smiled. 'She was furious. That was a few days before she died. She came home with a list of kids and she was going through it, pulling their records. She was trying to get as much evidence as she could before she went to the superintendent.'

'What did she find?' Hank tried to keep his voice neutral.

Dunc pulled a tissue out of the depleted box in the middle of the table and wiped his eyes. At the beginning, she didn't know what she was looking for, Dunc said. With the first kids on the list, she went through their entire records, spending hours on her laptop in the evenings. She was starting to narrow it down when she died, searching for specific items in each file instead of examining the whole thing.

'What specific items?' Hank asked.

'I don't know. But she was getting close. And more outraged.'

'Did she ever mention anything about a 504?' Hank knew about the federal law thanks to Judy's detailed tutorial after yesterday's science fair.

Dunc shrugged helplessly. 'Maybe? I don't remember.' He looked at Maggie and the tears started again. 'I was so irritated about it all . . . I'm so sorry.'

The apology was heartbreakingly genuine. But what was he apologizing for? Being a jerk or being a killer? Maggie leapt to her feet and went around the table. She wrapped Dunc in a hug. It hadn't occurred to her – would never occur to her – that her father was a suspect. Hank slipped silently out of the room before his face could reveal the truth.

THIRTY-EIGHT

Tyrone hated working Sundays. Stupid twenty-first century postal service, he grumbled on his way out the door this morning. Sheila usually felt sympathetic. But not today. Now she was glad for the empty house and the silent garage, where she could take all the time she needed to get into her Forerunner. Her beloved car which, thank Jesus, was high off the ground. If she had to crawl into a sedan, she'd never get out again. And if her husband caught her driving, she'd never hear the end of it.

She backed out of the driveway and fought with the steering wheel as her weak arms tried to turn it in the right direction. She finally got herself straight on the road and gave Mr Callahan's closed curtains a one-fingered wave as she drove away. Now all she had to do was make it across town to the steak and catfish place on Highway 165. She couldn't wait to tuck into one of the restaurant's barbecue offerings, or hear what Alvarado had to say about the missing retailer.

The restaurant wasn't on the crowded Strip. And it was open on a Sunday. That combination was hard to find in this town, so this spot was one of the few choices she could offer the ATF agent. She pulled into the respectably full parking lot and sighed. There was no way she could walk from a spot in the far row. She grudgingly pulled the disabled parking placard out of her purse and used it to park five steps from the door, praying that no one saw her. She was inside and seated at a table ten minutes before the arranged time, cane tucked out of sight next to the wall.

Alvarado slid into a chair across from her and eagerly took a menu. Her short, dark hair was a little tousled and her olive skin face had little makeup – only lip gloss and half-heartedly applied eyebrow pencil. Sheila wished for the days she could be as blasé. She now had to carefully spackle on her Fenty 485 foundation to cover the gray tinge still haunting her skin.

They waited impatiently for the server to leave them alone. Finally after a long list of specials, they ordered and were left in peace to talk about decidedly unpeaceful things.

'It's nice to meet you in person,' Alvarado said. 'I've been dying to know what Lamont told you.'

'Lyle was moving illegal product. Lamont didn't ever see it, but one of his friends did. Big stuff. M-1000 type stuff. Quarter sticks. And it looked homemade.'

Alvarado let out a 'fuck' loud enough to turn heads. 'Did any of it leave the premises?'

'I don't know.' She laid out Skyrocket's debt problems with the importers and the fights with his wife that employees witnessed. Alvarado's expression grew thunderous.

'So she did know.' The federal agent nearly cracked her water glass she squeezed so hard. 'She knew and she sat there crying pretty tears and disavowing everything. I will put her in prison, so help me God.'

Sheila didn't doubt it. Clearly the agent was not someone to be messed with. A woman after her own heart. 'So Lyle badly needed what his retailers owed him. What have you found out about William Buck?'

The fireworks retailer, he of the 'More Bang for Your Buck' chain of stores, had family who was refusing to consider he might be a murder victim and instead was launching a full-fledged missing camper manhunt out along the Buffalo River near Pruitt. The net result, Alvarado groused, was a refusal to provide a DNA sample. Sheila wished again that the cars parked in the warehouse lot had survived the blast. Some were recognizable, but two parked nearest the building were not. One of them might be Buck's vehicle. Or not. Evidence might be extracted at some point, but it was low on the forensic priority list, seeing as they still weren't even sure they had all the body parts. They also hadn't yet found the gun.

'We're asking for a warrant. To get his damn toothbrush or something with his DNA. And his phone records.'

Sheila thought about DNA as they fell silent and let the waiter set down their food. Alvarado dug in. Sheila nibbled a steak fry. 'I do have something else to share. One of the blast victims, Bryan Reynolds, had an extracurricular activity.'

Alvarado cocked an interested eyebrow.

'He was dealing pot, without the proper permits.' Sheila dunked the fry in her ketchup with a flourish. 'And storing what appears to be a large amount of cocaine.'

Alvarado put down her burger. 'That is not a low-risk side hustle.'

'It is not. That's why I'm concerned about the welfare of one of his criminal associates.'

Aidan Welby hadn't been seen in two weeks, which didn't mean anything. An apparent cocaine dealer with a large stolen stash to unload wouldn't necessarily be frequenting his normal places. He could be alive and well, Sheila said. Or his bits and pieces could be sitting in Tom Watanabe's morgue. Unfortunately, his previous convictions hadn't been serious enough to trigger automatic DNA collection, hence the currently ongoing attempt to sort out which toothbrush at the Welby homestead was his. Alvarado put down her burger. 'You're thinking some kind of business disagreement? He shows up at the warehouse to confront Reynolds and Reynolds shoots him?'

'I figured it was enough of a possibility to make it worth comparing the DNA.'

'Absolutely. If that's it, it wouldn't untangle the illegal fire-works mess, but it'd at least wrap up the homicide. That'd be nice.'

'What will you do next with the fireworks mess?'

Alvarado sighed. 'Homemade is very, very problematic. I really need to know if any of it left the warehouse. Which means . . .'

'You're going to take another run at Faye Halliday.'

'Hell, yes. Can I borrow your interrogation room again?'

She nodded.

'And your Deputy Karnes.'

'Sammy? Of course.' She finally took a bite of her sandwich. Alvarado leaned back in her chair and watched her. Sheila paused. 'Did you need anything else?'

'It'd be nice to have you there, too. You're the one who knows exactly what Lamont said. His statement is how we're going to hang her.'

Sheila thought about the long drive to the jail in Forsyth and then sitting in one of those awful, butt-numbing chairs in the interrogation room. She didn't think she could do it. She desperately wanted to, but even getting here for lunch had almost killed her.

'I'm happy to drive you.'

Sheila stared at her. The agent gestured at the handle of her cane, just peeking out from behind her chair. Sheila felt her face flush as she tried to draw herself up into a better posture. Alvarado quickly held up her hands.

'Look, sorry. I meant no offense. I just think it's gotten around, to women in law enforcement. About what happened to you.'

'What?' The word came out before she could stop it. 'It's gotten around? What the hell does that mean?'

It made the newspapers in places like St Louis and Kansas City, Alvarado said. Brief mentions, but enough to catch the notice of other female officers who all too often walked alone in what should be innocent places. She and her friends had certainly talked about it. Sheila stared at her. It wasn't news she ever thought would leave her little corner of the world. She didn't like that it had. But, as with so much else lately, she wasn't given a choice. She slowly forced her clenched hands to put down her strangled pulled pork sandwich. Barbecue sauce dripped off her fingers.

'I don't mean to be prickly. All of this has been . . . unpleasant. I just want to get it over with, with as little attention as possible and as fast as possible.' So far, she was failing miserably at both. 'Being forced to stay on the sidelines is, well, not something I'm enjoying.'

'So come with me.'

They sat there for a moment, Angie Alvarado sitting loosely relaxed and Sheila taking stock of the pain circling her middle like a heavyweight boxing championship belt. Finally, one of them made a move. A slow one.

'OK,' Sheila said. 'Let's go.'

THIRTY-NINE

Amber Boggs pulled up outside department headquarters and
got out.

'They told me not to handcuff her.'

'She's not under arrest,' Sam said.

'It sounds like she should be,' Boggs said.

'Yeah, they don't want her thinking she needs to call a lawyer.'

But they did want to spook her. And getting chauffeured by
the blank-faced Boggs appeared to have done that very effec-
tively. Faye Halliday huddled in the front passenger seat, hands
clasped between her knees and shoulders sagging forward into
the seat belt. Sam opened her door. She gave a start and
unbuckled herself. The circles under her eyes had gone from
puffy red to bruised purple and she looked as if she'd shed ten
pounds since he saw her three days ago. This was not a woman
with a light conscience.

Sam thanked Boggs and guided Mrs Halliday into the building,
where Agent Alvarado was waiting. He started down the hallway
to interrogation. Alvarado stopped and pointed in the other direction. 'We're going to sit in the conference room. It'll be more
comfortable.' Sam stared at her. That was where his bulletin
board was. And the other investigative material, plastered all over
the walls by various deputies. Alvarado shot him a look that said
keep your mouth shut and so he did. Then they entered the room
and he understood.

The table in the middle of the room had only four chairs
around it. Three faced a blank wall, stripped of the investigative
reports that he'd seen there a few days ago. The fourth chair
sat by itself on the other side of the table. It faced the bulletin
board full of pictures, which hadn't been touched since he'd
added to it earlier in the week. Fourteen alive and happy faces,
a Sharpie question mark, and a photo of a big gray dog
confronted the warehouse owner as she took a seat. They'd
studded the wall around it with photos from the blast site. And

it was *they*. Because in one of the chairs facing the blank wall sat Sheila. Dear God.

It took all his self-control to keep quiet. Hank was going to kill her. Mr Turley was really going to kill her. Hell, he wanted to kill her. He glared as he sank into a chair. Her face was pinched with pain, but she looked happy anyway. She nodded at him with only the tiniest smirk at the corner of her mouth. Anyone else would miss it. Which meant it was just for him, just as if she were wagging her finger in his face. *Don't you back-talk, I got every right to do my job*, her voice in his head clear as a bell. It made him smirk a little, too.

Fortunately, Mrs Halliday was busy staring at the carpet and didn't see him. Alvarado sat down in between Sam and Sheila and cleared her throat. 'Thanks for coming in, Faye.'

Sam was confident Boggs hadn't presented it as a choice. And now he knew whose sly idea it was to assign the task to the impassive deputy in the first place. He fought the urge to glance again at Sheila.

'We just have some more questions,' Alvarado continued. 'So let's start with the fight you had with your husband about a week before the explosion. And then the one you said you had just that morning. About the same thing, I hear. The debts you owe to the importers.'

Faye Halliday kept staring at the floor. 'We had some talks. It wasn't like we were arguing.'

Alvarado tapped a fingernail on the tabletop impatiently. 'You screamed at each other.'

'That's just rumors. Second-hand stuff.'

'No.' Every gaze snapped toward Sheila, including Mrs Halliday's. 'There is an employee who survived.'

Mrs Halliday slumped in her chair. 'That first fight was before Lamont quit? I thought he was already gone.'

'So you thought you could get away with not mentioning it.' Alvarado kept ticking a finger against the wood surface. 'Would've been so convenient if all the witnesses had been killed. Just like you thought all the witnesses to illegal homemade fireworks are dead, too.'

The word 'homemade' came out dripping with acid. It hit Mrs Halliday and she shriveled to nothing. Sam stayed quiet. That part was true. Anyone who'd actually laid eyes on the illegal product was dead. Lamont had only heard about it. But he wasn't sure Mrs Halliday knew that.

'So when did you start breaking the law, Faye?' the agent asked.

'I didn't.' She was trembling now.

'It's your business just as much as it's his business. So that room full of illegal product, that's on you, too.'

'Now hold on.' Sheila placed her hand flat on the table in front of Alvarado, then smiled at Mrs Halliday. 'Faye, you were fighting with Lyle about it. We have a witness. So you were trying to do the right thing. We need you to do that again. We need you to tell us who he was selling to. Who was buying this stuff?'

'We were just fighting about how much money we owed. And who owed us. That's all.'

She pressed her lips together and stared down at her hands. Sheila waited but got nothing else. After sixty seconds, she rolled her chair to the side. 'Lyle is dead. You might think you're protecting him, but all you're doing is creating even more pain for the other people who died. People in your employ. You have a duty to them, too.'

Alvarado rolled her chair in the opposite direction. 'Look up. Look at them. All fourteen.'

Mrs Halliday froze in place, head down and eyes focused on the floor. Alvarado slapped open a folder, pulled out a large photo and shoved it under her nose. 'Or you can see them afterward.'

Sam had already seen the woman in the morgue, but the photo of the smashed skull crowned with silvery gray hair still made him flinch. And it made Mrs Halliday heave and push away from the table.

'Don't you go anywhere,' Alvarado snapped. 'You know who this is. Who this *was*. This is what Lyle's illegal fireworks did to Paula Timmons.' She pulled out more eight-by-ten glossies. 'Or let's take a look at sweet Jordana Bennett. Or Randy Foulk. They found him in pieces.'

'Stop,' she wailed, putting her head between her knees and swiveling the chair toward the blank wall behind her. Alvarado kept smacking photos on to the table. Sheila appeared to be trying to stand. Sam didn't move. They'd forgotten him, there on the edge of things. That was fine. He waited for the next maneuver, watching carefully.

Sheila made it to her feet and leaned forward over the table. The gentle tone was gone. Brook-no-dissent Sheila was back. 'Tell us.'

Mrs Halliday lifted her head slightly but covered her face with her hands. She wanted no more glimpses of charred employees. 'I didn't know they were there. Until I heard about the explosion. Then I knew he must've actually done it. Brought them in from that guy, the one who makes them. I didn't want him to. I didn't think he actually would.'

'Had any been sold?' Alvarado said. 'Did any leave the warehouse?'

'I don't know,' she said through tears. 'I don't know how long the stuff had been there. I don't know if Ned had already made a delivery. It would've been him that Lyle had do it. They was good friends.'

Alvarado pressed her on the source of what she kept calling the 'incendiary devices'. They'd certainly gone off like a bomb. Someplace out in southern Kansas, Mrs Halliday said. Lyle had been approached last summer, right after the Fourth. She didn't know the name of the guy who made the stuff. He was just a 'hobbyist' looking to increase his sales radius, because no one wanted to come to him in the middle of the podunk prairie. Alvarado extracted a vague location – three hours away, off Highway 166. Then Sheila took over the questioning as the agent rapid-fired off a series of texts under the table without even looking at the phone screen. Sam smiled to himself. That hobbyist was about to get some unexpected visitors.

Mrs Halliday told him it was stupid. He agreed, until the returns came in for last year's Independence Day sales. Horrible. They'd made no money at all – all their retailers were buying straight from the importers. That was when he started seriously considering it. She begged him not to – and thought he'd listened to her.

'Who was going to buy it from Lyle?' It was the third way Sheila had phrased the question. Mrs Halliday kept shaking her head. Sheila scowled and sank back into her seat. She made it look a move fueled by irritation, but Sam could tell her stamina was gone. She kept her voice even, though. 'Then think, Faye. All your retailers. Who would buy that kind of product? Who do you think would be more likely to want in on that kind of deal? There's got to be somebody.'

That gave her pause. Everyone waited. Alvarado even stopped texting.

'Two. I can think of two.' Her head rose up slightly. 'I'm not accusing or anything. Just that they're more . . . cowboys. More willing to play fast and loose.'

Then she gave them names. Neither was William Buck, and both were alive and accounted for. So Sheila had to ask.

'What about "More Bang for Your Buck"? Is that guy a cowboy?'

Now she looked all the way up, meeting Sheila's gaze with surprise. 'Bill Buck? He's the main reason we're delinquent with our importers. He owes us so much money. There's no way Lyle would've offered him the opportunity to buy more from us.'

'Did he ever come down to visit the warehouse?'

Mrs Halliday looked at Sheila like she was crazy. Or stupid. Neither of which Sheila appreciated. She cocked an eyebrow and frowned.

'Sorry. No. Nobody came to visit. We're a warehouse. We're not exciting. And we don't have meeting space or nothing, either. There's no reason to come to us.'

Sheila reached into her stack of papers and slid out a four-by-six photo. Very gently, she placed it on the table and used one finger to slide it across. It showed something charred and blackened, but still easily recognizable. 'Then who is this? This is our extra skull, Faye. Who was in your warehouse that morning?'

That did it. She started to weep and no amount of softball questions or tissues would make her coherent again. They left her with the tissue box and went out in the hallway.

'I want to arrest her,' Sheila said to Alvarado. 'Give me a charge.'

'She says she didn't know the illegal stuff was there. Even if that turns out to be true, as a co-owner of the business, she holds federal licenses that limit what she can store. And her business is in clear violation of that. Which means she is, too. There will be more we'll throw at her later, but that's a solid start.'

'Excellent. We, of course, will be happy to hold her here for you. Sam, I'm going to ask you to take her over to the jail.'

'Sure. And when I'm done, I'm taking you home.'

'Thanks, but that's OK. Angie will take me back to my car.'

Alvarado gave him a nod that indicated she wouldn't let Sheila do anything that went against doctor's orders. Sam took her at her unspoken word and walked back into the conference room. He wanted to get this done quickly. He had one more stop to make before the end of the day. Because there was still one question Faye Halliday hadn't answered.

FORTY

Hank padded down the basement stairs in his stocking feet and stood in the hallway that led to the laundry room on his right and Duncan's bedroom on his left. An upstairs lamp was on and cast a pie-wedge of light down the stairs. It was the only illumination. He moved away from it and into the dark hall toward the bedroom. The ceiling was lower down here and he felt in danger of brushing his head against it even with inches to spare. He was five feet from the door when it opened.

They stared at each other in silence. Dunc did not offer him entrance.

'How's Maggie?'

'Not great. She finally fell asleep.'

They both stood there.

'You're not asking how I am?'

'That's not the question I'm here to ask.'

'Ah.'

The old man stood in his own slice of light. It bisected his face, showing newly carved wrinkles of pain on the half Hank could see. Dunc pulled his robe tighter. 'I figured. I've been waiting for you. You're here to do your job.'

'Yes. And I need you to tell me the real reason you and Marian weren't getting along at the end.'

'She'd started to do that juvenile justice committee again. There were people on there she said she wouldn't associate with again.'

'Why?'

'You say that like you already know.'

'Let me tell you what I know. I know she was scared of you. I know she apologized – again. And I know that you don't like Marvin Sedstone. Now you tell me what all those things lead me to think.'

'She was scared of me? Really?' His posture and his voice

both seemed to shrink, turning him even more into a dried husk. 'How do you know that?'

'Answer my question, Dunc.' *Confirm my fear.*

'She had an affair. With Sedstone.' It had been about five years before she died, when Duncan was busy and productive with work and not willing to carve out time for her.

'How did you find out?'

One of the guys in Rotary had seen them together. Nothing compromising, just noticing them in a restaurant up in Springfield and mentioning it to Dunc in passing. But Marian had told him she was on a girls' trip to Saint Louis that weekend. So he confronted her. 'She admitted it straight off. Looked me in the eye and said she felt like she deserved to be treated nicely. And since I wasn't doing that, she found someone who did.'

In a way, it was classic Marian – sticking up for herself just as much as she would stick up for others.

'I realized . . . that it wasn't a static thing, our marriage. That I needed to put more effort into it.'

'Really?' Hank crossed his arms. 'Just like that, you saw the light?'

Dunc rubbed his hand over his face. The rasp of his stubble was loud in the small space. 'I was mad, yeah. But I didn't want to kill her then, and I didn't want to kill her when she started the committee work again, either. Because I know that's what you're really asking.'

That was exactly right. And in all the investigations where he'd posed the question, he never once believed the answer. He didn't now, either. But his heart had never twisted so painfully with the asking.

'You had the most access to her. You were with her that morning. She had to have ingested the toxin four to six hours before she died.'

Dunc threw up his hands. 'And she drank coffee at school. And put the leftovers she took for lunch in the communal fridge.'

'What were the leftovers?'

He sagged against the door frame. 'So if I didn't poison her in the morning, I sent poison to school with her to eat there? My God. You're not just ticking off all your boxes. You really are suspecting me. I didn't kill her. How can you think that of me?'

Because Hank no longer knew the man who stood in front of him. He hadn't known Marian either, apparently. And now their messy, convoluted, motive-filled lives were forcing him into this corner. Making him ask these questions. Making him fracture an important relationship and sending dangerous fault lines out toward others that were even more valuable. He stood there and fought his own sad anger.

'What were the leftovers?'

'I don't know. She had a dinner meeting the night before. Brought it home in a doggie bag. Left with it in the morning.'

'What kind of meeting?'

Duncan sighed. 'A juvenile justice one. Multiple committee members were there. I don't remember which restaurant.' He flopped his arm wearily against his body. 'I wasn't mad at her for going. I wasn't mad at her at all. *I* was the scared one. I didn't want to lose her. I loved her. From the moment I met her, I loved her. Every day after that, I loved her. Every day. Even with the affair. Do you understand me?'

Hank nodded. He did understand. Completely. He watched as Duncan stepped back and swung the door closed, leaving only a thin crack of brightness at the bottom that didn't illuminate anything. Hank waited in the darkness and let his eyes adjust. He did understand what Dunc had said. He even believed him. But it didn't matter.

Love and murder were not mutually exclusive.

FORTY-ONE

Monday morning came too early. State investigators would descend on Whittaker's morgue and Hank would have to turn Marian's case over to Branson city police. The high school was within the city limits and they would be the ones to open an official homicide investigation. He'd hand over his list of suspects and step away. Try to step away. Possibly step away.

But before he maybe did that, there was something he needed to know. He found a bench in the cool morning shade and waited until the judge pulled into the almost empty parking lot. The courthouse was already Old Headstone's turf – Hank didn't want to have to sit in the sanctified space of his chambers, too. And this was not a conversation where Hank wanted him comfortable.

The judge saw him and changed course, pulling a rolling briefcase along behind him. He stopped with a cheery hello as he fished a pen out of the inner pocket of his sport coat. 'You need a search warrant this early? Is it for that horrible explosion investigation?'

'It's not about a warrant.' He gestured to the empty half of the bench. 'Please. Have a seat.' It wasn't a request.

That got him a surprised look. Their strictly professional relationship did not involve Hank telling the jurist what to do. Now he pointed again and waited for the judge to settle himself on the wood slats. His white, woolly eyebrows came together in irritation.

'I need to talk to you about Marian McCleary.'

Now one questioning eyebrow climbed toward Sedstone's hairline.

'About Marian and you. And your relationship. Not the professional one. The personal one.'

The judge turned and looked out over the parking lot. 'My boy, I have a very busy day ahead and—'

'Why did your wife file for divorce?'

'Excuse me?' The words had the weight of a marble grave marker.

'It's a simple question. She filed for divorce five years ago, then withdrew it four months later. Why?'

'We worked it out.'

'How?'

Sedstone started to stand. 'I fail to see how this is any of your business.'

'It's my business because you had an affair with my mother-in-law around the time that your wife decided she'd had enough of you.'

The judge sank back on to the bench.

'So why did your wife withdraw the divorce petition?'

The judge stared at the parked cars. 'I'm not going to dignify this with—'

'There's nothing dignified about any of it.' Hank swallowed the 'sir' he was reflexively about to use and hardened his tone. 'And there isn't going to be. So you'd better just answer my questions and get it over with.'

'She withdrew the divorce petition because I ended the affair.'

'*You* ended it?' Hank actually had no idea who ended it, but a self-serving answer deserved probing even if it was true.

'It was mutual. Marian said her husband had found out as well.'

'And how did you feel about it ending?'

Sedstone bristled again but deflated at the look on Hank's face. 'I was heartbroken. I loved her. She was the most amazing woman.'

'Then why not just go ahead and divorce your wife?'

'Because she wouldn't leave him.' His voice cracked. 'McCleary. She wouldn't leave him.'

'What was Duncan's reaction when he found out about the affair?'

Sedstone shrugged. After it ended, they both backed away from the juvenile justice committee. That had been something both his wife and Duncan McCleary had demanded. McCleary was angry, hurt – Marian hadn't said anything more specific than that. Hank sighed. He'd been hoping for concrete details.

'What was your relationship at the time of her death. Had you restarted your affair?'

Finally he swung his gaze away from the middle distance and looked directly at Hank. 'What? No. Why would you ask that?'

'Because she said you had lunch. She said the committee work had started again. Duncan wasn't happy about it.'

'She said? How did she say? This was two years ago. Why, why . . . I'm done. I don't know why you're dredging this up or why you think you can pry – you don't have any right.'

He struggled to his feet, an uncomfortably stiff old man with a pen in his hand and guilt on his back. Hank stopped him with three words.

'She was murdered.'

He lowered himself back on to the seat.

'What?'

'Marian was poisoned. Someone killed her. So I have every right to haul you in for questioning. This here,' he gestured at the parking lot and the late spring flowers on the trees and the bench, 'is a courtesy. Don't make me regret extending it.'

'You think I'm a suspect.'

'Of course you're a suspect. For all I know, you wanted to start things up again and she didn't, so you killed her.'

The pen fell from his hand.

'Oh, God, no. No, I loved her. I never would have hurt her. Ever.'

Hank's voice was cold. 'And how many times have you sat in court and listened to a man say that as you sentenced him for assaulting a woman?'

Sedstone let out a shaky breath. 'You're taking no prisoners, are you? You ambush me and tell me the woman I love was murdered and then expect me to sit here and be accused of—'

Hank turned to him, straight-backed and looming over the diminished judge. 'I expect you to answer this question. Truthfully. Had the two of you restarted your affair?'

He looked up at Hank. 'No. Believe me or not, but that's the truth.' He paused. 'Does McCleary know?'

'That his wife was murdered? Yes.'

Sedstone buried his face in his hands. 'I don't understand. Why now – so long after? She's been gone two years.'

'Dr Whittaker didn't do his job. For years. A state investigation will start today. Multiple cases will be reopened.'

'I don't want this out in public. I will not have her good name ruined.'

'Once all this is announced, you'll have no control over anything.' *And neither will I.* 'That's how murder investigations work. You know that.'

The judge stood, this time with stiff determination. He grabbed the handle of his roller bag and stepped away. 'Yeah, I guess I do.'

He trudged off, the rupture of their professional camaraderie complete. Hank watched him go and didn't even care. The only one who mattered now was his wife. The rest of them could find their own way out of the holes they'd dug themselves.

Former Medical Examiner Missed Multiple Homicides
Proper Autopsies Not Done; Authorities Open Investigation
into Dereliction, Mismanagement
By Jadhur Banerjee

Branson Daily Herald

SPRINGFIELD – State investigators descended on the Southwestern Missouri Forensic Pathology Office today after learning that cases initially ruled as natural deaths are in fact homicides. Authorities say the errors are due to the former medical director not conducting proper autopsies on decedents, including a Branson woman who died two years ago.

The former director, 69-year-old forensic pathologist Michael Whittaker, died earlier this month. He ran the office that served 15 counties in southern Missouri for two decades.

'He cut corners,' said Billy Townsend, an investigator with the state Board of Healing Arts, which regulates physicians. 'That's it in a nutshell, basically. If someone came in as a natural death, he just signed it off. Some of those needed full autopsies. We're here to figure out which ones, as best we can at this point.'

Thirteen cases have been reopened and two of those have already been reclassified as homicides, including the death of Branson resident Marian McCleary. McCleary, principal of Branson Valley High School, collapsed at work two years ago and died of what was then labeled cardiac arrest. Medical officials now believe she was poisoned.

'We're opening a homicide investigation into Mrs McCleary's death,' said Branson Police Chief Ed Utley. 'We would've done that at the time had Whittaker given us the proper information.'

McCleary's son-in-law is another high-ranking local law enforcement official, County Sheriff Hank Worth. He will not be involved in the investigation, Utley said.

Worth, reached by phone earlier today, declined to comment. McCleary's colleagues, however, had plenty to say.

'This is absolutely shocking. I can't believe it. Everyone loved Marian,' said English teacher Bo Cushman. 'I can't imagine what her family's going through.'

The Branson educational community will help in any way possible, said school superintendent Camille Getz. 'This is a very traumatic thing for everyone who knew her. We'll have resources available for any teacher or student who needs them. And of course, we'll assist the police any way we can.'

'I don't know how they're going to figure it out,' Linda Ghazarian, a Branson Valley teacher and friend of McCleary's, said through tears. 'It's been so long since she died.'

McCleary's case is not the oldest confronting investigators. Some deaths occurred more than five years ago, making it difficult or impossible to backtrack, especially in the case of cremation, said Oliver Bernstein, a forensic pathologist in Chicago who is not involved in the investigation.

'Once the body is gone, it's a tough road,' Bernstein said. 'All you have are the medical records.'

Whittaker's alleged negligence came to light when interim pathologist Ngozi Aguta noticed that a body in the morgue had completed paperwork but no signature, due to

Whittaker's sudden death from a stroke. Unwilling to sign off without reviewing the case personally, Aguta examined the body and discovered that it was an accidental death from medication toxicity and not a natural one. That prompted her to take a closer look at older cases, including McCleary's.

FORTY-TWO

'The newspaper said you're not involved in the investigation.'

Barstow backed up a step. Then another as Hank kept advancing.

'What do you think?'

The locker room wall stopped any further retreat. Barstow eyed him nervously. 'I think my sympathies go out to your family.'

Hank crossed his arms and kept his spine straight. He was three inches taller than the football coach and wanted to use every one of them.

'That's kind of you to say. But I'm here to talk about your unkind comments.'

'Um . . .'

'You were very angry at Marian. You had access to her the day she died. You—'

Barstow started waving his hands, protective palms out toward Hank. 'No, no, no. Don't even think that. I didn't kill her.'

'Her death got you everything you wanted.'

The hands stopped moving. 'No, it didn't.'

'Bullshit.'

Barstow yanked off his baseball cap and wiped at his forehead. 'No, really. We were going to make a deal.'

Hank was not in the mood for this. He leaned in. 'You did nothing but scream at her and try to undermine her every chance you got. You want me to believe you two sat down and talked it out? Again, bullshit.'

Barstow clamped shut a mouth more accustomed to yelling plays than playing nice. He twisted his cap into a ball, transferring his anger there so the words came out politely. They had been negotiating, he said. He would back off the GPA fight if Marian supported him for athletic director. Because she was the one with the parent booster club in her pocket. Not him. Those last two words came out marinated in two years of bitterness.

'And you dropped that goal after she died?' Hank said. He thought about the contempt and the disrespect that fueled this man's treatment of Marian, and he sharpened his knife. 'Because you're still not athletic director.'

The baseball cap disappeared into his clenched fists. 'I did not drop that goal. But at the point where she . . . passed away, she wasn't backing me. And those bastards on the booster club haven't forgotten it. So they won't support my application, and without that, the district won't put me in the job.'

'Why were you willing to give up the low GPA? That's what allowed you to keep all those kids on the football team.'

'At that point in time, yeah. So, you bet I was pissed off. I had everything all lined up for the next year and then suddenly she became principal and made the change. It totally screwed me.' But during the spring months of that school year, he started thinking. Looking at the whole lay of the land, so to speak. He pulled up the GPAs of players who would be coming up from junior varsity and things didn't look too bad. There were more kids taking honors courses, more kids getting decent grades. 'So it was becoming less of a factor. Or it would've been, after that one year. I just needed the one year.'

'The one where you won the championship?' That was the fall after Marian died, just as Hank and Maggie moved to town.

A grin spread across Barstow's face before he could stop it. He wiped it off as quickly as he could. 'That's how it turned out, yes.'

'I find it hard to believe Marian would've agreed to "one more year",' Hank said.

Barstow looked him in the eye. 'You're right. I don't know if she would have. But she was at least listening, taking a look at the upcoming players' grades, considering the whole picture.'

'When was the last time the two of you talked about it?'

His eyes narrowed. 'You ask that like you already know the answer. The day she died. There. Happy? I went into her office to talk about it. But I didn't poison her. Jesus, man. No way.'

Hank scowled. The man was a self-serving ass who was definitely not being entirely honest, but he also was one of the last to see Marian alive. Hank needed to put aside the urge to hit him and ask for the pertinent information. 'How did she seem when you saw her?'

Barstow thought. She'd seemed distracted. She had a sizable amount of papers she was looking through. And she was definitely ticked off.

'Not at me,' he added quickly. Hank rolled his eyes. 'I just mean she was that way when I walked in. She looked at me and started firing off questions about this one JV player. Jason Sutter.' He had gone from a below-average student who wouldn't have been eligible for the team to a kid with average grades in advanced classes. 'I told her that proved my point about the upcoming kids not needing a lower GPA threshold for athletics.'

He stopped. Hank gestured impatiently for him to continue. 'It was a good angle and I kept talking. But she just shut down. Like she'd changed the channel. She said, "That's not the point of this mess at all. And I'm finally realizing it." Then she told me to leave. She wasn't ignoring me, we would talk later, but right now – get out. So I did.'

Hank let the skepticism show on his face. 'You never respected her before that. Why did you choose to follow her direction then?'

'Hey. That's harsh. We just had disagreements. Two professionals with opposing positions.'

He stared at him, wondering whether it was the sugarcoating of a liar or genuine self-delusion. Either way, he was done. He stepped away, releasing Barstow from his corner. 'She was a professional. You were a bully.'

The last word echoed through the empty locker room as he walked out the door.

'I just got hand-delivered a set of used toothbrushes. You really shouldn't have.'

Sheila laughed in spite of it being a Monday morning with cloudy skies, lukewarm coffee, new abdominal bandages and nothing good on TV. 'There's also spit. Don't forget that.'

'Yes, I see. Only four of those, though.'

'That's because we can't find Aidan Welby. We swabbed the four others staying at his last known location. And we seized all five toothbrushes we found in the house.'

'So wherever this Aidan went, he didn't pack his toothbrush?'

Watanabe's tone was heavy with implication. Sheila pictured the charred skull sitting in the pathologist's morgue. She shifted painfully in her recliner and pushed the image out of her head. 'We're hoping one of them is his. The other four idiots refused to say whose was whose. So that's why you're getting all five. Hopefully four will match the cheek swabs, and the fifth will match the remains. Or not. Either way, it'll be more information than we had before.'

'Is Welby your only possibility?'

'We have one other. A fireworks retailer named William Buck. He didn't come back from a solo camping trip that started right when the warehouse exploded.' She explained Sam's theory. 'And now his family is fighting our request for his toothbrush. They're adamant that he's just lost in the woods. They say he never would've stopped off in Branson to confront Lyle Halliday.' Her voice insinuated the same thing Watanabe's had.

'Well, if there's anything else I can do, let me know. Or talk to Dr Aguta. It looks like she's going to be down in your morgue for a while longer yet.'

Sheila swished her now cold coffee and frowned. 'I thought she was leaving this week. We're getting some traveling hack until they can find somebody permanent.'

'The state folks have asked her to stay until they sort out the whole mess.'

The coffee whirlpool spun in her mug. 'What mess?'

'The former guy. Not doing proper autopsies. Aguta's even found two that were homicides incorrectly classified as natural.' He trailed off at her extended silence. 'You haven't heard about this?'

She couldn't speak. She stared out at her slice of sky and had no words. That bastard Whittaker. What had he done? She flipped frantically through the filing cabinet in her head – what county cases might be affected? She wasn't sure. If they'd been ruled natural, she wouldn't necessarily even know of their existence. Watanabe was still talking. She dragged her mind back to the conversation.

'. . . and after this, she's going to be able to run her own forensic pathology department right out of the gate, once she's done with her training. I'm quite proud of her.'

'You said state investigators are involved?'

They descended on Whittaker's old domain like a swarm of yellow jackets – angry, focused, and far too numerous. The announcement came this morning, but he'd known since Aguta told him last week. She'd been working with a local cop to get a handle on it before calling in the state regulators. He'd given his blessing to that, Watanabe said, because he understood her wanting to be sure.

Sheila sat there and watched with hard eyes as her coffee whirlpool slowed and died. A local cop. She had one absent-boss guess as to who that might be. Why did he have to go sticking his nose in everywhere he found interesting, even if he had no connection? How could he think that old cases should take precedence over the unidentified explosion murder victim and a community grieving fourteen deaths? She patted at her hair and tried to calm down.

Anger was making her tense, and tight muscles amplified the pain in her torso. She tried a few deep breaths, but that only made it worse. Screw it. Stay mad. She pushed aside her coffee mug and yanked open her laptop. She called up the Springfield newspaper's website as Watanabe kept talking. The big city paper should know which two cases in Whittaker's huge, multi-county area were now homicides. OK, one in Polk County north of Springfield. And the other . . .

The phone slid out of her astonished hand. The name burned into her retinas. She took it back. She took every thought back as she struggled to stand – yelling for her husband, her shoes, her wheelchair, her dormant sense of compassion. She needed all of them. Right now.

FORTY-THREE

A student summoned Arlene Ostermann from the back of the school office, and her brisk efficiency wasn't with her as she walked to the front counter. Her stride slowed even more when she saw Hank, but she didn't look surprised. Word of his presence was spreading through the school faster than a rumor started by a teenage girl.

'I saw it in the paper. How can you take it? This bombshell? Another murder? And for it to be Marian?'

All good questions. And ones he wasn't capable of answering. Instead, he asked for Florence Dettinger. Arlene's grief-stricken expression hardened. 'That's very interesting. I'll be happy to show you to her office. Especially since she was such a good employee for Marian before she died,' she said, her sarcasm blistering enough to peel paint off the hallway walls as they walked along. They reached the door for 'Florence Dettinger, M.Ed.'

Arlene didn't bother to knock.

She announced Hank and stepped out, leaving the door wide open. Hank had a feeling she'd love to have the whole school hear the coming conversation. He didn't disagree.

Dettinger looked puzzled for just an instant, then must've connected his visit to Marian's murder. All color left her narrow face. She tucked a strand of her brown hair behind her ear and tried to smile. Hank sat down without invitation.

'We haven't met, but I believe you worked for my mother-in-law, correct?'

She nodded.

'And I'm pretty sure you saw the news this morning. About her.'

She locked down her expression, then forced a look of sympathy. 'I am so sorry. That is just awful. And of course, we're putting resources in place to help any staff or students who need to talk about it. Thank you so much for checking.'

He relaxed into the chair and crossed his legs. 'That's not why I'm here.'

'Oh?' She shuffled some papers without taking her eyes off him.

'You've been running a racket. Bribery, most like. "Give me money and I'll let you into the classes you need."'

Her mouth went thin. She was going to fight. Good. He was in the mood for it.

'That is the most absurd thing I've ever heard. Students have the option to pay for an outside college readiness program, but that's it.'

'There's no program. There's only the payment. And if they don't pay, they don't get into the school's advanced classes. You control that.'

'I don't even understand what you're implying.'

Hank ignored that. 'And you also offer more test time. Special accommodations. You've been handing out 504s like they're hall passes.'

That got her. The clenched jaw went slack. He leaned forward. 'I now know what Marian knew. What she'd figured out right before she died. Right before she was murdered. You're a smart lady. What conclusion do you think I draw from all that?'

She spluttered and fluttered, trying to decide which allegation to deny first. She finally went with the lesser evil.

'I only give 504s to kids who need them.'

'The numbers in this school certainly went up once you started working here. Suspiciously so.' He was basing that on nothing more than Judy's chatty conversations and Marian's journal. Neither would be worth anything in court, but both could be proved correct by school records. There was nothing federal law liked more than making you document things.

'So you're blaming me for helping more kids? That's our job.'

'I'm sure there're some kids you genuinely did help. Kids who really need extra time for tests, or a quiet room, or whatever. That's great. But the ones who just want an edge up on college entrance exams? No.'

She waved a hand dismissively. 'What are you even basing this on?' *You got nothin'.*

She was semi-right. He had a private journal and a missing

list of highlighted names. Shaky at best. She didn't know that, though.

'I have the documentation Marian left behind.'

That made her the kind of worried she couldn't hide. He dug in.

'And then after she takes away your scheduling ability – and thereby your bribery income – and just before she's going to go public, she's killed.' He spread his arms wide. 'And *voilà*, everything goes back to the way you like it.'

'I did not kill her. I didn't.' She was saying the words before he even finished. Her hand smacked flat on the desk. 'Get out. I'm done talking to you. I want a lawyer.'

He sat there for a minute, looking around her office. He knew it was making her angrier. He didn't care. She had such motive. Such a nice, cushy set-up with its annually refreshing customer base of striving, anxious parental checkbooks. Marian would've blown all that out of the water. And if she truly was about to come to an agreement with Tom Barstow, that would have left her with more time to concentrate on the counselor in front of him. Which, if you were the counselor, would've been very bad news indeed. Kind of like what she was experiencing today. He smiled.

'That's fine. We'll be back. You are not to leave town under any circumstances, do you understand?'

She smacked both hands down this time. It was an excellent way to disguise the trembling, but he saw it anyway. He left without another word.

Ed Utley poured Hank a cup of coffee and lowered his bulk into the chair behind his desk. The Branson city police chief looked both sympathetic and annoyed, a tricky combination to pull off. Hank waited to see which one he'd start with.

'I want to say how sorry I am about your mother-in-law.'

Sympathetic, then. Hank took a cautious sip of coffee.

'All of us here are just staggered by the whole Whittaker thing. We would've investigated it thoroughly had anything suspicious been reported to us at the time.' Utley's chair let out a resigned squeak as he shifted forward. 'That being said, I appreciate you wanting answers, but you have to let us find them.'

And there it was. A smooth roll right into annoyed. Impressive. He watched Utley rest his hand on the file Hank had handed him minutes earlier. He took another slow drink. Better to let Utley air all of his complaints before trying to defend himself.

'Also, even without the jurisdictional issues, you can't be allowed within a country mile of this case. And you know that. The conflict of interest is as massive as it can possibly be.'

Hank nodded. Utley waited a beat and then sighed. 'So what am I supposed to do with all this not-gathered-during-an-official-investigation information you've given me?'

Hank finally lowered his mug. 'There are several viable suspects in there. I wanted to look into them before they knew Marian's case was getting reopened. Any Branson police detective trying to poke around would've tipped the killer off immediately.'

Utley frowned. Hank put up a hand. 'That's nothing on your guys. They're great. But I was reminiscing as a son-in-law, not interviewing as a cop.' He pointed at the paperwork under Utley's meaty hand. 'Everything I developed is in there.'

And it was. Every aching, painful, unfaithful tidbit. He waited as Utley opened the file and flipped through. When the chief's hand froze mid-flip, he knew which interview he was looking at.

'Judge Headstone? What in the name of holy hell are you thinking?'

Hank stayed quiet. Utley looked back down at the papers. 'Ah. Well, that certainly complicates things.' He eyed Hank. 'And your father-in-law knows that you know? About the affair?'

'Yes. But my wife doesn't. And that brings up a point I'd like to talk about.'

Now, the big ask. Utley was already scowling.

'If there's any way that part of it – the affair – can be kept quiet . . .' He spread out his hands, a mug of cooling coffee in one and his wedding ring on the other. 'Marian's been gone a long time. A posthumous trashing of her reputation isn't . . . well, it would hurt everyone involved. And if it turns out to not be relevant to the investigation . . .'

Utley slapped the file closed.

'I'm not asking you to *not* investigate that angle,' Hank said quickly. 'All I'm asking is that it be done discreetly. So that if the killer turns out to be not connected to the affair, it can just be . . . kept the secret that it has been.'

He knew how ridiculous the request was. He knew the scorched earth of a homicide investigation. He'd done the scorching, many times. And he'd always thought that the answer was excuse enough. Finding the killer justified prying and intruding and stirring up ghosts. That hadn't changed just because it was now his family in the path of the fire. But he had to ask. He had to try to protect Maggie from even more heartbreak.

Utley scraped a hand along his jaw. 'I get it. I do. I'll talk to my guys. But I can't promise anything. You know that.'

'Yeah, I do. And I appreciate you not throwing me out on my ear when I brought it up.' He rose to his feet and extended his hand. Utley stood and reluctantly took it.

'Well, there's always next time.'

'Fair enough,' Hank said. He left the office, taking one last look at Marian's green leather journal as Utley swept it up and out of sight.

Sheila found him at the office, staring into an empty desk drawer.

'My God, Hank. Why didn't you tell me?'

He tried to smile. His face wouldn't cooperate. He gave up and sank into his chair. 'Because this would happen. You'd be here trying to help, instead of at home recuperating.'

She glowered at him and rolled her wheelchair closer. 'I would smack you silly if I could raise my arms.'

That got him. A chuckle escaped, although his expression stayed tight and strained. He looked ten years older. Tight lines radiated from his mouth and eyes, and his face had that pasty pallor that white people turned when they got sick. He rubbed at his unshaven jaw and then slid the drawer closed.

'This was where I locked it away. Her journal.' Then he told her everything.

Good heavens, what agony. Her heart ached for Maggie. And for the bruised man in front of her. 'I'm so, so sorry you had to go through this alone. What can I do to help?'

'Keep on the explosion.' He shot her a look. 'I know you've been working it.'

'Ah. Who tattled on me?'

'Nobody. I just know you. And I know I abandoned that investigation. I'm sorry.' The pain in his voice right then was almost as great as when he'd been talking about Marian.

She waved off the apology, a move she never would have imagined her exasperated self making a day ago. 'A person can only carry so much. The one thing you should've done different is talk to me. You big idiot.'

That produced another smile, which was her intent. She went over the status of the explosion investigation, ending with Sam's efforts. 'He's got something rattling around that brain of his. Some kind of theory. He won't say what it is.' She raised an eyebrow. 'Seems to be an affliction with the men in this department. Not communicating like they should be.'

She rolled her chair back and started to turn. 'And that means things need to be whipped back into shape around here.'

It felt good to say it, and it was going to feel even better to do it. She spun around and wheeled toward the door. 'I'll be in my office.'

FORTY-FOUR

S am stood in the middle of the empty space. Dust motes danced in the light coming through the high windows and a solitary metal stool stood against the wall by the door. Alice and Kurt had searched this outbuilding as thoroughly as they did the rest of the Halliday property. And they found nothing but the utility trailer parked near the roll-up door. Sam spun slowly around and thought about that.

The building was old, probably built in the 1970s, same as the house. It was essentially a barn without the barn shape, just a rectangle with rafters under a pitched roof. It wasn't in disrepair but it certainly hadn't been kept up as well as the main dwelling. There were scrapes and scuff marks on the concrete floor, some of the siding was damaged, and the whole thing needed a lick of paint. Buildings like this dotted the countryside all over the Ozarks. And Sam was willing to bet none of them were empty. They might be tidy or they might be messy, full of everything from shiny farm vehicles to piles of junk – but they were all being used. No one owned a space like this for that many decades without using it to store *something*.

And that was what had churned at the corners of his mind ever since he read Kurt's search warrant return. An empty outbuilding made no sense. Unless it was empty on purpose. Ready for something to fill it. Ready and waiting. And what could a couple who ran a fireworks warehouse possibly have that would fill such a big space? Inventory they didn't want anyone else to see, perhaps?

He allowed himself a smile and left the building as lonely as he'd found it. He walked up to the house, still sealed off with crime scene tape, and let himself in. He wanted one more piece of information before he gave Faye Halliday an answer to the question she'd asked two weeks ago.

*   *   *

Judy Manikas's class was down the hall with the music teacher, so her room was quiet and she had thirty minutes to herself. She walked over to her institutional-beige filing cabinet and opened the drawer that had previous years' class information. Little Davy Rinconi. She flipped through until she found his file. She settled at her desk and sipped at her lukewarm tea as she paged through it. The 504 paperwork, assessments, report cards. It was all on the computer, of course, but she was old and not about to stop doing it the way she'd always done.

Davy had been a sweet boy. A joy and a challenge manifesting itself as a ball of kinetic energy. He had a very much needed – and extensive – 504 plan. She'd given Davy a lot of thought since her conversations at the science fair two days ago. She and his parents had worked together to craft the plan and the principal had signed off on it, because it was a small school and they didn't have a specific 504 coordinator. At the high school, clearly Florence Dettinger was the 'coordinator' who approved 504 plans that granted her paying students more testing time. But there had to be someone else, too. There had to be another staff member in agreement.

Judy had been so focused on Dettinger and the money that the counselor was extracting from success-obsessed parents that she hadn't stopped to consider the paperwork. She ran a finger along her own name on Davy's form. *We do have costs that need to be covered*, Dettinger had told her. At the time Judy thought of it as nothing more than her using the royal 'we'. But maybe she did mean it as a plural.

Maybe it wasn't Dettinger who so outraged Marian right before she died.

Who else would have access to a large pool of students besides a counselor? Who taught a subject that every student had to take? Who would've wounded Marian to the core?

Maggie didn't go to work. She faked a cold with Maribel and Benny and said she didn't want to get her patients sick. By evening, the kids were the only two in town who didn't know about Marian. Hank tucked them in and envied their ignorance. Then he forced himself down the hallway to the living room and his brokenhearted wife. She sat on the couch, curled up under a blanket. Her phone – shut off now after blowing up for hours – lay on the coffee table. She turned from staring at the muted TV and looked at him with unblinkered eyes.

'The spouse is always a suspect.'

Hank slowly put down the third Percy Jackson book. 'Yes.'

He sat down on the other end of the couch. She stayed still, her gaze not leaving his face.

'So?'

He could say it was out of his hands. He could say he didn't know who would become suspects – that was up to Utley. He could flat-out lie and say *not your dad, maybe other spouses but not him*. Or he could throw the truth at her like a pot of scalding water, *your mom was unfaithful so that makes your dad the main suspect*.

But he couldn't do any of that to her.

'I don't know. I don't know what's going to happen. I just don't know.'

She nodded. 'OK. Will Chief Utley keep you updated?'

'Honestly? Probably not.'

She shifted a little and eyed him thoughtfully. He reached out. She pulled the blanket tighter and turned back to the TV, leaving his hand hanging in midair.

FORTY-FIVE

The kids were cranky and slow and refused to listen as Hank tried to get them ready for school. Benny wiggled and cried and demanded his normal routine, which couldn't be done without Duncan. Hank told him that, like Mommy, Grandpop wasn't feeling well – and begged him to please put on his pants. Benny ran instead, fleeing toward the kitchen on his spindly four-year-old legs. He skidded to a halt in the living room as they heard scuffling steps on the stairs. Hank stopped cold, pants dangling from his hand as Dunc emerged from below. He looked several inches shorter as he curled into his bathrobe, his spine a miserable question mark instead of its normal defiant exclamation point. His face was blotchy and his eyes were shot through with red.

Benny backed away.

Dunc flinched but covered it quickly. 'All you got to do is explain to your dad how we do it. There's no need for a ruckus.' He turned to Hank. 'It's got to be both legs at the same time. You hold the pants while he sticks his legs out.'

Benny hopped on the couch and stuck his legs out. Hank wrestled the pants on to him and hustled them out the door in time for the preschool carpool and Maribel for the bus. He walked back in the front door to find that Dunc hadn't moved.

'I wanted something to eat. If that's OK with you.'

Hank's insides twisted. 'Of course it is. It . . . you . . . you're . . .' He couldn't find the right words. There were no right words. Just wrong ones that would make things worse.

Dunc scoffed and took a step toward the kitchen. 'Yeah, I'm something to you, that's for sure.'

He was halfway across the living room when his bathrobe pocket rang. He fished out his phone, looked at it and then raised his eyes to Hank. He kept staring at him as he answered.

'Yes, this is he . . .Yes, I'm available today . . . Where? . . . No, that won't work. It's not my house, you see . . .'

Hank's gut writhed even more.

'The community center? . . . It's empty right now? . . . Yes, I can be there . . . Uh, huh. Bye.'

He slid the phone back in his pocket. 'You provided my contact information. How considerate of you.'

Hank knew he could point out that city detectives had the option to interview Dunc in full public view at the police station. That they were doing it someplace private only because the sheriff asked for a favor. But saying that wouldn't fix anything, he thought, as Dunc finally peeled his gaze away and shuffled his slippered feet toward the kitchen. And from the other direction, he heard the soft click of a bedroom door closing. Maggie had heard the whole thing.

'Whatcha got, kid?'

Sam took a breath. He hadn't expected Alvarado to be here, too. She and Sheila were besties all the sudden, sitting all cozy at the conference table with mugs of tea and stacks of investigative reports. He cleared his throat.

'Why didn't he wait?'

They both stared at him. He'd been very sure of himself this morning. That shouldn't change just because the fed was here, he told himself. He sat down and straightened his uniform shirt.

'That's what Faye said the day of the explosion. When she came running up to the scene. She kept yelling it.' He paused. 'And it's bugged me ever since.'

He'd talked to all the Halliday neighbors in the last twenty-four hours, and two had seen stuff getting moved out of their storage building last weekend.

'Yeah, it was empty when Kurt and Alice searched it,' Sheila said.

'Because that's where the illegal fireworks were supposed to go.'

They both stared at him. He spread out his hands. 'Think about it. You don't empty a building like that. You just don't. You move stuff around to fit more, you maybe toss some stuff. But you don't clear it to where all that's left is a utility trailer and the dust in the corners. Unless you're moving something else in.'

'OK, that makes sense,' Alvarado said. 'So Lyle was going to move it from the warehouse to this outbuilding and just never got a chance to.'

Sam watched a smile tug at Sheila's mouth. 'Lyle isn't who we're talking about here.'

'Faye had to have known,' Sam said. 'The neighbor to the west said he saw her come and go that weekend. Not with the trailer or anything, but she was around. She knew what was going on. You can see the outbuilding doors from her kitchen window.'

Alvarado leaned forward. 'But that doesn't prove she knew what Lyle was going to put in the building.'

'Why didn't he wait?' Sam pressed his palms on the table. 'Why didn't he wait to bring in the illegal fireworks until the outbuilding was ready?'

'That's what you think she was asking? At the explosion scene?' Sheila said.

He nodded. 'She knew it was coming. All that homemade stuff. She was fully aware. I'm sure of it. She just didn't know it was already at the warehouse.'

So it wasn't a case of an innocent wife with a nefarious husband. It wasn't even a wife who realized a husband went against her request to not sell illegal fireworks. That would've been *Why did he do it?*

Sheila pushed back from the table. 'Let's all take a walk.'

Faye seemed to sense that something was different. She sat motionless in the interrogation room chair, a field mouse desperate for invisibility from circling hawks. Sam laid it all out. She didn't even blink. Then Sheila rolled her wheelchair forward.

'And I've been going through your business records. The money in, the money out. And I haven't found any payments to people who would've constructed that room in your warehouse. No contractor, no electrician, not even a generic handyman.'

Alvarado shifted in her seat. 'And that leads me to think you and Lyle did the work yourselves. How'd you get light into there? Did you jerry-rig some wiring? Maybe use extension cords and overload some circuits?'

Faye slowly made her first movement, a small shake of the head.

'I don't believe you,' Alvarado snapped, smacking her hand

on the cold laminate surface between them. Faye jumped like startled prey. Alvarado jabbed a finger at her. 'You cut corners, then loaded the place with the equivalent of unstable bombs and populated it with innocent employees.'

'No,' she shrieked. 'There was no ceiling on the room. It was open to the lights already on the main warehouse ceiling. We didn't wire anything.'

Sheila pondered that. She was no explosives expert, but Faye's answer seemed to leave only one possible cause on the table.

Alvarado slowly lowered her hand. Her next request told Sheila she was thinking the same thing. 'Tell her about your phone call.'

Sheila laid her notepad on the table. 'While Deputy Karnes was chatting with your neighbors, I talked to a nice lady named Lindsay Buck. I believe you know her husband, Bill. He's currently missing somewhere along the Buffalo River south of here in Arkansas. At least that's what she's been hoping. But two weeks is a long time to be gone, and she's becoming more open to the possibility that Bill is not in the backcountry somewhere – and is instead in the university morgue.'

This realization had been helped along by Sheila's blunt advice: 'He's dead or he's not. Giving us a sample of his DNA isn't going to change that one way or the other. But then at least you'll know. Otherwise, all you got are miles of empty woods and no way to collect a life insurance policy.' She'd delivered it in her comforting voice, which was very similar to her don't-fuck-with-me voice, just with a few token *there, there, ma'am* murmurs. And it had worked. Mrs Buck agreed to hand over a toothbrush – and also, she and her husband shared a family calendar on their cloud internet account and would Chief Deputy Turley be interested in the note Bill had down for the day of the explosion?

Sheila eyeballed Faye in the interrogation chair and then read from her notes. 'It says, "Bear Creek Road. Take a right off 65." Bill Buck planned to stop by that morning. His wife said he left home all packed for his camping trip, including with his Sig Sauer P320, which was apparently a typical thing for him to take.' She raised an eyebrow. 'And Lyle must've had his Smith & Wesson 686 revolver, because we didn't find it when we searched your house. We know he owned it because we found the old permit paperwork from back when it was required.'

Alvarado sat back in her chair. 'Two men in the middle of a financial dispute, two guns – one of them a revolver, for Christ's sake – and a room packed with unstable pyrotechnics. I think we have our answer to the explosion.'

And if the skull's DNA came back as William Buck, they had their murderer.

FORTY-SIX

Judy picked up her phone and put it down again. It was still the middle of the school day. She couldn't call Linda now. But Lord, she needed to talk to her. One, she could finally discuss Marian's murder with her friend now that it was on the news and everybody knew. And two, Linda had access to the high school's computers. She could look up the 504 plans and tell Judy who the second signature was.

God, what if it was Bo Cushman? Every student had to take English – he probably taught half the kids in the school. Had easy access to their parents. Nobody would think twice if he was the teacher signing off on the 504 plans with Florence Dettinger. She groaned. Marian had thought so highly of Bo.

She fidgeted and paced her way through the afternoon, handing out extra math worksheets instead of conducting the science project she'd originally planned. When the bell rang, she shooed the gaggle of disgruntled second-graders out the door and grabbed her purse. She was halfway to the high school when she saw a figure walking along the road, gray hair and white New Balance tennis shoes gleaming in the sun. She'd forgotten Linda walked home along the golf course when the weather turned nice. She pulled alongside and rolled down the passenger side window.

'I was hoping you hadn't left yet. I need a favor.'

Linda bent down to look in the window and Judy cringed. Dark circles ringed her eyes and splotches of red dotted her cheeks. She chided herself – she'd known about Marian for a week, but poor Linda just found out yesterday. 'Get in, honey. I'll drive you home.'

Linda climbed in and Judy pulled the car forward a bit so she wasn't blocking traffic. 'How are you doing? It's a shock, isn't it?'

Linda nodded.

'Do you want to talk about it?'

Linda's hands balled into fists in her lap as she said no.

'OK. That's fine.' She reached out and patted Linda's arm. 'I do need your help. Relating to Marian. I need you to look up something in your school computer for me.'

Linda seemed to have stopped breathing. Judy gave her arm a stronger pat. 'Linda, come on. Breathe.' She waited a second. 'OK, I need you to focus for me. I'm going to take us back to the school, and we're going to look up some students. And that's going to give me information that's important.'

Information she could take to Hank Worth. She shifted the car into drive, waited for a break in traffic, and pulled back on to the road. Linda twisted toward her. 'You said you'd take me home. Don't take me back to school.'

'Linda, this is really important. I need you to look up some student records. I don't know anybody else I can ask. It won't take very long.'

'Take me home. Right now.' The words came out sharp and jagged. Judy looked over in surprise.

'Linda. Good heavens. This is for Marian.'

Linda started fumbling for the seat-belt buckle. It popped loose and she reached for the door handle. Judy yelled and slammed down the locks. Linda wailed and lunged for the wheel.

Utley. Hank saw the name pop up on his phone screen and felt nauseated. He slumped into his chair in the otherwise empty Branson sheriff's substation. What had happened during Duncan's interview? It rang three times before he found the strength to answer it.

'I didn't expect to be hearing from you,' he said.

'Yeah, I didn't expect to be calling you, either,' Utley said. Wherever he was sounded noisy and chaotic. Had they hauled Dunc into the police station anyway? 'But I need you to . . . wait.' He pulled the phone away from his ear and started issuing orders to someone else. 'Get him in here. Do not let him leave campus. You know what – don't let any of them leave campus. I'm not gonna be hunting these people down all afternoon. You . . . you there, little guy. Get on the intercom and tell your teachers that everybody stays. Kids can leave, teachers stay.'

'Who do you want to stay? Barstow?' Hank couldn't help himself. He almost wept when he said the name. Any name but Duncan. Please.

Utley came back on the line. 'Yeah, Barstow. But I'm pretty sure he's gonna be just a mop-up interview.'

'What? Why?'

He was up and pacing without even realizing it.

'You come across somebody named Linda Ghazarian during your unsanctioned investigation?'

'Linda?' His voice sounded hollow.

'She's not at work, not at home, not answering her phone. I was hoping you had another way to contact her.'

He wasn't close enough to the chair as his knees gave out. He sagged against the desk. There was only one reason Linda would be important to Utley. 'Linda's the other signature, isn't she?'

'Yeah. Since you told us what the scam was, we knew exactly which forms to look for. And on ninety percent of what we've found so far, she's the teacher signatory.'

Linda the trusted friend. Linda the experienced colleague with a sizable pension only a few years away. Linda with the grandkids who needed college tuition. Linda with the home on the golf course. Linda who vilified Coach Barstow, who told Hank she never heard Marian talk about Dettinger and the scheduling problems.

But she had. She knew. She knew Marian had figured it out. And she had even more to lose than the young counselor did.

'Where's Dettinger?'

'Yeah, that lady. Her signature's on one hundred percent so far. We got her down at the station. Denied the murder before she clammed up, though.'

'She denied it to me, too. I don't believe her, though.'

Utley scoffed. 'It could easily be either one of 'em.'

'No,' Hank said. Only one of those would've made Marian so upset.

'I know someone who might be able to reach Linda,' he said. 'I'll give her a call.'

He struggled to his feet and dialed Judy. The call went through with the canned sound that meant he was on a car speaker. Then the screaming started.

The Kia Sportage jerked to the right and went off the pavement. An astonished Judy slapped at Linda's hands and tried to steer left. Then her brain snapped into gear and she went for the brake.

Just as her foot reached it, Linda gave another vicious yank and the car slammed into the rock wall built along the shoulder. The force of the collision and the braking threw both women forward and to the side. The front right of the hood crumpled against the rock as Judy's seat belt locked her shaking body into the seat. Linda took her hand off the wheel and started to hyperventilate.

From somewhere, a male voice kept shouting. Judy couldn't understand it through the buzzing in her ears. Linda pushed on the door. She was out and gone before Judy could find breath to speak. *What the hell was she doing? Had she gone completely mad? There was no . . .* But there was. Judy wheezed against the tight shoulder strap as realization hit. There was a reason for her friend to go crazy at the mention of 504 plans. It hadn't been Bo Cushman. Linda must be the signatory.

She fumbled to get out of the seat belt as Linda disappeared up a driveway farther down the road. She finally got herself free and was pushing open her door when the shouting finally pierced her rattled head.

'What the hell is going on? Where are you? Are you OK?' It sounded like Hank.

'She's flipped out. I just asked her to look up the signatures for me. I think . . . I think she's in on it with Florence Dettinger.'

'Judy, I need you to tell me where you are. Is Linda with you right now?'

'We're up by the quarry. The one by the high school. She just ran off.'

She swung her trembling legs out of the car and pushed herself to her feet. She had to stand there for a second before she was able to will herself to move. She looked at the empty road and then started for the driveway, hobbling after her friend as Hank shouted warnings to an empty car.

FORTY-SEVEN

S am lowered the binoculars and looked over at Ted Pimental.
Molly March was behind him and another deputy, Bill
Ramsdell, was off to the side in a cover position. It was
overkill, especially considering their target might currently be
on a morgue slab instead of in this dilapidated shithole of a cabin.
But it never hurt to be careful.

Aidan Welby's stoned roommate, once he sobered up, had
offered this location, way out in the far east of the county near
the community of Protem. Halfway to nowhere in terms of popu-
lation and convenience. Where you went to do nothing but hide.

They crept around until they had the place surrounded. Sam
took a deep breath, tightened the straps of his body armor and
walked to the front door with the warrant in his hand. No one
answered his knock. He moved to the left and peered in a window.
Nothing. His phone vibrated in his pocket. He ignored it and
moved back to the door. The rusty knob was locked. He quickly
picked it, and he and Ted swept in. It was a single room with a
tiny bathroom in one corner. There was a camping stove near
the window and a stained, sagging mattress on a metal bed frame
next to the back wall. That was it. Ted swore softly. 'I bet he's
the one who's dead. The other guy is lost in the woods somewhere
and this dude is the one who got shot and then blown up in the
explosion.'

Behind him, the mattress twitched. Sam slowly moved one
hand to his holstered Glock and pointed the other at the bed. Ted
pivoted and saw nothing. Sam drew his gun. 'Put your hands out
where I can see them.'

There was no further movement. Ted grinned and moved
toward the end of the bed. Sam repeated his order. At a nod from
Ted, he said it a third time as the older deputy grabbed the metal
frame and yanked it away from the wall. There was a yelp and
a scrape and the hands of a bare-knuckle brawler shot out from
underneath the mattress.

Ted hooted in delight and flipped the whole mess up on its side, exposing a bruised and dirty Aidan Welby. Ted cuffed him, sat him in the middle of the floor and called in Molly and Bill.

'Who'd you go ten rounds with?' Ted asked as he cuffed him. Welby glared and stayed quiet.

Sam leaned down. 'You got any cocaine in this place, Aidan?'

His answer didn't match the angry red that flooded his face. 'I don't know what you're talking about.'

Sam eyed the man's bruised cheek. 'Oh, did somebody take it?' Welby winced.

'You know, you really got to stop jerking like that when you're surprised,' Ted said. 'It's a habit that's doing you no favors.'

Sam straightened and smiled. 'I bet the folks who took it also did that to your face. Was it theirs to start with? Before you stole it from Reynolds's place?'

His face went white. 'I ain't talking.'

'So that's a "yes" then,' Ted surmised as Sam tugged his phone out of his pocket. The vibrating had been a text from Sheila. He hauled Welby to his feet and slapped him on the back.

'Congratulations. You're officially not dead. Turns out the other guy wasn't lost in the woods after all.'

Ted whistled. 'They ID'd the extra body from the explosion?'

'Yeah. They confirmed it was the guy who owns the chain of fireworks stores. It means Lyle Halliday almost definitely is the one who shot him. Nobody else would've had motive.' He read the follow-up texts and chuckled. 'Sheila's pretty happy about it. Thinks we can wrap that case up.' He pulled out his handcuffs. 'And she's going to be extra happy when I tell her that we found you.'

He put Welby in his squad car and was in the middle of sending Sheila an update when a call came over the radio that froze his fingers in mid-text. A frighteningly flat-voiced Hank reported a car accident and a suspect at the top of the quarry cliff. Sam swore. His boss hadn't been able to leave the other case alone after all.

The siren howled as Hank sped past the high school and the wreck of Judy Manikas's car. He turned into the driveway leading to the quarry and stopped. He didn't see either woman. Ahead of him were dump trucks and bulldozers busily carting dirt and gravel from side to side. The walls towered on either side, limestone climbing more than four stories high on one side and even taller on the other. A man in a hard hat jogged toward him, pointing off to Hank's left and a dirt track that led up a slope to the top of the quarry. He shut off the sirens.

'. . . went up there. The bigger lady kept yelling for the other one to stop.' He reached the squad car. 'That's all employees-only up there. They can't be just walking around. It ain't a hiking trail.'

'You can get a vehicle up there, though?'

'Well, yeah, of course. Our equipment, not—'

'I need all your guys to stop. Everybody stops their vehicles until I come back down. And when the city police get here, you do what they say.'

'We ain't in the city limits.'

'Yeah, but it's their killer, so they're going to show up. Trust me.'

The hard hat stared at him slack-jawed as he made a sharp left and took the dirt track too fast. Dust billowed behind him as the car rose in elevation. He curved around to the right and the trees gave way to a large cleared area clearly well-used by heavy equipment. On one side, the ground sloped down into the woods. On the other, it dropped fifty feet straight down. And Linda stood on the edge.

Judy knelt in the dirt, gasping for air. The dust Hank brought with him enveloped her briefly and moved on, puffing away on the spring breeze. It didn't reach Linda before it went over the cliff, much more gently than she might.

'Linda. Come on back. Let's get away from the edge.' Hank rounded the front of his car and approached with his hands in front of him. She didn't turn around. He stepped closer.

'Don't.'

He froze. Judy wheezed softly behind him. What the hell should he do now? What the hell did he want now? She stood there, the architect of his family's agony – and possibly its destruction. Did he want her to just go ahead and jump? Would that help? Would it even matter? The damage was done. The damage she had done was done. He thought of Duncan. He thought of Marian. And he lowered his hands. Then he thought of Maggie the doctor and raised them again.

'Linda, let's step back from the edge, OK?'

Still looking out over the quarry, she shook her head. Hank shot a look back at Judy. She nodded.

'Linda, honey,' Judy said. 'Whatever's wrong, we can work it out. I'm sure there's an explanation. Just come over to help me up. Can you do that for me?'

That was good. Brilliant. He gave Judy a thumbs-up as Linda slowly started to move. She turned to face them and looked over at Judy but didn't budge from the brink.

'I only wanted to make her sick.'

Hank kept his eyes on her as Judy mumbled in confusion.

'Why did you want her to be sick?' He struggled to keep his voice unemotional.

'So she'd have to take time off. So she'd stop focusing on me. On the 504 plans. Everything Flo and I were doing was going to come crashing down.'

Behind him, Judy sucked in a breath.

'How did you do it?' His hands were still out. He fought the urge to curl them into fists.

'I spiked her coffee. With ground-up foxglove. The next thing I knew she was dead.'

Judy sagged to the ground. Linda stared at her with blank eyes. She still hadn't looked at Hank.

'How could you not say anything?' Judy could barely get the words out.

Linda lifted a limp hand. 'It went away. It got called heart failure, and . . . everything went back to normal.'

The hand dropped back to her side and she inched back. 'I never thought that would change. I never thought anybody would know.'

Hank, still six feet away, reached toward her. 'Don't move. Please. Just step this way, over to me. C'mon, Linda. We can sort all of this out.'

'I prayed for her. Every day. And you. Your family.'

A full confession at the time it happened would've been more helpful than two years of empty prayers. And how dare she wrap his family up in her greed? Hank forced himself to take a deep breath and push the thoughts out of his head.

'We can stand up here as long as you want, but please step over to me. Or Judy.' *Just get away from the damn cliff.*

The limp hand again. 'I can't . . . go back. I can't face . . . everyone will know . . .'

'Linda, please.' Judy was begging now. Thank God she was willing to, because that was a bridge too far for Hank.

'Listen to me,' Judy said. 'You have a family. Think of them. You don't want to do this to them.'

'I already have. I can't face them knowing. I can't . . . erase it.'

'They love you. They—'

Her gaze finally swung to Hank as her hand waved Judy into silence. 'She's a second-grader. All happiness and rainbows.' She stepped backward. 'But you know. Love breaks. Things break it and that's the end.'

'Then you put it back together.' He took half a step. 'It can go back together.'

She gave him a sad little smile. 'You're no child. You know that's not true.' And then she tipped backward into the void.

FORTY-EIGHT

He left his shoes in the garage but otherwise didn't bother. He walked through the house, shedding quarry dirt with every step, until he stood outside Duncan's bedroom door. He knocked and stepped back. The old man swung open the door and his window cast the day's last rays of sunlight into the basement hallway.

'What the hell happened to you?'

'I tried to catch something.'

'"Tried?" So you failed?'

'Yeah. That's about right.'

'Well, you look like shit. If that's supposed to make me feel better, it kinda does.'

Dunc crossed his arms and waited. He was dressed more nicely than normal – a crisp white button-down shirt, khaki slacks, the leather belt Maggie got him for Christmas. It hit Hank that he'd done it for the police interview. He'd dressed respectfully for men he knew would ask if he'd murdered his wife. Even though he knew he hadn't done it. Hank suddenly needed to sit down. He put his hand on the wall instead.

'I came to tell you . . .' He concentrated on the textured drywall under his fingertips and tried again. 'I came to tell you that you're no longer a suspect. That we know—'

'Oh, really? You get to determine that? You turn me over to BPD and *then* decide that now it all can just go away? You just decide to wave your magic wand where you wouldn't before?'

'No, that's not . . . we know who did it. She confessed.'

Dunc stared at him.

'I swear to you. I came straight from the scene. She . . .'

Hank couldn't even say it.

'Someone confessed? After two years of keeping quiet? I don't believe you.' Every word was louder than the last. But the next one was a whisper. 'Who?'

'Linda Ghazarian.'

Hank wasn't sure how much time passed before Dunc was able to speak. 'Linda . . . killed my Marian?'

Hank explained. Or tried to. The high school scheme. The poisoning. He hadn't wrapped his head around it. Probably never would. From the look on Dunc's face, he wouldn't be able to, either.

'And you'll tell everyone? Announce it? That she did it?'

'Oh, yes. It will come from BPD, but yeah. So the stuff at the high school, too. That will all come out.'

Dunc nodded. He was regaining a little bit of color. Some of the lines on his face were easing, but new ones were furrowing in different places. Cut by different emotions, Hank supposed. Dunc seemed to feel it, and rubbed at his cheek.

'Is that all that will come out? Nothing more about us? About Marian?'

Opposing thoughts collided in Hank's head. He knew what his father-in-law was really asking. He opened his mouth, but couldn't speak.

'Don't tell Maggie. Please don't tell her. About the affair.' He dropped his arms to his sides, extending his hands just slightly toward Hank. 'I don't want her to think badly of Marian. Please.'

It was an incomplete request. Hank straightened and took his hand off the wall. 'Just Marian?'

'For Marian. And yeah, for me. Jesus, you put me through all this and then you make me say it?'

Hank started to take a step forward but forced himself to stop. 'If I don't tell her, then I'm the one she'll think badly of. For suspecting you at all. She'll think I had no reason to.' He thought of the quiet distance his wife had put between them during the last few days. 'And I'm not going to sacrifice my marriage for you.'

He turned and headed quickly for the stairs, forcing himself to ignore the dusty handprint – and the lonely old man – he was leaving behind.

Hank trudged up the stairs, trying to haul his thoughts away from the bottom of the quarry.

If Linda had only held on, she could've blamed Marian's murder on Florence Dettinger once they were arrested. With both of them pointing fingers, it would've been damn hard to prove it was one over the other. He followed that line of thinking through. Say they had charged her. There would be a court case and a trial. Marian's diary would be evidence. And the affair would become public knowledge. Out of his hands. He almost wished that was the way things had turned out.

He reached the last step just as the kids came bursting through the back door with Maggie close behind. He hadn't realized they were on a walk. She saw where he was coming from and her face hardened.

The kids ran for the kitchen. They stood there and stared at each other.

'It was Linda Ghazarian. She laced your mom's coffee that morning.'

The dog leash slipped through her fingers. Suddenly forgotten, Guapo disappeared with his prize. Hank waited.

'Linda? Mom's friend Linda? She murdered my mother?'

He nodded and again explained the 504s and the parent payments.

'So you took her to jail, right?'

'She's dead.'

'Excuse me?'

So he explained that, too. Up to the point where he dived and slid to the edge, almost going over, just in time to see her body break on the gray ground so far below him. He kept that bit to himself. She looked at the front of his clothes smeared with dirt and guessed part of it anyway.

'Are you OK?' Her tone was muddled and uncertain. He couldn't tell if it was her clinical physician voice or her I-love-you voice.

'Yeah.' *No, not even close.* He gestured toward the stairs. 'I told your dad.'

She wrapped her arms around her middle and looked out the window. 'I can't believe it was Linda. I can't believe . . .' She turned back to him. 'I can't believe you suspected my dad.'

'Honey, everyone gets looked at during a homicide investigation. You know that.' This is where he should say it. He tried and nothing came out.

'You turned him over to the police department.' It was an accusation.

'He met a couple of guys for coffee down at the Community Center. It's perfectly reasonable they would want to get information from the spouse of a murder victim.'

He knew he'd phrased it wrong the second he said it. She stiffened.

'Perfectly reasonable?'

'I'm just saying that he was helping with the case. That's all.'

'You're trying to gloss over the fact that you honestly thought he could have killed my mom.'

'That's not what I'm trying to do.' His voice broke. 'I'm trying . . .'

I'm trying not to lose my mind. I'm trying not to lose you. And I'm trying not to break your heart. And the last two were incompatible. He shrugged helplessly. 'I was trying to do right by your mom.'

She blinked in surprise. She opened her mouth to say something but then clamped it shut. He took a step away. He couldn't keep standing here. At this point, she probably wouldn't even believe him if he told her about the affair. He headed for the front door.

'It's OK. I don't blame him.'

Duncan stood on the stairs. He shoved his hands in the pockets of his slacks and cleared his throat. 'What I mean is, he didn't do anything wrong.'

The old man's tone didn't quite match with the words. It had an edge that said all was not forgiven. Maggie seemed too concerned with his well-being to notice. She hurried over and guided him to the couch. He didn't sit, instead turning to Hank. 'He was just doing his job. So please don't be mad at him.'

Maggie looked from one man to the other. Then she sat, pulling her dad on to the couch next to her. They began to talk about Linda. Hank changed direction and headed to the kitchen, where he corralled the kids and bundled them into the minivan. Then he got behind the wheel and couldn't think of a single place to go. He didn't want to take them for pizza or to run errands. The whole town knew about the murder and was in the midst of finding out about Linda's confessional plunge, and he didn't want either subject broached in front of his children. One idea came to him. He sent a text and then drove the two miles to the only place where no one would pass judgment on him tonight.

'You come right on in.' Sheila was waiting for them at her front door. She sent the kids into the kitchen and they followed more slowly as she used her walker.

'You OK?' she said.

'I must look really bad if you're worried.'

'I didn't say I was worried. Curious. That's all.' She gave him a sideways smile that let him know she was teasing.

'How're the kids?'

'Oblivious. I'm trying to keep it that way.'

She grinned. 'I think I can help with that. I called in a little order. Should be here any second.'

A low-pitched engine rumbled up the street and stopped in front of the house. Then came the flop of footsteps on concrete that could only come from a size fifteen shoe. Sam let himself in. He held two tubs of ice cream and a six-pack of Negra Modelo beer. Hank looked at him and Sheila and suddenly couldn't see for the stinging wetness in his eyes. These two people knew. They knew he'd done what he had to.

And at this moment, they were all the family he had.

ACKNOWLEDGEMENTS

This book has been brewing for a while. I knew years ago that it would bring Marian McCleary to the fore. Even though she died before the first book, she's always been a crucial character; it was time she got her due. Back in the first Hank book, I made her an educator for a reason—I wanted her to be special. I come from a long line of teachers—my mother, both grandmothers, sister, sister-in-law, aunts, uncles, cousins. The list is long, and I would argue, incredibly distinguished. They've taught every age group from preschool to college, in rural areas and crowded urban centers, poor kids and rich ones. And it is *hard*. It is also immensely rewarding, and I wanted this book to address both of those aspects, but mostly I wanted it to serve as a love letter to teachers. Especially the one who taught me to read and write in the first place. Thanks, Mom.

In addition to her and my dad, I had the support of many others in the writing of this book. I had the sharp eyes of Carol Adler, Paige Kneeland, Mike Brown, and the immortal Chris Hauger, who all read the manuscript and offered feedback, corrections, and advice that made the finished book so much better than I could've done alone. Luci Hansson Zahray, the Poison Lady, gave me the means to kill someone who'd already been dead for five books. She's always willing to share her immense knowledge of toxic plants with the entire mystery community, and this book wouldn't have been possible without her help. And a special thanks to Janis Herbert and Tina Ferguson, who go the extra mile so often they should be considered elite marathoners by now.

I'm lucky to have wonderful bookstores who champion local authors. Face in a Book in El Dorado Hills, California, and Capitol Books in Sacramento both benefit the community in countless ways. The Sacramento Literacy Foundation does the same, working to raise literacy rates. A while back, Randy Getz generously bid on a character name at a Foundation fund-raising auction. I was happy to include his daughter's name in this book, and I thank Randy for his support of children's literacy. The other jewel in the regional writing community is Capitol Crimes, the Sacramento chapter of Sisters in Crime. Support, education, drinks, laughter—we have it all. Thanks, everyone.

I've been fortunate to get to thank my agent Jim McCarthy in every book I've ever written. I've been with him since the beginning, and I'm still one lucky writer. Thanks, Jim. Another thank you goes to Vic Britton, my editor at Severn House, who brought the book across the finish line and is a delight to work with. Also at Severn House, Jo Grant, Rachel Slatter, cover artist Jem Butcher and copyeditor Penelope Isaac are much appreciated.

The last people I want to thank are the ones who are always there from the beginning. They are my support, my anchors, my comic relief, my everything. Joe, Meredith, and Carolyn, thank you always.

And a final thank you to my readers, without whom there would be no Hank, Sheila or Sam. Your support and reviews keep making the books possible. Thank you.